MONEY
DEVILS
1

ALSO BY ASHLEY & JAQUAVIS

The Cartel 7: Illuminati

The Cartel 6: The Demise

MONEY DEVILS 1

A CARTEL NOVEL

ASHLEY & JAQUAVIS

ST. MARTIN'S
GRIFFIN
NEW YORK

First published in the United States by St. Martin's Griffin, an imprint of St. Martin's Publishing Group

MONEY DEVILS 1. Copyright © 2020 by Ashley Antoinette Coleman and JaQuavis Coleman. All rights reserved. Printed in the United States of America. For information, address St. Martin's Publishing Group, 120 Broadway, New York, NY 10271.

www.stmartins.com

The Library of Congress Cataloging-in-Publication Data is available upon request.

ISBN 978-1-250-19767-2 (trade paperback)
ISBN 978-1-250-19768-9 (ebook)

Our books may be purchased in bulk for promotional, educational, or business use. Please contact your local bookseller or the Macmillan Corporate and Premium Sales Department at 1-800-221-7945, extension 5442, or by email at MacmillanSpecialMarkets@macmillan.com.

First Edition: 2020

10 9 8 7 6 5 4 3 2 1

Money
Devils
1

PROLOGUE

"*Se pou nou jwenn em kounye a,*" the man said smoothly in his native Haitian language—Haitian Creole to be exact. His accent was heavy, and his raspy voice sent chills up the spines of many men in Miami. In translation he simply said, "Let's get them now." His voice was calm and steady; however, his heart was filled with anxiety. Fear didn't trigger his internal butterflies; rather, sheer eagerness and a burning passion for revenge had his blood racing.

Two Haitian men were inside a van parked directly across the street from a popular restaurant. One man sat in the driver's seat, while the other sat in the back, right next to the van's sliding door. An AR-15 semiautomatic was in the man's hands. He was waiting for the perfect time. They had been sitting there for the past hour and a half after receiving a tip about their enemy's whereabouts, and they'd wasted no time getting there to handle unfinished business. They'd been looking for him for quite some time.

The man in the back seat cocked back his rifle, preparing for what would be a gory scene. Anonymity didn't concern them, so they'd passed on wearing ski masks or other disguises. They wanted to send a clear message: DO NOT FUCK WITH THE HAITIANS IN DADE COUNTY.

This had been an ongoing drug war between their crew and the other side for a very long time, and the only way to end it was to kill the other side's leader—none other than the notorious Carter Diamond, boss of the feared drug syndicate the Cartel. The Cartel controlled the Port of Miami, which meant it controlled the flow of the country's imported drugs. Its power and influence were so strong that it was almost a death sentence to go against them. Yet Matee and Milo did when they'd set up shop and started selling drugs in Carter's territory, a crucial mistake that ignited the war they were currently losing by a landslide. Just a few months prior, a drive-by shooting claimed many members of their Haitian mob while at a birthday party for a member's child, and their niece had been one of the victims. Not only that, a bullet had grazed Milo's daughter during the attack. Milo had thanked God every night his daughter wasn't murdered, but his thoughts always swung from grateful to being enraged over the possibility of "what if?" *What if his precious daughter had been taken away from him?* The hypothetical drove him nuts and vengeance became his burning desire. Getting back at the Cartel, but especially Carter Diamond, was personal to them. The Cartel had crossed the line of morality even for a drug war, and revenge was the only thing on both of their minds. It was a sad day for their family and a tough pill to swallow. Although it wasn't intended for her, a young life was lost, and all bets were off at that point.

Milo and Matee understood there was no honor in the streets. They had been trying to find the head of the Cartel for so long, knowing that ending him would be the only way for them to win the war. No matter how many soldiers they killed, Carter could recruit more and more. He had an endless supply of street mercenaries and his power was overreaching. His money was longer and stronger so there was no match. So Milo suggested they shift from killing soldiers to solely hunting for Carter Diamond.

And today, it was their time. They had their man.

However, they were racing against the clock. Carter Diamond was currently on trial for tax evasion and he could serve jail time if convicted. That would take their chances of murdering him from slim to none. They had to get him before his possible conviction, which would be next week.

As they looked through the front window, the man at the wheel cranked the ignition. His dark, smooth skin was the same color as tar and long locs hung past his shoulders. A Haitian flag–themed bandana was wrapped tightly around his head, keeping his locs from falling into his face. The man in the back wore locs, too, and resembled the driver very closely. They were blood brothers only a few years apart. Milo, the driver, was the eldest, the more levelheaded of the two. He looked down into his lap and released his firm clutch from the steering wheel to grip two chrome pistols, one in each hand. He rarely went into the field or got violent, but this matter was personal. Milo was the brains of the operation and typically acted as the silent partner to their drug organization. The tension in the street was so high and both sides had lost much. As they watched Carter closely, Milo could hear his brother's heavy panting. Matee was like an animal that stalked his prey. He looked back and saw Matee's chest rapidly rise and fall with each breath. He could literally see the adrenaline pumping throughout Matee's body. Tears began to form in Matee's eyes and Milo knew his little brother was locked in. He wanted Carter Diamond dead in the worst way. Milo, mindful of how hotheaded his brother was, understood he had to calm Matee before they made their move.

"Matee," he called out, but Matee didn't snap out of his rageful trance. "Matee!" he called again, louder this time. Matee slowly shifted his eyes and looked at his brother with a demented gaze.

"*Konsantre!*" Milo spat with a stern expression and a piercing stare. This meant "focus" in Haitian Creole. He spoke in their native tongue, knowing that would resonate better with his hell-bent brother. He grabbed Matee around the back of his neck and turned him so they were eye to eye. He whispered harshly, peering directly into his brother's soul through the windows of his dark eyes.

"*Konsantre,*" he said again, giving Matee a firm shake to get him to snap back to reality. In a calmer tone, he repeated once more, "*Konsantre.*"

Matee nodded quickly in agreement as he slightly leaned forward, gently pressing his head against his brother's. They would do this as adolescents, a soothing technique Milo used with his troubled younger sibling. Matee finally blinked and returned to the present as a lone tear fell from his left eye. Just the sight made Milo's insides shake and he had an urge to cry along with his brother, but he didn't. He was the stronger of the two, so he had to remain stout to keep Matee stable. Nevertheless, Milo felt uneasy seeing the most ruthless man he had ever known on the edge of insanity. That was a bad combination. It was only a matter of time before a mental explosion happened. He hadn't seen Matee drop a tear since they were little boys. The death of their precious niece had his mind foggy, but his goal was crystal clear. Matee wanted Carter Diamond to feel the pain he'd caused his family and to experience it in the worst way possible.

Milo also wanted to exact revenge—he could feel his trigger finger begin to itch—but he wanted to be strategic about it. He suddenly began to regret bringing Matee along for the potential hit. During the past few months, they had stalked and waited patiently. Even now, his eyes were trained on the restaurant's entrance, closely studying the tall, dark, handsome man in a well-tailored Italian suit who'd just emerged. It *was* him, the urban legend, Carter Diamond. A smooth, chocolate man with the grace of a professional ballplayer, he was all that he was cracked up to be and then some. Diamond's salt-and-pepper beard was perfectly lined and his bright smile shined from a distance. Some could hardly believe the gracious man was as vicious and coldhearted as they came. Not many knew about his dark side, but those who knew, *knew*.

Milo and Matee intently watched Carter talk to the valet attendant and then stand on the curb to wait for his car. Other patrons walked in and out of the restaurant.

"We get 'em now, bruva," Matee said, not taking his eyes off Carter. Matee's jaw clenched tightly, the muscles visibly flexing as he ground his back teeth against one another. He was thirsting for retribution, ready to shoot with reckless abandon. The cold steel in his hands had never felt better.

"Make sure you hit him in de head. We can't afford to miss this mu'fucka. All head shots, you 'er me?" Milo instructed as he slid the van onto the streets, merging into traffic. "Listen close. We going to slide right up on 'em. Let 'em have it as soon as I slide the door back."

Milo slowly drove past Carter, who was on the opposite side of the street. He smoothly made a U-turn. Now they were on the same side of the street as the restaurant and were creeping up to the restaurant's front curb where their target stood.

"Here we go . . . here we go," Milo drawled under his breath.

His eyes locked on Carter, not even blinking, fearing he would lose sight. He then reached up to push the button that automatically slid the van's door open. They were two cars behind in the valet line and had the perfect angle to assassinate the Cartel's leader.

"*Pare . . . pare*," Milo mumbled, meaning "get ready."

Matee licked his lips and focused as he squeezed the rifle's handle and extended his pointer finger just next to the trigger. His nose began to run and sweat beads formed on his brow. His animalistic nature had clicked on and he was in pure savage mode. His heart raced ferociously as the van inched up, now only one car back from Carter. They watched as Carter looked past them to focus on the Bentley behind them, which was his car. Carter then looked back to the restaurant's entrance and motioned, waving someone over. They couldn't make out what he was saying, but soon out came his Dominican wife and a young girl. The car in front of them cleared the way for them to pull up right next to Carter. As Milo slowly edged forward, he could see the young girl's face and the guilt began to tweak his heart. She seemed to be the same age as his oldest daughter. He began to breathe deeply, knowing this child could catch a bullet that wasn't meant for her.

"Hold on, Matee. No kids," Milo whispered as he pulled up to the curb.

"*Fuck sa a femèl chen ti kras,*" Matee said, meaning "Fuck that little bitch." He was zoned in and didn't care about his brother's protest. He only saw red.

Matee finished sliding open the door and there stood Carter, his wife, and his daughter. Without hesitation, Matee raised his gun and yelled, "*Sak pase!* Remember me?"

He put his finger on the trigger and pointed the gun at Carter, slightly smirking as their eyes met. He then twitched his gun to the right, aiming it directly at the young girl.

"Breeze!" Carter yelled as he realized what was about to happen. Matee's twisted smirk turned even more sinister as he thought about the pain Carter was about to feel. Matee's lip began to quiver in demonic pleasure and his eyes got as big as golf balls as his attention focused on the young girl.

The young girl froze in fear. There was nothing she could do.

Carter lunged to protect his daughter, but the crack of gunfire sounded before he could reach her.

Milo quickly pushed the gun away at the same moment Matee pulled the trigger, causing him to sway. Bullets sprayed throughout the air and sparks flew from the rifle's barrel. Milo's last-second push made his brother hit the valet worker instead of Carter or his family. Milo then mashed the gas pedal to the floor, making the tires screech and a cloud of smoke appear. The van fishtailed into the middle of the street and it quickly fled the chaotic scene.

The vehicle's unexpected jerking motion thrust Matee across the van. "Fuck! What de fuck are y'u doing?"

"No children!" Milo yelled, swerving in and out of traffic. The thought of Carter Diamond's daughter almost being shot made him feel unexpected empathy. That was a pain no man should feel, and his moral compass wouldn't let him lean all the way into the devil's playground.

"Fuck! Fuck! Fuck!" Milo screamed as he repeatedly hit the steering wheel out of rage and frustration, his mind racing. They'd likely never get a chance like that again to kill their sworn enemy and shift the balance of power.

Matee sat in the back seat, shaking his head in disbelief. He looked at the rearview mirror and caught a glimpse of his brother's eyes. Their stares matched in intensity and both decided to remain quiet. It was unspoken, but they both knew things would never be the same. They were at a point of no return. Carter had seen them and now knew exactly who they were. This street war had reached its boiling point. It was no longer about the lower-level drive-bys and drug territories. It was personal on both sides. Carter and Matee had locked eyes and there was no room for misinterpretation. It was crystal clear and etched in stone.

They would be enemies for life.

• • •

Milo stood in the doorway of his children's room. The modest three-bedroom home was in the middle of Little Haiti, a small area in Miami he and his family had made infamous for years. It was a two-story home and Milo was on the second floor where the bedrooms were. It was just before midnight and he had been standing there for the past fifteen minutes while counting his blessings. His heart melted as he watched two of his four daughters sleep peacefully in their bunk beds. He walked over and kissed them on their foreheads as he did every night. When he reached his second-youngest daughter, Honor, his heart skipped a beat at seeing the bandage on her cheek, the result of the drive-by shooting from a while before. She was still healing up. The doctor assured him that she would be okay. She would just have a scar once it healed.

He cringed every time he saw it, knowing his involvement in street life had nearly gotten his baby girl killed. At that exact moment, he realized he had done the right thing by stopping Matee from shooting. The possibility of another young girl getting killed was too heavy a burden to bear.

He gently rubbed her hair and the thought of losing her made his eyes water. A tear trickled down his cheek and he quickly wiped it away, not wanting his wife to come in and see him at a weak point. He looked back at the door to make sure she wasn't there and shook his head, attempting to rid himself of the feeling. He bent down and kissed his two-year-old and youngest, Ashton. He lived for his girls, and shame came over him. He was the only man in the house among his wife and daughters. They all were depending on him, and the life he was living put all of their futures and stability at risk. If something happened to him, their entire world would be turned upside down.

He headed out and walked to the next room where his other two daughters rested. He saw Sutton and Luna, his oldest two, who were in separate beds. Both were preteens and he began to think about how fast they had grown up. He dreaded the day they fully understood who their father was. When the drive-by had happened, he hadn't been ready to expose himself as a gangster. They only knew him as Daddy and that tragedy had made his daughters grow up faster than he had planned. He carefully walked over to kiss his sleeping beauties, then left. As he reached the hallway, his smiling wife was waiting for him with her arms crossed. The small gap in her teeth, which Milo loved, triggered his own smile. Her dark chocolate skin and petite frame leaned against the wall, and he walked over, hovering above her.

She rested her head on his chest and her eyes automatically closed. A feeling of security covered her as it always did when he was near and she said a quick prayer under her breath, thanking God he made it home that night. She knew the life he led usually ended tragically with either a funeral or a long prison sentence.

Milo leaned down to kiss the top of her head as he listened closely to her prayer.

"Amen," she whispered.

"Amen," Milo repeated. "Why aren't you asleep?"

She shrugged as she looked up at him. "I couldn't. I was worried."

"Sweetheart, there is nothing to be worried about. I had someone outside the home all day protecting you guys," Milo assured her.

"I know. I seen them. The girls did too," she responded with disappointment in her eyes. Milo shook his head, feeling ashamed. He had robbed his children of their innocence and that was something he could not reverse.

"They mentioned it?" he asked, concerned.

"No, but niggas around the house with AK-47s is not normal. They know that something is different. It's like we're living in a prison, Milo."

Milo dropped his head with dishonor. "Damn."

"And Sutton isn't a baby anymore. She knows that her father doesn't have a regular job. She also knows that it's a street war going on. She isn't dumb and kids talk, ya know," she said, referring to their oldest daughter. Milo's mind began to churn and the image of what happened earlier kept replaying in his mind. He kept seeing that van door slide open; but instead of Carter's daughter's face looking back at them, it was Sutton's. He'd always stayed away from Matee's world and handled their operations from the tactical aspect. Unlike Matee, he was college educated, and he was the more studious of the two brothers. Before he'd gotten sucked into a life of crime, he'd been on his way to becoming an accountant. However, the birth of his daughters back to back had pushed him into his brother's business, and what was supposed to have been a temporary hustle of selling pure cocaine had eventually become his lifestyle. This had never been for him or in his plans. He'd thought himself much too smart for that, but life's ills had a funny way of crushing aspirations. What was supposed to be a short-term stint in helping his brother had led to him being the head of a ruthless drug syndicate.

Just as he was about to say something to his wife to reassure her of their safety, a loud barrage of knocks sounded, startling them both. Milo quickly told his wife to wake up the girls and all go into the same room. He reached for his gun that was in his waist band and held it up. He watched her whisk the girls into the safe room with a worried look on her face. He placed his finger to his mouth, signaling her to keep quiet. He feared the worst and couldn't imagine who was knocking at his door at that time of night. His mind instantly went to

Carter Diamond and an inevitable retaliation. His adrenaline began to pump, and he went into protector mode. He looked at the small-caliber pistol in his hand and decided to grab something bigger. He rushed into his bedroom and dropped to the ground, lying flat on his stomach. He reached under the bed and pulled out an AK-47 assault rifle. As he stood, he cocked it, prepping it to be ready for any action warranted.

He hurried out of the bedroom and glanced at his wife, who was huddled in a corner with the girls in the safe room. They were all confused and trying to understand what was going on as their mother whispered to them, instructing them to be quiet. He crept down the stairs while the knocking was still going rampant, making their girls shriek in terror with each loud thud. Milo got to the first floor and stood in front of the door. The urgent knocking continued. He took a deep breath and exhaled slowly as he approached the door. He was prepared to blow away whoever was on the other side.

Quickly unlocking the door, Milo pulled it open and pointed the assault rifle at the man standing in his doorway. It was Matee.

"What de fuck are y'u doing here!" Milo asked as he lowered his gun and exhaled harshly, trying to calm himself. He tossed his rifle onto the couch and rested his hands on his hips while shaking his head in irritation.

"We hit dem at court! That's de only way!" Matee yelled as he brushed past his brother and entered the home.

Milo looked at his brother as if he were crazy, shaking his head in disbelief that his brother would come to his home and disrupt his family time. "What the fuck are you talking about? We can't do that! You're going to get yourself killed." His dismay then turned into disgust as he noticed the redness in Matee's eyes, immediately knowing his brother had been doing blow, his drug of choice. Milo never partook in drugs himself; he only was interested in making money from them. He hated that his brother had this bad habit and it broke his heart every time he saw Matee high. Their undocumented immigrant parents had worked so hard to build a life for them, but the streets had consumed Matee, and eventually Milo too. They were probably rolling over in their graves because of what their sons had become.

"Matee . . ." Milo said, shaking his head.

"*Matee*," Matee repeated, mocking his brother's "proper" voice. He hated the fact Milo could turn his accent on and off and he couldn't.

In Matee's mind, Milo was ashamed of their roots and thought he was better than him. However, that wasn't the case. Milo just understood that to be successful in this country, he had to adapt to American customs and ways. Therefore, he'd tried extremely hard in school and worked on his English feverishly until he'd learned to hide his accent completely. Also, while Milo's locs were neat and well kept, his brother's were dyed and unruly. Milo and Matee were as opposite as could be but bonded by blood.

Milo glowered at his brother as Matee sniffled and shifted his weight from one foot to the other. "You need to stay off that shit! You come knocking at the door in the middle of the night, like a madman. You're out of control!"

"Well, me had to get mind off t'ings, y'u know? I have to kill Carter. I want him dead! No more waiting. Not doing it y'u way anymore! I make the rules now!"

Matee began to pace the room, obviously bothered by something. He mumbled things under his breath.

Milo was confused, trying to make out what he was say-ing. "Lower your fucking voice." Milo kept his own voice quiet as he glanced at the stairs, hoping his family couldn't hear his brother's rant.

"Fuck dat!" Matee said, fire in his eyes as he charged to-ward Milo. They were now face-to-face, staring at each other. "We had dat muddafucker and y'u let em go!"

"You pointed the gun at a little girl. You're fucking insane. I couldn't let you do it."

"Fuck dem! Dey had no remorse when dey shot Tata," he said, referring to their niece. The sound of her name made both of their hearts flutter. Grief caused both of their eyes to water, reminding them they'd had to bury a little Haitian girl at the hands of the Cartel. "We hit 'em at de' courthouse," Matee repeated firmly and confidently. Matee was hell-bent on killing Carter and the only place where he knew for sure to catch him was at his trial.

"You know this is never going to end, right? We hit some-one from their side and then what? I'm not burying another child! I can't do this anymore. I have a family to protect and this is getting too crazy. I'm out!" Milo said, fed up with the life. He wanted out of the drug game and all the murder and malice that came with it. He had four little girls and for the first time, he was going to put them first, not his brother. He could see the devil in Matee's eyes, and he knew what came with that chaos.

Matee squinted his eyes and leaned his head to the side while staring directly into his older brother's soul. "Out?"

"Yes, I'm done. This stops today. I'm out! If you go to that courthouse, you're going to get killed. Whoever you take with you is going to die as well. Either that or get lifetime sentences. You're leading your own people into a fire you aren't going to be able to pull them out of. You can't go on federal property and execute a hit. It just can't happen!"

"It's happening," Matee said, not budging whatsoever.

"You're fucking crazy," Milo said as he threw his hands up, not understanding the thought process of his brother. He knew at that moment Matee was on the brink of insanity, willing to lose his own life just to take Carter Diamond's.

"I can't do this anymore," Milo said as he turned around and walked to his door. He opened it and stepped aside, giving Matee a clear pathway to exit his home. Milo had tears in his eyes because this could very well be the last time he would see his brother.

Matee saw the pain in his brother's eyes and he instantly grew disappointed, knowing his brother was waving his white flag like a coward.

"*Kapon,*" Matee said, which was the worst thing you could call a man in Haiti. It meant "coward" or "without merit." Any other time, Milo would have taken offense, but in that moment, the word didn't matter to him. If being a coward meant keeping his family out of harm's way, that would be a badge he would wear proudly and without any reservation.

Matee slowly walked past his brother with disdain and heavy disappointment in his eyes. He stepped out of the house and looked onto the street where a line of trucks was parked back to back. Three Haitian men leaned on the lead vehicle, all with guns in their hands. The others were standing around casually talking and not paying too much attention. Some had been there all day watching Milo's house; the others had pulled up with Matee.

"You're no longer one of us, *kapon!*" Matee yelled, a mean grimace plastered all over his face. He had the eye of the tiger and he wouldn't stop until Carter Diamond's blood was on his hands.

As he approached the door, one of the henchmen opened it for him, allowing Matee to smoothly slide in. They all stared at Milo as he stood there looking on. He was their boss, too, but Matee was their leader. Matee was in the streets and he led by pulling, not pushing. He was a street general and a king. For the soldiers, the choice to follow him was a no-brainer.

Settling in the back seat, Matee rolled down the window so all the goons could hear him loud and clear. "He's not with us anymore. Move out!"

Everyone paused, not fully understanding what Matee was saying. Matee noticed the hesitation and opened the door. He stood, half his body out of the car, and looked around at his crew. "I said move de fuck out!"

Just like clockwork, everyone began to move. Matee reached into his top pocket and pulled out a small glass vial that contained pure cocaine. He popped it open and put it into his right nostril. He took a deep sniff, shooting the drug into his system.

They all were disappointed to know Milo had tucked his tail in the middle of a war. Without saying anything, Milo knew he had been exiled for his decision not to ride. All attention was on the upcoming court day; that was where it would all end for the Cartel.

Milo closed the door and locked it. He was now alone and considered an outsider within the organization. He no longer had the armor of his mob and would have to be his girls' sole protector. Understanding the Cartel's reach, he immediately began to reassess his newfound situation. He grabbed the rifle from the couch and went upstairs to put it away. When he entered his bedroom, he put the weapon away in the closet and entered his girls' room where his wife had them all in one bed. His oldest daughter, Sutton, and his wife were the only ones awake. His wife rocked the youngest, Ashton, in her arms as she slept peacefully. Milo wished his wife had that same peaceful expression rather than the grimace of worry she wore. He noticed the same look on his daughter's face too. Then, looking closer, Milo saw tears in Sutton's eyes as she hugged her mother tightly. He knew they'd overheard Matee's yelling.

He dropped his head in shame at the fear in their eyes, but it also confirmed he had made the right decision. At that moment, he vowed he would never touch a drug again. He was out of the street game for good.

He took a deep breath and leaned against the doorway and locked eyes with Sutton.

"Are we going to get shot, Daddy?" she asked as she began to fully understand the life her father led.

"No, sweetheart. I promise. We are going far, far away from here," he said with conviction. He then looked over at his wife and spoke. "Pack up all that you can fit in a bag. We are leaving."

His wife began to do as she was told with no retort or pushback. Milo then walked into the bathroom and stood in front of the sink's mirror. He rested his hands on the sink and began to stare at his own reflection. He was tired of the fast life and wanted a change. A big one. He reached into the sink's drawer and grabbed his clippers. He proceeded to shave his head, gradually exposing the skin on his head, which he hadn't seen since he was a little boy. As odd as it seemed, it felt like the weight of the world fell off with each loc as it hit the bathroom's floor. Allegiance to his Haitian mob had blinded him to his true self. Milo wasn't just a thug whose calling was a life of drug dealing. He was much more complex, and he began to see himself clearer as he shaved himself. With hair trimmings scattered on his face, shoulders, and chest, Milo continued to stand there staring at himself. He was above what he was doing, and he vowed from that point forward that he would use his mind to achieve his goals, not for murder and drugs.

In the wee hours of the morning, he packed up his family and all the money he had stashed from his drug empire and headed west. He, his wife, and his four little girls drove across interstate lines and they would never return. Milo had purchased a modest investment home in Houston, Texas, that he'd kept secret. He figured that would be a good haven to take his family to until he figured out his next move.

It was the end of one story and the beginning of another.

Within the next few weeks, a historic street war would ensue back home in Miami. Carter Diamond would be killed at his trial and many lives would be lost because of that. Miami remained a bloodbath for years and Milo never looked back. He hadn't known it then, but that night would be the last time he would ever see Matee alive. He always felt bad, but he never regretted his decision because he knew he likely would have met his demise as well. He'd decided to leave for his girls and he would do it the same way again. He had seen the devil in his brother's eyes and he knew it would eventually consume him. The necessary evil called murder associated with that life was too heavy on his soul. He didn't want to succumb to the devil's pie. However, he never foresaw that the devil comes in many forms, even when one thought he wasn't present. The biggest trick the devil ever played was convincing the world that he didn't exist. The devil had a way of forming himself in the thing one loved the most. In Milo's case, that was money.

CHAPTER 1

Milo sat in a federal penitentiary thinking about the night he and his family had left Miami for good. His facial hair was now salt and peppered because of the gray that had grown in over the years. His build was slightly slimmer than it usually was. Crow's feet had formed just between his temple and eyes on each side, showing his mature age.

He waited patiently for his visitor. It had been years since the last visit, so he was excited for today. The guest list said his visitor's name was Dana Cook, but that wasn't the case. He watched a beautiful young lady approach the opposite side of the glass. Before she sat, she looked at him and her face lit up. The sight of her brought warmth to his heart and a smile to his face. She took a seat and picked up the phone that allowed them to talk through the glass. He did so as well.

"Hey, baby girl," he said. It was his daughter Ashton. She

had to sign in with an assumed name because of her felony conviction. Felons weren't allowed to visit other inmates in federal prison, so she had to do what she had to do to see her father. She hadn't seen him since they were arrested together years back.

"Hi, Daddy," she said as tears began to form in her eyes. She was so glad to see her hero. He had aged over the past few years, but his eyes never changed. She had been anticipating today for years and exhaled deeply now that she was there. The tension that had built up in her chest instantly eased. Her stint in Miami had been so life changing and dramatic. Now, she just needed her father. Seeing him did wonders for her soul; and at that moment, she realized how vital he was in her life. She didn't know exactly what to say to him, considering she was the reason he was in prison in the first place. The day that had changed everything flashed before her eyes yet again, a point in time that replayed in her mind constantly.

• • •

The tension was thick and steadily growing by the second. The young woman's anxiety was building inside of her chest, creating uncomfortable, sporadic flutters. Sweat beads formed in her palms as she stared at the clock on the coffee shop's wall. It was the top of the morning and the city's early risers moved around the downtown district of Dallas, Texas. This spot was strategically chosen because there was no camera inside and the entrance was outside the scope of the surrounding businesses' cameras too. The shop was half full. A few baristas worked hastily behind the counter as they scrambled to make espressos and lattes for the line of customers.

The chatter was constant throughout the shop and everyone seemed to be in their own world as they got their morning fix of caffeine.

Tick.

Tock.

Tick.

Tock.

It seemed like the clock's hand ticked a tad bit slower than what she was used to, like time was moving at a snail's pace. She was ready for this meeting to be over. She looked down at her foot that nervously tapped the ground inside of her red stiletto heel. Although she was a wreck on the inside, her facial expression was that of a calm businesswoman. Her navy-blue Versace pantsuit was the perfect fit and her hair was neatly pulled back with her baby hair resting on her edges. Her nonprescription glasses sat on the bridge of her nose as she tried her best to look as nonthreatening as possible. Ashton LaCroix was her name and she was having the most interesting eighteenth birthday one could imagine.

She looked at the older man who sat across the room reading a newspaper. He had deep, dark skin and his neat salt-and-pepper beard revealed his maturity. He lowered the newspaper slightly and his eyes peered just over the top of it. He locked eyes with Ashton and showed no facial expression. He then slowly nodded, offering her calm. As always, it seemed to work almost immediately. Ash's heart rate began to slow as she closed her eyes, took a deep breath, and exhaled.

The older man winked, doubling the feeling of stillness only he could have provided. The man, who was thirty years her senior, was none other than Milo LaCroix, her father. He also was the mastermind behind this blackmailing scheme.

As the clock struck high noon, a fifty-odd-year-old man walked in. He was tall, slim, and had a head of white hair that was balding near the crown of his skull. His pale white skin and oversized glasses matched the description of every other financial broker in town. His frame didn't seem to have an ounce of muscle on it; he was as intimidating as a fluffy white kitten.

He seemed to be in over his head and a fish out of water. As a partner and top broker at the biggest brokerage in Texas, he always was in a position of power and privilege. However, now he was putty in the hands of unknown con artists. He had never been threatened with blackmail before and Ashton knew he had too much at stake to risk not paying. He had to give in to their terms.

His eyes quickly scanned the room, his jittery hands holding a small leather briefcase. His uneasiness was written all over his face as he spotted Ashton, who sat in the corner of the coffee shop. Ashton gently touched the red rose brooch that was on the lapel of her jacket. The man slowly approached her and took a seat across the table from her. He looked at the young African American woman and a wave of disgust came over his face.

"Why are you doing this to me, you slimy bitch? You have no idea who I am and who you're fucking with!" he harshly whispered as he stared a hole through her. He had rage in his eyes, along with worry.

"Oh my, Mr. London," Ashton said as she smirked and gently touched her chest again. It seemed as if all the tension left her body once she spoke. "This is not personal. It's just business. Moving right along . . ." Ashton reached down into her briefcase at her feet and pulled out a large envelope. She sat it on the table and folded her hands on top.

"In this folder is your freedom. It contains various video clips of you going to meet an eighteen-year-old male intern. I counted around nineteen times from the months of September through January. It also has the hotel records that were purchased with your credit card for each visit. Not to mention, the raunchy text screenshots and photos of you in drag. You've had a steamy past six months, don't you think? You like them lace panties, huh?"

Ashton calmly laid out the mounds of photographic evidence of infidelity and homosexuality. She stared at Mr. London and the embarrassment seemed to be almost instant. His pale white face turned plumb red and he quickly flipped over the pictures, nervously looking around. He didn't want anyone to know his deep dark secrets and for that reason, he was being blackmailed by a complete stranger.

"How did you find out this information? How do you even fucking know me?" he questioned through clenched teeth as he intensely stared at the beautiful young woman in front of him.

"That's information I can't share, Mr. London. What I can tell you is if I don't get a money transfer by two P.M. today, all these photos and videos will be on your church members' Facebook pages. Plus, your wife will get a special delivery. Not to mention the email blast that will be in each and every one of your colleagues' inboxes. Now, I know you don't want that to happen; and to be quite frank, I don't either."

"You dirty bitch." Mr. London sneered as he gathered the pictures and stuffed them into the envelope.

Ashton smiled. "Here is the bitcoin address that I need the funds wired to. Exactly $400,000, and this problem will go away." She slid over an index card with a series of numbers and letters.

"How do I know these are the only copies you have?"

"You can rest assured that this little problem will go away as soon as I get confirmation of the funds. We have no desire to prolong this any longer than we have to, sir. Once I confirm the funds, all of this will be destroyed."

"This is bullshit," he whispered harshly, hatred in his eyes. Veins formed in his forehead, a mixture of fear and rage all over his face. After an intense stare down, Mr. London broke eye contact and then reached for his phone in his inner jacket pocket. Ashton sat there patiently with her hands collapsed inside one another. She glanced over at her father who studied them closely, watching over Ashton as she committed her first crime. It was his youngest daughter's rite of passage and entry into the family business of white-collar crime.

Mr. London snatched the card with the bitcoin address on it and stood. He shook his head just before he exited the café. Ashton closed her eyes and took a deep breath. The intensity of the exchange was newfound territory for her. She looked over at her father. He smiled and winked at her, letting her know she had done a good job. She watched as he slyly stood and gathered his newspaper. As always, he was cool as a cucumber, calm and collected. He neatly tucked the paper under his arm. There was a ding, which prompted him to look at his cell phone. He smiled after staring at his screen for a few seconds. It was a notification the funds had transferred into his ghost bitcoin account. He glanced over at his daughter and discreetly nodded, letting her know that their job was done.

Almost instantly, Ashton felt relief as she felt the tension in her shoulders slowly begin to melt away. She had just completed her first mission and she couldn't be prouder of herself. She couldn't wait to get home and celebrate with her three older sisters and father. Ever since she'd learned what type of business her family was in, she'd wanted in. On that day, she had finally gotten her wish and she couldn't wait to see her favorite sister, Sutty, and get her approval. Her father's and Sutty's approval were what she longed for and in that moment, she felt like she had finally arrived.

She watched as her father casually exited the place and just as planned, she would wait a few minutes and then leave after him. Ashton heard her phone vibrating and quickly reached down into her Louis Vuitton bag that sat in the chair next to her. She pulled her phone out and saw she had gotten a text from her sister Luna, whose nickname was "Gadget."

Gadget
Good job Ash. Just got confirmation. The bag is in. $

Ashton
OMG. That was tense. My heart pounding . . . smh

Gadget
Welcome to the big leagues. Oh yeah. HBD Bitch! Lol.

Ashton
Love ya

Gadget
ILY too. See you tomorrow

Ashton smiled from ear to ear and quickly pressed Send to text her sister back. She couldn't wait to get home and celebrate her first caper with her family. They had a rule to always wait twenty-four hours after a job before they met, just to ensure if they ever were tailed by the authorities or a disgruntled victim, they wouldn't lead them back to the family. Throughout the years, she had watched her father groom her older sisters into con artists; and because she was the youngest, she never got to participate. However, on that day, she had arrived. It was so hard for her to keep her cool while in front of their target. The adrenaline rush of getting six figures from blackmail was a new feeling for her. She then understood why her sisters were addicted to their family's secret hustle. Her father, Milo LaCroix, was a mastermind and set up the perfect play for Ashton's initiation.

What the fuck? That pale mu'fucka looked like he had smoke coming from his ears, Ashton thought as she took a few deep breaths. She closed her eyes and tried her best to slow down her rapid heartbeat that was caused by the intense exchange. She felt anxiety inside of her chest and felt her internal temperature begin to rise. She sensed her forehead begin to sweat and quickly stood up to go to the bathroom to gather some type of composure. She stood in front of the mirror for a few moments then turned on the faucet, dipped her head, and splashed the cold water in her face. She stared at herself in the mirror as she patted herself dry with a paper towel and felt a sense of pride. She thought about the smirk on her father's face just moments before and couldn't wait to meet up at home to get his feedback. She was a daddy's girl and she wanted nothing more than to make him proud, even if by way of white-collar crime.

Ashton headed out and stopped at the counter to purchase a bottle of water. The nerve-wracking experience had her mouth dry, her tongue feeling like sandpaper. After she downed the water, she gathered her things and headed out the door. She couldn't wait until the next day when she could celebrate with her loved ones. She'd sacrificed her birthday for the family business and she couldn't be happier about it. In her eyes, she had officially become a woman.

The following morning, Ashton was heading into the upscale subdivision where her father resided near downtown Houston. His home also acted as their hub and meetup spot after a job. Ashton pulled into the circular driveway at her father's immaculate home. She saw her sisters' cars there, too, so she knew they were present. As she parked, a swarm of police cars pulled into the driveway. She never saw them coming. Federal agents then surrounded the car, screaming at her.

"Put your fucking hands up now!" one police officer shouted as he approached the car with his gun drawn and pointed directly at Ashton's head. Ashton quickly threw her hands up, her heart racing rapidly. She didn't know what was going on. It all began to make sense when she saw her father getting brought out of the house handcuffed. Two federal agents escorted him, one on each side of him. Ashton was yanked out of the car and handcuffed as well. Just as quickly as her career as a criminal began, it ended. She would later find out that the bottle of water she'd purchased at that coffee shop had linked them back to the crime. Mr. London had gone to the authorities and told them everything that had happened. A small mistake had landed her and her father in jail for years, the job blown all because of her carelessness. If she hadn't purchased that drink, they would have been in the clear. She gave the authorities a paper trail that led straight back to them. It was the beginning of a domino effect that would crumble their family for years to come.

• • •

Milo placed his hand on the glass, knowing what his daughter was thinking about. He saw the guilt in her eyes. Ashton placed her hand on the opposite side of the glass as well, aligning it with his.

"It wasn't your fault," he whispered, as if he could read her mind. His words soothed her, and she took a deep breath and exhaled. She closed her eyes, feeling relieved he wasn't disappointed in her. A weight lifted from her shoulders. He had taught them so well and she knew better than to leave any evidence or links that would eventually put her or her family in harm's way. Ashton nodded and tried her best not to drop a tear.

She had gotten a blocked call from an unknown caller a few weeks before. The caller had simply left a message saying her father needed to see her immediately and gave her instructions on how to do so by using a fake name. A week later, Ashton had received an envelope with a fake ID, as well as a date and time to visit. Milo was a very powerful and resourceful man and had an expert-like skill to get things done, even if behind bars.

"How have you been?" Milo asked as he studied her face closely.

"I'm okay . . . I'm okay," she said, not wanting to tell him about all she had been through in Miami. She had just left there and had no plans of ever going back.

"Now, why do I have a feeling that you aren't being hon-est with me?"

"It's nothing that I can't figure out myself. How are you holding up?"

"I'm always good. I'm just reading a lot and working out. Trying to walk this time down," he answered, referring to the ten-year stretch that he had left. Once the feds had begun investigating him, they found a few more instances of blackmail that he'd facilitated. He had to take a plea to keep his other daughters' names clear. Ashton was the only one that was directly connected because of her small mistake. How-ever, he couldn't save her from the wrath of the feds. He felt responsible for sending his daughter to prison, even though it was her mental error that crumbled their operation. He im-mediately noticed that she seemed to be more hardened since the last time he had seen her. He knew that her prison stint had done that. He could only imagine the drastic changes that she had to go through. He had roots in Miami and word had gotten back to him about who she was associating with. The information that he'd received had him very concerned. He had made it very clear that he never wanted any of his daughters to come and see him while he was imprisoned. This was why he requested for her to come and see him.

"I see you got some grays since the last time I've seen you."

"That comes with the territory," Milo said as he rubbed his hand over his now short-cut, waved hair. He smiled, showing her his infamous smile, and that sight warmed her heart. "I wanted you to come here today because I've been hearing some things," Milo said, shifting the conversation to a more serious tone. Ashton's mind instantly began to turn, wondering what exactly her father was referring to. She had done so many things since she had been out, specifically in Miami. Her natural instincts prompted her to play dumb.

"What kind of things, Daddy?" she asked as her mind thought back to her Miami life.

"Baby girl, I changed your diapers. I was there at your first steps and I heard your first words. I know you like the back of my hand. I know when you're bullshitting me. I think you know exactly what I'm talking about," he said calmly.

She had a wild time in Miami and honestly didn't know where to start, so she froze, not knowing exactly how to answer him. So, she said nothing.

"You're playing with fire. You have no idea the history between our family and the one that you were mixing with. Don't think because I'm in here that I don't have my ear to the streets. Your father isn't as square as you might believe. I was a completely different person before we moved to Texas. It's a deep, embedded hate between the LaCroix and the Diamonds that spans back years. Things happened that you have no idea about. Things that I would never speak on. I'm going to say this once and once only. Stay away from the Diamond family."

"Yes, sir," Ashton said as she looked in the eyes of a man that she loved but also feared. She couldn't remember the last time that he had a stern tone with her, so she knew he meant business.

"That's my baby," Milo said as he slowly eased up and began to smile, lightening the mood. "How are your sisters? Have you spoken with them?"

"No, I haven't. You know how funny-acting they are. None of them have said a word to me since the incident.

Not a letter, a visit, or anything. I think they blame me for mama—"

"Don't say that," Milo said, cutting her off when she mentioned his wife.

"They just don't fuck with me, Daddy," Ashton said, being as blunt and direct as possible.

"Those are still your sisters. Nobody wins when the family is at odds. Remember that."

"I know, but . . ."

"There is no but. You have to go and make that right. I didn't raise you girls like that. We are all we got."

"Yes, sir," Ashton responded as she dropped her head. Just as her father was about to speak again, a guard yelled "time!" Milo looked back, then refocused on his daughter and smiled.

"I want you to know that I love you with all my heart and I always will. I'm sorry for everything that happened. I have to go, but please know that I think about all of you every single day, and one day, we will all be back together. I have to go now. I love you."

"I love you too, Daddy," Ashton said as she looked at her hero. She watched him smile and place the phone on the hook. He kissed his fingers and then touched the glass. Ashton smiled and watched her father exit the booth. His words hit home. Even though he was locked up, she felt obligated to follow his orders about reuniting with her sisters. Ashton left the prison and knew going back to Miami wasn't an option. So, just as her father requested, she would head back home to reunite with her sisters. She was unsure about how it would play out, but at that point, they were all she had.

CHAPTER 2

"Are you comfortable, Ms. LaCroix?" the driver asked. "Is the temperature okay? You need some music or a water? There's water if you need it. If you're thirsty."

His eyes found hers through the reflection of the rearview mirror and then bounced back to the road nervously. She was beautiful. A sequined emerald-green dress graced her body.

She marked him with her stare. "Silence would be nice."

Not one to mince words, Sutton LaCroix spoke what she felt. Annoyance. She was annoyed because the driver with wandering eyes was not only putting her life at risk, but he was also distracting her from her thoughts. Very important thoughts, indeed.

She pulled out her phone and pulled up the group chat with her sisters. She hit a button, tracking their locations to ensure they were in place. Three chauffeurs were a necessity. There was no bubbly being popped on the way, no girl talk and gossip, no fun to be had. This was business. Three drivers for the three sisters in case they had to get out fast and go their separate ways. Sutton always thought of every aspect of every situation. Every possible exit strategy was already mapped out inside her head. Anything that could go wrong had already been expected. "Expect everything, lose nothing" was what she told herself.

She opened her Chanel clutch and removed the diamond earrings that were inside. Her neck tensed as she held her breath, turning to the side to place each delicate stone in her ears. Gravel crunched beneath the tires of the car as it rolled to a stop. She released her breath then pulled out her compact, opening it to find her reflection was intact before snapping her bag closed as the door opened. She exited and lowered her gaze, smoothing the back of her short haircut down as she walked to the entrance. The cameras positioned above the door would catch the back of her head instead of her face; no recognizable markings were anywhere on her body. Tattoos. Piercings. Those were sure ways for a witness to identify someone; and although Sutton ensured that she would never be under anyone's lineup, precautions were necessary.

"Welcome to Techcon. Fingerprint please, right thumb."

The two men stood at the door, clad in black suits and white shirts. Off-rack, for sure. Sutton's eyes went to the devices that were positioned in their ears and then her gaze slid down to the 9mm standard-issue handguns that were half-hidden behind the suit jackets.

She smiled as she placed her thumb on the sensor.

"Melissa Stanford. Welcome," the man said. Sutton smiled and then proceeded into the dinner. She lifted a hand to the diamond earring on her right side and pressed the back.

"Two guards at the front," she said. The faux earrings

were genius. With a one-mile radius, she could communicate with her sisters with ease.

She grabbed a champagne flute from the tray of a server walking by and glanced back at the door.

"Honor, I said understated. That dress has everybody's eyes on you, bitch. What is it? Dior?" Sutton asked.

"Saint Laurent," Honor answered.

"I hope you spill something on it," Sutton snickered.

"Hating ass," Honor said, laughing. "You wanted me to distract his security, right?"

Sutton stood on the second-floor balcony, overlooking the main floor below.

"Oh, you're going to distract them alright," Sutton said. "Are you in?"

There was silence on the other end for a few seconds as Honor went through the security at the front.

"I'm in," Honor confirmed.

"Me too." The soft-spoken voice trembled a bit and Sutton frowned. She heard the nerves of her younger sister Luna.

"Fuck you nervous for? This was your idea. Get your head together. Nerves are the precursor to mistakes. Come on, Gadget. Get it the fuck together," Sutton hissed.

"Nobody's nervous. Shut up, Sutty," Luna barked back. "Everybody ain't a fucking sociopath. With your lack-of-emotions-having ass."

"Just be ready. We need you to get to the laptop. This damn dinner was $100,000 per plate. I want that list," Sutton whispered. "We'll let everybody get good and faded, we'll sit through dinner, and then we make our move. Honor, you're up."

Sutton watched as Honor took a seat at her table. It wasn't by chance that she was seated right next to the man of the hour.

Lathan Naples was a tech juggernaut. With the design of his new social app, Connexxxion, he was taking the industry by storm. Sutton had spent months vetting him. She knew everything about him, from his credit score to his mother's maiden name. Sutton could recite his social security number backward, and she had kept track of every single flight he had checked into during the past twelve months. No detail had gone unnoticed, down to his fetish for designer socks, which he wore tonight. Pink ones with green polka dots, a bad choice if Sutton had to say. She even knew the names of the two dogs he kept behind the gates of his Napa Valley mansion. A single man with no kids, he was one of the most eligible bachelors in the country.

Sutton smirked when she saw Honor introduce herself. He was taken at first glance. Most men were. Rarely did Honor give men the honor of gracing them with her attention, but she granted Lathan a gracious smile as he pulled out her chair for her. Her curves were hypnotizing, and her skin shimmered like sand under moonlight. Her femininity was admired by everyone at the table, but the contrast of the sleeve of art covering her left hand and forearm confused them. She was both good and bad, a paradox of morality, riding the line between what people assumed her to be and who she truly wanted to be. A bad bitch had just been seated at the table and everyone was in awe.

"She's a star," Luna said into the microphone.

"That she fucking is," Sutton whispered. She spun abruptly, headed to her table, and crashed right into one of the guests. Champagne spilled all over the man in front of her.

"I'm so sorry," she gasped. A passing server stopped immediately, and Sutton grabbed a cloth napkin off the tray. She pressed it into the fabric of the designer suit.

"It's fine," the man muttered, taking the napkin from her hands and wiping the drink from his lapel. "It'll give me a reason to break out of this shit early."

Sutton lifted her focus from the suit to the man. Her light brown eyes widened slightly as she stood upright, settling on him. The sternness in his crinkled brow made her heart wrench in alarm. Like she was in trouble with this man, like she had offended someone who was used to nothing less than high regard. The champagne to the fabric of the cranberry Dolce suit certainly was a bit disrespectful.

"Nice eyes," he said.

It was always what people noticed first. Skin the shade of tree bark, and eyes the color of autumn leaves, Sutton was stunning. Her eyes sparkled at first glance.

"So I've heard," she responded. "You can send me the bill for cleaning. If it's destroyed, my assistant can have it replaced."

Her eyes were on Honor and she smirked in satisfaction. Her sister was already charming the entire table. Sutton dropped her card in the front pocket of the man and then moved around him. He was a sight and Sutton's thoughts veered toward inappropriate as she bit her bottom lip, wondering if he tasted like almonds since his skin matched the color of them. His scent followed her as she walked away. She glanced back, wishing she could indulge in the bit of flavor he added to the otherwise bland guest list, but she wasn't

there to fraternize. Business required absolute concentra-
tion, especially in her line of work. She found her table and
took a seat as she anticipated the night's events. If all went as
planned, they would leave here with a bag.

• • •

"You're amazing. You're so beautiful. It's hard to focus on
anyone else in the room."

Honor LaCroix. Bad bitch. That bitch. Not his bitch, so the
hand on her thigh beneath the table annoyed her soul. His net
worth rang up like a cash register in her head, however, keeping
her patient and motivating the forced smile on her face.

"I'm glad you're enjoying the visual," she answered, voice
super sweet, extra sugar. "Everything is really beautifully done.
I can't wait to see the reveal of the next generation of your
company's flagship phone. It's a real game changer, I hear."

"You hear right," Lathan bragged. "We're cutting edge in
communication right now. The reveal tonight will be stunning."

Brag much? Honor thought, but her smile never slipped.

"You're such an innovator. Of course, I was a fan of the
product, but being lucky enough to be seated next to the man
himself, I'm even more impressed. I can't wait to see it."

It didn't matter the type of man, they all loved her stroke,
both dick and ego. Honor was the best at finessing men.
There was something about the way she fanned their flame
that made them crazy about her. She knew how to make
a man feel like a man. Lathan was so engaged that he had
turned sideways to face her direction, eyes solely on her as
one hand draped over the back of her chair.

She fingered the necklace on her neck, running her

thumb beneath the chain and causing the pendant to rise and fall against her cleavage. His eyes followed it.

"My mother gave it to me. It's made of amethyst." She leaned forward and lifted her neck, sweeping her hair over one shoulder to move it out of the way. "You want to see? It's really beautiful. Touch it."

Lathan reached for the necklace and Honor smiled. "It's perfection."

"It really is," she said as she stood to her feet. "Would you excuse me? I need to find the ladies' room."

The sway of her hips commanded his attention until she was out of sight.

"Got it," she said as she fingered the diamond earring. She pushed open the restroom door just as Luna was coming out, swapping the necklace without missing a beat.

• • •

Luna hurried to the elevator and pressed the number three. "Did you get a good print?" Luna asked.

"His hands were all over it," Honor answered. "Hurry and get the list so I can get the fuck out of here. He's disgusting."

Luna peeled off the thin layer of hospital-grade skin adhesive and then delicately laid it over her pointer finger. It was the same thing they'd used to get into the event under fake identities. According to the guest list, the LaCroix sisters were never there at all.

As the elevator doors opened, she slid out, discreetly moving down the hallway until she reached the double doors at the end. She pressed her thumb to the pad and waited until the digital lock turned green before pushing her way inside.

"I'm in," she reported.

"The laptop is there?" Sutton asked.

Luna rushed over to the desk. "It's here," she confirmed. She opened it and used the same fingerprint to access the machine.

"Download the list," Sutton said.

Luna inserted the flash drive she carried and then her fingers danced across the keyboard. "Working on it," Luna answered. "I just need a little time. He's keeping track of all the guests. Every single person who he fingerprints at the door pops up on this screen," Luna reported. "Their driver's licenses appear as soon as they enter."

"Just hurry," Sutton said. "Get me what I need before the speech starts. He's headed to the stage now."

Luna's fingers tapped the keys as she broke through the firewall, scanning the files that were supposed to be hidden in plain sight. To the average eye, they would have been un-detectable, but to the Carnegie Mellon top alum, the firewall stood no chance. She pulled up the list and began to upload it to her flash drive.

"Oh my God, Sutty, the names on this list . . ."

"I know," Sutton said. "I can only imagine. Pigs are com-fortable rolling among filth. Copy the list and the origin and then get out of there. I'm about to ruin this man's night."

• • •

Sutton arose from the table and her long legs carried her across the dance floor as she headed for her mark. Lathan Naples might have been a genius, but he was a monster as well. The vice of this rich man was about to make the LaCroix sisters even richer women. His app was becoming the most popular social media trend globally. It allowed people to communicate worldwide with just a touch of the purple icon on their phone screens. It was also built to facilitate anonymous groups for men who indulged in sex with children. The groups were invite only, and their only form of communication was conducted through Connexxxion. Their host was none other than Mr. Lathan Naples himself; and in about three minutes' time, the LaCroix sisters would have every single name and private direct message that had ever been sent within the group in their possession. The price for their discretion? Five million dollars . . . each.

Before she could make it across the room, she felt a tug to her fingertips as she was pulled in the opposite direction. Before she knew it, she was in the arms of the man in the nice, but now wet, suit. She looked at him through the skeptical slits of her eyes.

"When you move too fast, you might slip," he said. It wasn't what he said, but how he said it that made Sutton stay put. This was no ordinary guest. She noticed the tattoo under his shirt collar and then took in the ink on his hands as they held hers.

"I don't slip," she answered. "And I don't dance." She pulled away.

He pulled her back. "What do you do, then, Sutton LaCroix?"

She stopped, swaying. The card she had given him had her alias, not her government name. She was at a loss for words. How did he know? And more importantly, who was he?

"Don't worry, I keep secrets real well," he said. He left her in the middle of the dance floor as he moved around her. Sutton's eyes followed him, and he nodded in acknowledgment as he fell into a conversation with the city's mayor.

Oh, he's arrogant, she thought. She would have been amused had there not been so much at stake.

She turned her focus back to Lathan; but before she could take one step, Luna's voice filled her ear.

"We've got a problem."

Sutton turned and covered her mouth with her clutch as she held the earring to reply.

"Don't tell me that."

"The fingerprint scan at security just pulled up Ashton LaCroix," Luna informed her. "It pulled up her government and rap sheet. She's flagged by security."

"What?" Honor chimed in. "How is she here right now?"

Luna's eyes found the door and sure enough, their baby sister was walking into the building. She was stunning in a rose-gold gown that hugged her body like Saran Wrap and her hair was long and flowing in huge Hollywood glam curls. She was breathtaking and Sutton was both proud and enraged at the same damn time.

"It's off," Sutton said.

"What? We can still finish the play," Honor hissed.

"You know the rules. We control the environment. Ashton is a problem. Get out of there now. Meet me in the south bathroom."

Sutton's six-inch heels clicked across the marble floor as she made her way toward Ashton. She didn't stop to speak as she passed her, and Ashton didn't acknowledge her. They were like strangers passing in the night.

"Bathroom. South elevators. Now," Sutton whispered without missing a beat.

The crowd thinned as she navigated her way to the rest-rooms farthest from the ballroom. When she pushed her way inside, Honor and Luna were already waiting.

"What is she doing here?" Honor asked.

"I don't know," Sutton said, pinching her brow as she paced.

"Isn't she supposed to be in Miami?" Luna asked.

"I don't know," Sutton answered again. She was burning a hole in the floor. Back and forth. Forth and back. She couldn't wrap her mind around Ashton's reappearance.

"Is she working someone here? She has to have a mark. Who's her mark?" Luna asked.

"Damn it, I don't fucking know!" Sutton snapped.

The bathroom door opened and the 5′5″ beauty walked in, silencing them. Tension filled the room as Sutton, Luna, and Honor squared off with their youngest sibling.

"I swear if you weren't my sister, I'd be all over your ass right now," Honor said.

"Wow. That's how you greet family? I haven't seen you in years. I can't get a welcome home before you bite my head off?" Ashton asked.

"Ash, you just fucked up a whole bag! You picked the worst possible time to show up," Luna added.

"I'm working my own job. I'm not here to fuck anything up," Ashton said. "I'm just looking for a rich sucker to fill my time."

"Tired of chasing drug dealers in Miami? What? You fucked up down there and now you're here to bring bad luck on us?" Sutton asked.

"I'm not in the way. You can still do whatever it is you came here to do," Ashton defended.

"Only we can't," Sutton shot back. Sutton peeled off the silicone imprint that was over her thumb and flicked it at Ashton. "As soon as you scanned your goddamned thumb, your entire record came up. We're wearing fake prints. We were never here, but our fucking baby sister's name is on the guest list. They flagged you, Ashton! You're hot. You know the rules. If anything doesn't go as planned it's a done deal. You're a liability."

"Surprise, surprise, isn't she always?" Luna said, sighing. "I couldn't get the entire list to download before I had to get out of there. What are we going to do?"

"We're back at square one. The night we've been planning for the past twelve months is dead. Good job, Ashton," Honor said.

"What's the play, anyway? Maybe I can help. Who's the mark?"

"Lathan Naples. He's a pedophile with pedophile friends. Your grand entrance interrupted my download. There's a list of names that's worth cash money."

"You bitches and your high-tech-ass schemes. I can get the list. It don't take all that to get in a room with a man and his laptop. Throw the nigga some pussy and—"

"You've helped enough," Sutton answered. "We aren't running playground tricks, Ash. We're not throwing pussy at niggas for chump change. This isn't a hustle. It's a corporation. We fix shit."

"We break it first, though," Honor said as she leaned in to the mirror to refresh her lipstick.

"We create the problems then solve them," Sutton stated.

"For a fee," Luna added.

"I'm the CEO of a multimillion-dollar company. We're

good at what the fuck we do. We aren't winging it. Do me a favor and go home. We'll see you in the morning. If you're back, you need to know the rules."

Sutton stormed out of the restroom. Luna followed. Honor took her time completing her look before adjusting her breasts and doing a shimmy in the mirror. She smudged her lipstick and then turned to Ashton.

"See you at brunch, baby sis. Same time. Same place," Honor stated. Honor walked to the door and opened it. She paused. "Oh, and Ash?" Ash lifted misty eyes to her older sister.

"I'm glad you're home."

• • •

Ashton stood outside of the venue waiting impatiently. The dinner was long over and only the elite of the guest list remained inside. She shuffled anxiously as her glamorous dress swayed with every movement. She checked the time on her phone. "Great," she hissed. The drizzle of the unexpected rain turned a bad night into an unbearable one. She huffed and marched back toward the building. She was soaking wet by the time she made it to the grand foyer.

"Ma'am, the function is over. We can't let you back inside."

Ashton blew out a breath of exasperation. "You've got to be kidding me," she snapped. "It's pouring outside."

"I'm sorry, miss, it's protocol," the guard informed her.

"My driver left. There was some mix-up and he picked up the wrong passenger. I just need to wait for an Uber. It's ten minutes away," Ashton pleaded.

"Miss, if you don't leave, I'm going to have to have you escorted off the premises."

The sound of laughter echoed through the empty halls as a group of men sauntered toward the exit.

"Now, miss." The guard grabbed her forearm and Ashton resisted, pulling away. His aggressive tone garnered attention from the group.

"Hey, is everything okay out here?"

The man of the hour, Ashton thought. *About goddamn time.*

She had waited intentionally to catch him leaving. Strait-laced men couldn't help but play Captain Save-a-Ho when they saw a beautiful woman in distress.

"I'm just trying to wait somewhere dry for my Uber," Ashton said.

"Hey, man, let her go. That isn't necessary. It's fine," Lathan said.

Ashton was released and she gave Lathan a grateful smile. "Thank you. It should be here any minute."

Lathan stopped walking and let the rest of the men exit without him. "I have a minute. I can wait with you," Lathan offered.

"Thanks, but I'm really okay," Ashton replied.

"How about I wait anyway. Make sure this guy doesn't give you a hard time," Lathan answered.

Ashton nodded. "Okay."

"So what did you think of the app?" Lathan inquired.

"I think it's made by a bunch of Silicon Valley brats who have no idea how social media has cursed the human race. They don't have an ounce of personality, so they create these alternate digital realities to hide behind."

"Wow, that's . . ." Lathan paused and rubbed his smooth baby face. ". . . presumptuous, don't you think?"

Ashton shrugged. "Maybe, or maybe they jerk off to

pretty girls at their computers because they've immersed themselves behind screen names and JavaScript."

Lathan chuckled. "You're a tough critic. I didn't catch your name."

"Tracy," she said, extending her hand. "And you might be?"

"The Silicon Valley brat who created Connexxxion," he stated. "Lathan Naples."

Ashton winced and covered her face with both hands. "I just made a complete ass of myself," she groaned. "I'm so sorry." He laughed and lifted his hands in surrender.

"No apologies necessary," he replied. "Perhaps I have missed some time in the real world while creating this app."

"I feel like an asshole," she said, blushing.

"I've been called worse, trust me."

Ashton glanced at her phone and sighed in frustration. "Great," she muttered.

"Everything okay?"

"My Uber canceled," she said. She threw out the bait knowing he would bite.

"I have a car. My driver can take you wherever you'd like," Lathan offered.

"Oh no, I can't ask you to do that," Ashton stated. "I can call another Uber."

I insist, she thought, his next words running through her mind before he got a chance to even speak them.

"Don't be ridiculous. I insist," he said.

Doesn't matter if a man is black, white, or blue, they're predictable as shit, she thought. She smiled graciously.

"Really? It's not an inconvenience?" she asked.

"Not at all. A pleasure, in fact," he said. He walked out of the building, holding the door open for her before leading the way to his car. A suited driver stepped out of a black SUV and opened the back door for Lathan. Lathan paused to allow her to enter first. When they were safely inside, he said, "You wouldn't want to grab a bite to eat, would you?"

"Sure," she agreed.

"I have my laptop with me. I just need to stop by my suite and put it away. If that's okay with you," he said.

"That's fine," she agreed.

Ashton was a stunning girl. She knew it. She had always known it and she used her beauty to lower defenses effortlessly. By the time they arrived in his suite at the five-star hotel, she and Lathan were laughing like old friends.

"This dress is soaked. Do you mind if I borrow a shirt? Maybe we could eat in," Ashton suggested.

Lathan's laughter faded and the room filled with tension as Ashton slipped the straps to her dress down. She peeled the fabric down her body, revealing skin so brown it seemed edible. She was the color of brown sugar and she exposed herself unapologetically, letting the dress fall in a heap at her feet. The lingerie she wore beneath was perfection. Lathan swallowed the lump in his throat.

"Wow, I . . . wow," he stammered.

"Or you can eat out," she said, lifting one stiletto heel onto the couch.

Lathan loosened his tie and blew out a sharp breath. He rustled his hair.

"It's not JavaScript." Ashton smirked. "It's not hard at all. Just bend and lick. Come here."

Like she had a leash around his neck, he came toward her.

"Are you sure about this?" he asked.

"I was sure when we walked through the door," she answered.

Lathan kneeled and dove into her face-first.

Complicated isn't always best. A little pussy makes a man weak every time, Ashton thought as she palmed Lathan's head while he pleasured her.

He might have been a tech geek, but his tongue worked with the precision of a surgeon, bringing her to orgasm within minutes. A flash of guilt swept through her because she had someone who lived in her heart, but there was work to be done. Since she had sabotaged the lick her sisters were working on, she had to make up for it. Sex was a quick sell, so fuck it. A little trick always led to a treat.

"Why don't you come out of that suit? Get comfortable," Ashton said. She reached inside his jacket and pushed it back and off his shoulders. "I'll fix a nightcap."

She walked to the minibar and retrieved two glass tumblers. "These things are usually pretty limited," she said as she looked over her shoulder at him. He was stumbling, almost rushing out of his clothes.

Eager ass.

She unscrewed the top of a bottle of vodka and killed it. She would need it to work up her nerve. She hadn't fucked for profit ever. She was witty enough to outthink her mark, running game so well played that they never knew they had gotten defeated until she was long gone. She didn't have time for a long con, however. She needed to microwave this lick to get back in her sisters' good graces. So, pussy it was.

She pulled out two more small vodka bottles and poured one into a glass. She poured the other down the sink then filled the second glass with water.

He was eager. Sitting on the couch rubbing what she was sure were sweaty hands against his thighs and bouncing a bit on the cushions.

"Relax, Lathan, I don't bite." She smiled. "Unless you like that."

"This is unbelievable," he stammered. "Stuff like this doesn't happen to me. You're so beautiful."

Ashton straddled Lathan and he planted his hands beside him.

"You can touch me," she whispered. He awkwardly put his hands on her breasts.

Ashton smiled, handing him one of the glasses. "Okay, let's talk. Relax you a little. You're uptight," she said. "Where were you born? Were you born into the world of computers and nerds or do you come from humble beginnings?" she asked.

"I was born in South Dakota, actually," Lathan said as he took a gulp of the drink.

"Oh yeah? I have a college roommate from South Dakota. What parts?" Ashton asked.

"Aberdeen," he answered.

"Oh okay, my friend was from Sioux Falls," Ashton said. "Do you have siblings?"

"One sister, Emery," he said. "How about you?"

"Only child," she said. She took the water glass to the head and winced.

"It's strong right?" Lathan asked.

"Brutal," she replied. "Want another?"

"Hey, why not. Let's party like it's 1999, right?" Lathan asked.

Ashton chuckled. "Let's," she agreed. She walked back to

the minibar and poured one shot, one water. She drank the water down before even walking back to him.

"Wait for me," he said. She handed the glass over to him and he drank it without thinking twice.

"I think you're so smart," she gushed. "Like, computer science and coding and all that must be a heck of a challenge. It's all numbers, right?"

"And some other things," Lathan answered.

"I'm into numerology and astrology. I'm partial to the number seven. How about you? I can tell a lot about a man just by his favorite number," she said.

"Threes and zeros," Lathan answered, pointing at her. "Favorite numbers."

"Any particular reason why?" she asked. "That's very specific."

"My father's birthday is November thirtieth. He died on January thirtieth," Lathan answered. "So I always remember those days, you know? The number thirty is significant to me."

"Seven's my number," she said and moved closer to him. "You seem much more relaxed, Lathan," she said, smoothing his hair. She stared in his eyes. "So, how long is it going to take you to kiss me?"

"Can I?" he asked.

She would actually feel a bit of remorse if she didn't know who this man was and what he did behind the mask of social media. He went in for her lips and Ashton lifted her head. His lips landed on her neck.

"Lower," she instructed. He kissed the valley of her throat. "Lower," she repeated.

He palmed her breast and then took her nipple into his mouth.

She pulled a condom from her bra and handed it to him. He strapped up. She took little Lathan for the ride of his life. She over sexed him. Gave little Silicon Valley the orgasm of his life. He could barely keep his eyes open by the time she was done. Ashton showered and then slipped back into her dress. She scoffed as she looked down at him. He wouldn't wake up until morning and by then she would be long gone.

Ashton grabbed his laptop and sat down on the couch. His light snores told her the coast was clear and she opened the machine.

"Password reset," she said, clicking on the link.

Just as she suspected. The questions were cliché.

"City you were born in," she whispered. "Aberdeen." She typed the answer. What was casual conversation for Lathan had been intel for Ashton. He had given it to her effortlessly. She logged into his laptop with ease and then quickly accessed the dark web through his browser. She emailed herself the list of gentlemen her sisters had been after, then she closed the laptop and headed for the door.

She wouldn't walk into brunch empty-handed. She would prove her worth and show Sutton there was more than one way to skin a cat.

CHAPTER 3

"Somebody's hungover," Luna said as she pulled out a chair to the circular table, joining Sutton. The popular Sunday Brunch was filled with Houston's elite. The cowboy-themed event took place each week and the sisters never missed it. It was girls' day, a chance to reconnect, catch up, and put business aside to tap into their sisterhood.

"I finished an entire bottle of Brignac Brut solo last night," Sutton said. Oversized Chloé sunglasses hid the evidence of red, regretful eyes as she leaned her temple against her finger. "I haven't messed up a job in a long time. I'm meticulous about my shit. From start to finish, we plotted this thing out for months, again and again, and Ashton blows into town to tear it apart without thinking twice. I could kill her."

"Ashton has always been known to do things her own way," Luna said, shrugging. "Her way got Daddy locked up. There's no telling what she fucked up down in Miami or who followed her back here. She's here for a reason. She's running from something. I don't need her bringing whatever that is to our front doors."

"At least we weren't marked," Luna said. "We got out. No harm, no foul, but we need to go back to the drawing board to figure out how to get that list. A bitch spent hella bread anticipating that bag. I just bought a Bentley coupe. I need to replenish my bank account. If I had known this job would be a bust, I would have gotten something a little more modest."

Sutton chuckled. "Your black ass driving around in a Bentley coupe. You live for the stunt."

"You know it," Luna countered. She flagged down a waitress. "Can we get four lemon drop martinis?" She held up her Amex platinum card and the waitress swiped it from her fingers.

"Sugar rims as usual?" the waitress asked.

"You know it," Luna answered. The waitress walked away.

"You really think she's going to show?" Sutton asked.

"She wouldn't miss it. She lives to get under our skin. It's her birthright as the baby." Luna looked up and as if Ashton had been waiting for an introduction, she walked into the room. The LaCroix girls had always been beautiful and as Ashton and Honor entered together, the men in the room turned to admire them. Honor's size 18 body was full of curves and the spandex nude-colored dress hugged each one dangerously. She had always been a bigger girl, but her days in the gym and a little lipo in the right places had turned her into the thing fantasies were made of. She was beautiful and a whole lot of woman. Men ogled her every time she left the house. Even men who were seated with little metal bands around their ring fingers couldn't help but gawk at the sisters with wandering and unintentional eyes. They just shined. It wasn't just a physical beauty, which neither lacked, but they commanded a room. Their father had taught them to be as noticeable or as invisible as they needed to be depending on the predicament. This day, they had decided to be the center of attention.

"They seem to be getting along," Luna said, noticing the smiles and laughter floating between them.

"Ashton knows Honor is soft on her," Sutton said.

Luna reached across the table and grabbed Sutton's hand. She rubbed her thumb lovingly across Sutton's knuckle. "She's our sister. Some rules don't apply when it comes to her. It's okay to forgive her, Sutty. Daddy wouldn't want us to box her out."

Before Sutton could respond, Ashton and Honor were taking their seats.

"I'm surprised you showed up," Sutton said.

"I wouldn't miss an opportunity to see that glowering face, Sutty," Ashton said, sarcasm dripping from her tone. She rolled her eyes and pulled her cloth napkin from the table, setting it in her lap. "Hey, Gadget." The warm tone came out of nowhere and a huge smile broke across her face.

"Hey, Ash," Luna replied, blowing her baby sister a kiss. "I should be kicking ya' ass, but I'm a little happy to see you, so I'ma let that shit you pulled last night slide. How long have you been in town?"

"A week," Ashton answered.

"And you're just getting in touch with us?" Honor frowned as she reached for her cocktail.

"I've been getting settled. I wasn't avoiding you."

"And we just happened to be in the same place at the same time last night?" Luna was skeptical.

"Who was your mark?" Sutton asked, cutting the small talk.

"Straight to the point," Ashton scoffed. "I wouldn't expect anything less."

Sutton sat stone-faced and unmoved by Ashton's return to town. It was an unexpected and uninvited reunion.

Sutton's brow lifted in curiosity. "Well?" She had always been impatient.

"An athlete. An NFL prospect that went to school with Lathan Naples. He's entering the Draft this weekend and I thought I would get my hands on him before his name is called as the number-three pick. You know? Give him that real shooting-in-the-gym feel," Ashton replied. "Be real ride or die." She shrugged and smirked as Honor shook her head, laughing.

"This damn girl is so cutthroat and I love it," Honor said, snickering.

"I learned from the best," Ashton said. Honor held up her martini glass and acknowledged Ashton with a toast.

"We aren't out here fucking niggas for handbags," Sutton said. "Social media has changed the entire game, Ashton. These hoes are out here fucking and sucking to get a coach flight and get clout on a nigga Instagram. There is no real money in using pussy as currency. That's not what we do. That's not our end-game. I run a business. We run a multimillion-dollar company. We're publicly traded, Ashton. A lot of things have changed since you went to prison. You would know that if you had responded to any of my letters."

"Prison isn't a place where you hold on to what you

miss outside those walls, Sutty. I couldn't write you back. I couldn't call. I couldn't miss you guys. I couldn't even think of you. My family didn't exist as long as I was on the inside. You have no idea what I dealt with, what I've been through," Ashton argued.

"And I never plan to learn," Sutton said coldly, seeing the fire in Ashton's eyes. The emotion. It was that quality that was dangerous. Ashton couldn't turn it off. She made emotional decisions and took things personally. It led to errors every time and Sutton left no room for those. "We leave the tricks for the kids," she schooled. "This is a sophisticated hustle, not amateur hour."

"You want to explain to me how it works?" Ashton asked. "I'm all ears."

"We're problem solvers. Our company is a one-stop shop for investing, management, and public relations. Our clients are some of the richest in the world, and also the most problematic. When we see a solution to a PR nightmare, we handle it. We make sure our clients stay in the good graces of their beloved followers," Sutton explained.

"Only they have no idea that we're the ones who kick up dust for them in the first place," Luna said, leaning into the table and lowering her tone.

"Plant the mouse then sell the trap," Ashton said, scoffing. "Daddy taught me that when I was four years old."

"Daddy taught us all," Honor said.

"I just turned it into a business model," Sutton said. "So that I didn't have to see any more of my sisters taken away in handcuffs."

Ashton leaned in and pressed a coffin-shaped nail into

the table. "I want in," she said. "I want in so fucking bad my pussy's wet."

Honor spit out her drink mid-sip as she and Luna burst into laughter. She used her napkin to clean up her mess, but she was so amused that tears filled her eyes.

"I'm not bullshitting," Ashton said.

"You have a stake," Sutton said. "You're our sister, we'd never leave you out. What you don't have is a job at the company. You're a felon and you're a fucking liability. You'll sit back, be pretty, and collect the money that we make, but you won't be involved."

"Sutty, I'm ready. I'm just as capable of hitting corporate licks as I am of hitting street ones," Ashton said. "I just took down the fucking son of Carter Jones."

"It would have been more impressive if it was actually Carter Jones," Sutton responded, not even looking Ashton in her eyes. Her blasé attitude only angered Ashton. Sutton knew it. She didn't care. She was pushing buttons on purpose to prove Ashton wasn't ready for the big league.

"Sutty!" Ashton pleaded.

"My answer's no." The sisters paused as the waitress came back to the table.

"You ladies ready to place your orders?" she asked.

They took their time putting in their food preferences. Sutton could feel Ashton's eyes marking her. As soon as the waitress walked away, Ashton was back on it.

"I think you're going to let me in," Ashton said.

Sutton scoffed. "Is that right, baby sis? Hell would have to freeze over for me to let you get anywhere near this company."

Ashton reached for her jumbo Chanel bag and lifted the double flap. She pulled out her phone and AirDropped the file she had stolen from Lathan's laptop.

Sutton's phone buzzed on the table. Honor's and Luna's chimes went off next. The three grabbed their phones.

"What is this, Ash? It's redacted," Honor said.

"It's the list of names in the secret trafficking group on Lathan Naples's app. I have the file and I have pictures directly from his laptop," Ashton bragged. "Your little sophisticated con was cute. I took a more vintage approach. Guess whose method worked better?"

Sutton's nostrils flared and she scoffed. She hated to be one-upped. It didn't happen very often, but when it did, she was the sorest of losers.

"How do we know it's even real?" Sutton challenged.

"It's real," Luna confirmed. "I saw some of it before I had to get out of there. The file was too massive to download quickly. How did you get access to his laptop for that long?"

"I put him to sleep and then had my way. Sweet-talked him out of the answers to the security questions. I may not be high tech, but I'm good as fuck at the finesse."

"What does this list have to do with bringing you in?" Honor asked.

"She'll give us the original files if I put her on," Sutton answered.

"That's a bet!" Luna exclaimed.

"You don't decide," Sutton said. "I'm the oldest. Daddy left me in charge. It's my job to keep us safe. All of us, including you, Ash. You are not ready. What we do isn't for you."

"I'll play by your rules. I just want to get back right with my family, Sutty. You know I can't sit around and not earn my keep. Let me help."

Sutton took her time answering. She took her time doing everything. Even with her back against the wall, she never let another motherfucker in the world see her sweat. She sat there, one elbow resting on the table as she rubbed her fingers together in a balled fist. Her tell. She was irritated. She had been doing the same thing since she was a little girl and they knew it was only a matter of time before she exploded.

"Sutty—" Luna began to speak but Sutton opened her hand, putting it up to silence Luna.

"Fine, Ash," she said, conceding. "Make sure you get that hot pocket checked."

Sutton then smiled, stubbornly, as the tension melted from the table.

Honor snickered. "Bitch put that pussy on Lathan's little nerdy ass and voilà!" They laughed as Luna held up her glass.

"Daddy's girls," Luna said.

"Daddy's girls," they toasted.

Sutton knew she wouldn't be able to keep Ashton out of their family's business. She had a right to be involved. Her last name alone entitled her to a piece of the pie. Sutton didn't worry about any of her sisters the way she worried about Ashton. She was the baby. They were years apart in age. Ashton was almost like her child. Seeing her baby sister sent away to prison was what made Sutton incorporate their hustle. The LaCroix of the past had held court in the streets, starting with her uncle Matee and her father, Milo. Their family's name had been strong in every major city in the South, but war had brought them to their knees. With a dead uncle and a father in prison, Sutton couldn't let her sisters follow the same path. Thus, the family enterprise was born. They used their street instincts and focused on the corporate dollar. They were sharks at every table where they sat, and their beautiful faces only helped them lure in prey. Sutton told herself she would keep a close eye on Ashton and an even tighter rein on her. It was the only way to make sure everyone stayed safe.

The waitstaff arrived with four platters of food. It was more than they could ever eat. They had a tradition of ordering one of everything on the menu. They shared the food family-style as the music from the DJ relaxed them. The sisters were always the center of attention and as they turned their table into a party, their energy infected the room. It was like old times. Even after years of separation, the bond and love Sutton had for her sisters hadn't waned. She would go to war for them on any given day. She feared the day she would have to.

• • •

"Ms. LaCroix, I have Lathan Naples here for you."

Sutton's pen stopped and she looked up from the third-quarter financial report. "Put him in conference room B and buzz me again in twenty minutes," Sutton said.

It was strategy. The person made to wait always psychologically conceded. Anything past five minutes established a hierarchy. Sutton wanted it known who was in charge when she entered the room.

She spun in her executive leather chair, the back of it so high that it hid her from anyone entering the room. Downtown Houston was at her feet as she peered out of her floor-to-ceiling windows. Her office sat on the thirtieth floor. She had worked hard to get here. She had spent her twenties being ride or die for drug dealers while she finished her doctorate in business. In her thirties, she had turned on those same cheating-ass niggas and hit licks with her father. From bank jobs to stash houses to art galleries, any job they took on was executed to perfection. She built the LaCroix Group from the ground up, starting with rappers and socialites, hoping one day they could clean all their dirty money through a legit company. Then Ashton and their father were arrested. Their convictions made Sutton go harder, pulling her remaining sisters all the way into the real world and leaving the streets behind. At thirty-nine years old, she was at the top of her game. *Forbes* and *Black Enterprise* recognized her as the one to watch. She had never felt more accomplished. The only thing missing in her life was someone to share it with. She had always lived her life by rules. She had deemed men to be distractions. One bad heartbreak at eighteen years old had turned her off the idea of settling down. Dick and disloyalty, that was what she believed a man would bring, and they weren't worth her slowing down the pace of her success. Her business model was to never stay in one place too long, to always be able to leave anyone behind. Every three years, she and her sisters opened a new office in a new city to avoid extortion charges. Love didn't fit into that plan. A kid for damn sure didn't fit. The rules were in place for a reason, but as her fortieth birthday neared, she could suddenly hear her biological clock ticking. She couldn't help but wonder if she had made the right decisions. Being raised by her father had taught her resilience, making her strong, but she wondered if her lack of a mother had made her too strong. She lacked balance. The empathetic bone that women drew emotion from was absent in Sutton. Things the average woman dreamed about hadn't crossed her mind her entire life until now. She stood there contemplating her past until her assistant let her know her time was up. She grabbed the manila folder off her desk and strutted out of her office and down the hall. She passed Luna's office, stopping briefly to speak.

"You need backup in there?" Luna asked.

"No, I've got it. Get ready to blow a bag. You call our girl at Saks?"

Luna smiled. "She has the entire winter collection put up for us," Luna answered.

"And the SEP transfers are scheduled?" Sutton was the type to check then double-check to make sure no one missed a beat.

"Yes, ma'am. Four transfers into retirement investment accounts are scheduled to go out at 9:00 A.M., right after Lathan Naples wires the money," Luna stated.

"And Daddy's commissary?" Sutton asked.

"Taken care of."

Sutton smiled. "Let me go collect the bag, then."

She entered the conference room and walked around the long executive table. "Mr. Naples, so sorry to keep you waiting. I don't want you to think I don't value your time."

"I'm a very patient man, no worries," Lathan answered.

He was smug. Sutton liked the arrogant ones, the successful ones, the ones who had elevated so high up on the food chain that they never saw her coming. This would be fun.

She sat and crossed her legs, gripping the arms of the swivel chair. "I'd like to represent your company. I'm sure you did your research on the LaCroix Group. We offer a range of services that could be beneficial to you."

"I have done some research. Your accomplishments are

well noted but I have people in position in-house who are on salary to provide me with the same services you offer."

"Those people aren't comparable to what I offer," Sutton answered.

"My CFO is a graduate of Stanford Business School. My head of publicity graduated *summa cum laude* from Howard. They're diverse, bright, and the best," Lathan bragged. "It's why I hired them."

Sutton scoffed and folded her hands in her lap. "Lathan, I'm going to keep this brief. You have a brilliant mind. Your app is genius. It's the new Facebook, but you have a PR problem," she answered.

"I have no such thing," Lathan countered.

"Are you sure?" Sutton asked. She stood and walked to the window that faced the rest of the office. She pulled the string that closed the blinds and then walked back to her seat, picking up the remote control in the middle of the table. She pointed it at the 80-inch screen at the head of the table.

PLAY.

"Harlan Imes, Vincent St. James, Oscar Dockbright, Merlin Rockefeller, Dalton Hilton," she said, reading from a list of names, his list of names. "Shall I continue?"

Lathan was visibly unnerved.

"I don't know the significance of those names," he said, trying to play it cool. "But if you're done wasting my time . . ." He stood and Sutton did as well, putting both hands on the table as she leaned forward.

"Sit down, Lathan," she said. "I have all twelve hundred thirty names of elite gentlemen around the country who belong to your secret group on Connexxxion. A group that traffics underage boys and girls for sexual enjoyment."

"I have no idea what you're talking about. My app is a social media platform. I'm not responsible for the groups formed within its constructs."

Sutton sighed and pressed another button. The images on the screen caused his eyes to bulge. "She can't be a day over thirteen years old."

She enjoyed his panic. The terror that flashed in his eyes equated to dollar signs for her.

"Th-this is extortion," Lathan stammered.

"This is business," Sutton stated. "Now take a seat." They both lowered into their chairs. "Right now, I'm the only person who has seen this. Well, and that pretty little piece of pussy you let into your hotel room last night," Sutton said.

She saw the regret streak through him.

"Like I said, you're in need of new PR," she said. "You're not here to determine if you're going to hire the LaCroix Group. You're here to discuss how much you're going to pay for our services. We were hired the moment we got our hands on this list."

"How much do you want?" Lathan asked.

"A twenty-million-dollar deposit and a one percent stake in the app," Sutton said. Most would have gotten greedy and asked for more, but Sutton understood the valuation of Lathan's company would only continue to grow and that one percent was worth more than any cash payoff.

"That's absurd!" Lathan protested, swiping his hand over his head.

"Look at it like this. It's twenty million or twenty years in a federal penitentiary and your face plastered all over the news. I'm sure your buddies on this list would hate to be exposed. There are some powerful names here. I'm almost certain they would see you as a loose end should you be put on trial for this . . ."

"I can explain. This isn't what it looks like," Lathan hissed.

"Less explanation, more cooperation, Mr. Naples," Sutton said, flipping over the manila folder and removing a piece of paper. She slid it across the table. "If you'll sign the agreement and get your superb team on the phone to wire over my money, we can conclude this meeting. I'll have my attorney fax over a nondisclosure so you feel confident that your little secret is safe with me."

"What about the girl from last night? She knows. How can you guarantee that she won't expose the information?" Lathan asked.

"Because *she* is a partner in this firm."

Lathan turned toward the door as Ashton walked in. When he realized he had been set up, his eyes pricked with tears.

"I believe you're well acquainted with my sister, Ashton LaCroix," Sutton introduced.

"You told me your name was Tracy," Lathan said.

"And you told me you were a good guy. Turns out you're an asshole pedophile who deserves a bullet between the eyes. You're lucky that's not the route I decided to take. Pay up."

Lathan signed the document, writing so hard he tore through the paper.

"Now make the call," Sutton said, nodding to the phone in the middle of the conference table.

Within twenty minutes, the transfer was in. As Lathan exited the room, Sutton stopped him. "Oh, and Mr. Naples?"

He turned to her.

"Shut down the group immediately," Sutton ordered. He pushed out of the door, enraged.

"Redact Lathan's name from the list and send it to the Federal Bureau of Investigation," Sutton said to Ashton.

"But he just paid for our secrecy," Ashton said, shocked.

"He did, the rest of them didn't," Sutton answered. "They're fucking disgusting. Send it immediately and then meet me in your new office. We've got some decorating to do." Sutton's high heels clicked against the floor as she made her exit. "Welcome to the LaCroix Group, baby sis."

CHAPTER 4

It was midday and the sun beamed down on the surface of the oil rig, which was owned and controlled by Sinclair Enterprises. It sat in the middle of the ocean and the beautiful blue water just below them was a sight to see. The state-of-the-art rig stretched just over four hundred feet, about the size of two football fields. Six people had just gotten out of a helicopter and walked onto the platform. They all were wearing professional attire and had clipboards in hand, all except the two men who led the bunch. All wore yellow hard hats and they followed the gentlemen as they explained the sophisticated logistics of their operation. The two men out front were father-and-son duo West and August Sinclair Sr. One wouldn't guess them to be father and son because of the shades of their skin; however, blood wouldn't have made them any closer. West Sinclair was a thirty-something-year-old black man, and his father, August Sinclair Sr., who everyone simply called "Senior," was a tall, slim Caucasian man with long legs and a diamond-encrusted belt buckle that glistened in the light. His full beard was snow white and his teeth matched the shade. His eyes were deep-sea blue and his voice was deep, textured, and even. West and Senior led the way, taking their time while giving the group a mandatory tour. Both West and Senior wore snakeskin cowboy boots with spurs, a Texas staple that symbolized wealth. They both wore big straw hats as well, rounding out their cowboy look.

As they moved about the rig, the group of people held clipboards while making observations and jotting down notes. West wore Wrangler jeans with a dress shirt; his sleeves were rolled up as he described the daily routine of their workers. Senior was letting his adopted son lead the conversation. West expertly broke down the logistics of the company's operation, making sure he covered every possible regulation and assuring them their rig was run with care and up to code.

"We run maintenance on all of our machinery once a week to ensure safety," West said as he tipped his hard hat to a maintenance worker who was on a ladder tending to a lift.

"That's right. Here at Sinclair, we make sure employee safety is our top priority," Senior added as he stopped and turned to face the group of inspectors that trailed him. Just as West was about to follow up about their new lighting systems, the sound of loud music sounded. Also, the roaring of an oncoming speedboat engine filled the air. All eyes went toward the water as the shiny, sleek watercraft sliced through the water, causing a steady splash. The logo SE was on the side of the speedboat, making it crystal clear who the boat belonged to. Senior's biological son, August, drove the boat.

He was shirtless, belligerent, and loud, splashing a big wave of ocean water onto the platform as he whipped next to it recklessly. He almost crashed the boat into the rig but missed it by only inches.

The speakers blared Pop Smoke and a half dozen girls danced and twerked their asses to the beat. Another girl held a bottle of champagne to August's mouth and poured it down his throat as he gripped the steering wheel. Instantly the inspectors all looked at each other, growing confused. The expression on Senior's face told a thousand words. His naturally pale face turned plum red and his insides boiled at the sight of his drunken son. He was instantly embarrassed and ashamed. West noticed his father's rage, although he remained expressionless. He knew him well enough to know that his fire was going on his insides and quickly moved to try to rectify and calm the situation. He leaned into his father and put his lips near Senior's right ear.

"I got it, Pops." West patted him on the back.

Senior clenched his jaw tightly and shot a look to his son. He wanted to say something to him, but he understood it wasn't the right time. He just plastered a fake smile on his face and looked at the inspectors.

"Let me direct you guys over here to the new drills we had installed," Senior said as he pointed toward the southern part of the rig, which was opposite of where August was. West gave the group a huge smile and spoke.

"Pardon me for a sec." He removed his cowboy hat and placed it on his chest. As he watched the crowd move away, West's smile slowly became a frown. He spun on the spurs of his heels and beelined directly to August, who was drinking champagne as he looked down at the young, sexy, ebony girl twerking on him. He watched her ass wobble on his pelvis area. Her big cheeks shook, waves traveling through her ass like a tsunami.

"Aye! Aye! Aye!" the group yelled in unison as they cheered the girl on. West walked briskly over to the edge of the dock and looked over his shoulder to the inspectors to make sure they were out of earshot.

"What the fuck are you doing, bro?" West said under his breath and harshly as his face frowned in displeasure.

"Bro! What's good?" he asked as he briefly took his eyes off the fat ass in front of him.

"Why in the fuck would you pull up to the rig like this?" West hopped onto the boat and stepped in August's face. The girls immediately stopped dancing. He then reached past August to push the boat speaker's off button, causing the music to die.

"Chill the fuck out, bro. I just needed some gas and decided to pull up," August said with a dumb-looking smile across his mug. West shook his head in disappointment as he realized August was wasted.

"You have to move smarter. This ain't it, kid," West said as he shook his head and stepped off the boat, back onto the rig.

"Man, you sound like the old man. You gotta relax."

"No, nigga, you relax!" West said, raising his voice, getting totally out of character. He'd temporarily reverted to his true origins. He was decades removed from anything street, but at times it came out. It was very rare, but when it happened, August knew he was dead serious.

West noticed himself getting loud and looked around

as he clenched his teeth, so much so that his jawline muscles were on display. He gathered his composure and cleared his throat. In a lowered tone, he added, "We are running a billion-dollar company and you try to find a way to sabotage it every chance you get. You gotta tighten up."

August had just popped a few pills, so he wasn't listening to anything West was saying. His mind was on that ass that was a few feet away from him.

"A'ight, man. I hear you," August replied to appease his adopted brother.

West looked over at one of the workers and stuck two fingers in his mouth, whistling to get their attention. When the worker looked, West put up one finger, signaling the sign for gas. The worker instantly headed to fetch the rolling gas pump that could supply enough gas for the speedboat to make it back to shore. West put his hands on his belt buckle and shook his head at his careless brother. The rig worker approached the edge and began to prep the rolling gas station to fill the speedboat.

West looked over at August and talked in a low tone. "Get out of here before you cost us a violation. I'll be by later this evening," West said quickly.

"A'ight, bet," August said just before he took a huge swallow of champagne. West walked away, leaving them at the edge, and headed toward his father who had continued giving their visitors a tour.

．．．

The sun was just setting against the purplish and orange-hued sky. The view from the downtown Houston condo provided a perfect skyline of the city. The glass front provided no privacy for the people inside. However, they didn't care who watched. In the middle of the studio-styled layout was a king-sized bed. An ebony woman with a huge ass slowly rode August's face. Her thick legs and thighs were spread and his mouth lined up perfectly with her love box. His hands rested on her cheeks, massaging them as she waved her body in a snakelike motion. Her short hair was cut in a Caesar style and her baby hair rested perfectly along the edges of her hairline. She looked like a chocolate version of Betty Boop with her big, full lips that were painted in red lipstick, and her big, fluffy eyelashes stuck out an inch from her eyelids.

She moaned as she moved her hips in circular motions, ferociously grinding against August's pale face. It was the same girl from the boat earlier that day, but she was the one driving this go-around. She motorboated his face as he licked away. A petite-framed Latina woman was giving him oral while massaging his sack. She used her free hand to please herself as she rested her body against his thigh. They were all in unison as soft moans and slurping sounds filled the spacious high-rise. As the Latina girl took August in and out of her mouth, she looked up at the big, chocolate cheeks grinding and she rubbed them, following it up with a firm smack. An echoing slap sound resonated. This made the ebony girl moan in pleasure and subsequently turned her on even more.

As their threesome was underway, they were so tuned in to the sexual acts that they didn't see the man walk into the middle of the room. It was West. He looked away, not wanting to see what was going on. He let himself in because he had a spare key to his brother's spot. He didn't know he would be walking into a full-fledged orgy.

"Okay, that's enough," West said as he turned his back to the action and stared out of the window onto the city's horizon.

"Agh!" the ebony girl yelled as she hopped off August and covered herself with the bedsheet. The other girl shrieked as well and jumped in terror. August sat up in confusion and saw his unwanted visitor turned away from them. He still had the woman's nectar dripping from his mouth as he frowned, trying to figure out what was going on.

"What the fuck, bro?" August yelled as he threw his hands up.

"Young ladies, it's time to go. Sorry to interrupt." West turned around and waved toward the door. Both girls looked at August and tried to make sense of what was going on. He quickly backed his brother.

"You heard him. Get lost." August stood buck-ass naked and walked across the floor, heading toward the bathroom. He didn't have a care in the world and let his Johnson swing freely. He didn't put up a fight because he knew exactly why West was there. The stunt he'd pulled earlier was the reason, because West never visited the condo.

West didn't say a word, waiting patiently for the women to get dressed and leave before he addressed the situation. He followed them to the door and opened it for them, nodding to them as they exited like the true gentleman he was. As soon as he closed the door behind them, he barged directly to the shower where August was. His brother stood under the running water with his hand resting against the wall, letting the water cascade down his body.

"What the fuck were you thinking, man? That had to be

the dumbest shit you've ever done and with your track record . . . that says a whole fucking lot."

"I know, West. I know," August said as he shook his head in guilt.

"'I know,' my ass. Do you know I had to promise the head inspector a million-dollar donation to his wife's charity just for him to overlook your bullshit? Huh?"

"I fucked up," August admitted. He turned off the water and looked at West. West grabbed a towel and threw it at August's head before he walked into the living room. August followed while wrapping the towel around his waist. "I was drunk as shit," August revealed.

"And high! I saw that shit in your eyes. Your pupils were big as pennies. Who the fuck drinks and gets high before noon?" West asked, shaking his head in disbelief, trying to make sense of August's stupidity.

"Did you see that bitch's ass?" August imaginatively outlined the girl's hourglass shape with both hands. He tried to make light of the situation to ease the tension. He ended it by playfully humping the air. West couldn't help but crack a smile and they both burst out laughing.

"Pops is hot though, bro. You have to move smarter. You are making the family business look bad. This isn't some mom-and-pop operation that you can just play with. This oil business is a multibillion-dollar industry and Sinclair Enterprises is at the top of it. You have to think before you act sometimes, bruh," West said in a concerned tone, rather than one of condescension.

"I know. I know. I'll go and talk to Pops in the morning and smooth shit over," August said, not being new to having to clean up a mess that he had made.

"Good, because he's on fire, you hear me?" West said as he walked over to the china cabinet that was in the corner of the flat. West began to pull out a small glass and then poured himself a glass of Scotch. August slipped on a pair of slacks and began to think about things other than his fuckup.

"Yo, you going to New York this weekend?" August asked as he buttoned up his shirt. He assumed West would be there considering his brother had a few athletes under contract who were projected to go in the first round of the NFL Draft.

"Yeah, I'll be there. The Lions have been blowing my phone up, saying that they might move up to get Jay," West said, referring to his quarterback client who was projected to go between the fifth and seventh pick.

"That fucker has a cannon for an arm," August said as he put gel in his blond hair.

"Yeah, he does. He just has to stay healthy and make it to that second contract. That's where the real money is." West finished up his drink and set his cup down, pointing at his brother as he headed toward the exit. "Make sure you clean up that shit with Pops. That million-dollar donation has him tight. And check on Ma too. She asked about you this morning."

A sports agency was one of his many business ventures and he was one of the very few African Americans who was head of a reputable one. Although August knew his brother hated going to public functions where there would be a lot of sack-chasing women and younger crowds, West understood it was a necessity for acquiring future clients. He was getting money at the highest level on many fronts, and representing athletes and negotiating their deals was one of them.

"Love you, bro," West said as he disappeared into the

hallway, leaving August there alone. August began to think about how he would turn up in New York too. So in August Sinclair fashion, he pulled out his phone, planting the seeds for any groupies he might have on the East Coast. He instantly opened his Instagram account and prepared to go live. He put up the camera and pointed it back at himself for the best possible angle. He waited for a few seconds before he spoke to let his followers join in first. He patiently watched the numbers climb by the second. He had over a million followers and a strong social media presence. He didn't do anything to be famous . . . he just was. All the socialites and entertainers followed him because of his extravagant lifestyle and his willingness to show it.

"Okay. . . . A'ight, so look. New York this weekend. I'm looking for a few of the sexiest ladies in the city to jump on the Private with me. What up?"

"What up, RiRi?" August said as he saw a famous female singer had logged on and watched along with the others. The pop star sent him a heart eyes emoji in the comments for everyone to see. August grabbed his other phone and began to shuffle through his playlist, finding one of the singer's latest songs. He pressed play and made it sound on his Bluetooth speaker while playfully swaying back and forth. He was vibing to her new popular song. In return, his viewership climbed and climbed rapidly. Before he knew it, many celebrities and influencers were giving him shout-outs in the comments and cheering him on as they all listened and watched him. He made his way to his dresser drawer and opened it up, exposing rubber band–wrapped money in neat stacks completely filling the drawer. He pulled out a stack of all hundreds and placed it to his ear boastfully. This continued for the next few minutes as he played more songs, getting a text from the singer with a link to some unreleased tracks. She'd asked him to play snippets on his live and August was doing just that. She knew his influence would get the buzz going for her upcoming album. She used August's influence for her album awareness. This was something money couldn't buy. It worked like a charm because everyone was tuned in to see what new music was on the way.

"Who wanna go to New York with me this weekend? Let me know. Share this video . . . tag me. Let's go." He burst into playful laughter, tossing the money into the air. The bills slowly fell like snow onto his condo's floor. He looked at his viewers and over a half million people were tuned in. He logged off and began putting his plans into motion for the weekend in New York. He was about to make it legendary.

. . .

"You see this shit?" Luna asked as she held up the phone, showing August on his social media as he flaunted money. He had just gone live and invited random girls to go to New York with him. The girls were at the LaCroix Group offices preparing to head out for the day and Gadget had stumbled across something interesting. August Sinclair. Luna always stayed on top of who and what was trending; and since she saw this man trending once again, she logged on to see what he was talking about.

"Look at this white boy's numbers," Honor said as she watched them climb by tens of thousands by the second.

Honor stared at Luna's phone screen. "Who is that?"

"August Sinclair."

"He's playing that new RiRi record and people are going

crazy. Look, it's almost at a million viewers." Honor held her phone up and pointed to the corner of the screen where the view count was displayed.

"What does he do?" Sutton asked, loading up her brief-case to end the day. She stood behind her desk as her other sisters were visually invested in August's live feed.

"That's the thing. No one knows. He just flashes money, yachts, and jets on a daily basis," Honor said, trying to best describe the lure of his popularity. "He's always in pictures with the Kardashians in Calabasas. Plus, he is always front row at all the nationally televised Lakers games."

"Those fifty-thousand-dollar seats?" Sutton asked, getting more and more interested by the second. She didn't like to not be in the loop of the movers and shakers of the entertainment industry. She knew celebrity row was a great place to get clients, referring to the Lakers' courtside seats.

"Yep, he's there every time, front and center where the cameras can see him," Honor confirmed.

"Gadget, who is this guy? Look . . ." Sutton said. How-ever, Gadget had already popped open her laptop and begun to type. She cut her sister off, already knowing what was go-ing on.

"I'm on it, sis. Okay . . . here he is." Gadget slightly turned her screen so her two other sisters could see. "His name is August Sinclair. Heir to August Sinclair Sr., who is CEO of Sinclair Enterprises. Which is—"

"The biggest oil rig in Texas," Sutton interjected as her ears perked. She walked around her desk, her eyes glued to Gadget's computer screen. She knew immediately what com-pany Gadget was referring to when she heard the name. This was a company she'd had on her radar for years but never had too much intel about them. Sinclair was a tight-knit, family-owned company no one knew too much about, other than the Sinclairs were one of the wealthiest families in Texas. Her mind instantly began to spin and work overtime, seeing a possible entry point for their firm. A client like this was what firms aspired to get. Sutton understood the chess move of acquiring a client of that magnitude, not only for the potential business, but also for the future acquisitions of more big-name companies.

"It says here that he has a net worth of two point four billion dollars, just himself alone," she added.

"Oh yeah," Sutton said as she began to ponder the possibilities. "Where did he say he was going this weekend?"

"New York," Honor answered while smiling, already knowing what her sister was thinking.

Sutton smirked and ran her tongue across her teeth. "Gadget, get a full profile on this guy. I want to know everything about him. Where he banks, where he eats, where he fucks, and who he's fucking. I need to understand what type of person he is and what are his vices. This is our way into Sinclair Enterprises, ladies." Sutton leaned back on her desk and crossed her arms. She was already orchestrating a plan inside her mind.

"I'm on it." Gadget started to type away, beginning her intel. Her first task was to search the black market and get his financial records to understand how much he really had in the bank. After that, she would create a virtual paper trail and take a full analysis of his spending patterns. This would allow them to understand him more as a person. Gadget would deep dive into August's life and by the end of it, they would know and understand him better than he knew himself.

"Guess we are going to New York this weekend?" Honor asked as she smiled. Sutton looked over at Honor and winked, confirming their next target.

CHAPTER 5

"Tell me again why we didn't rent a PJ?" Honor asked as she sat in the airport terminal, legs crossed, with her eyes glued to her phone.

"Because niggas who rent private jets eventually work at Walmart when they hit fifty-five because they did stupid shit with their bread when they were young," Sutton said.

"Ha!" Luna shouted in laughter. "The fucking accuracy."

"First class will have to do, dear sister," Sutton said, smiling as she shook her head. Honor had always been high maintenance. Thanks to their father, she had been introduced to Louis Vuitton at three years old; by twelve, she was carrying her first Chanel. Only the best for his girls. Sutton had always preferred the money over the gifts. Five thousand dollars on a handbag or five racks in her bank account? Even as a kid, she saw the value in a dollar. She liked to see her money sit and collect interest. The dividends excited her more than the attention of a luxury bag. Those habits had followed her into adulthood. And now, she had both.

The girls giggled as Sutton lifted her wrist to check the time. "Where is this girl? We're about to board." She looked around the crowded airport. Ashton was late. "Call her and see where she is."

Luna placed the call and hung up seconds later. "Her phone is going straight to voicemail."

"Attention passengers on Flight 732 headed for New York, we are now boarding our first-class passengers."

Sutton stood and grabbed her carry-on. "I guess she's not coming. One thing about Ashton, she never misses the chance to disappoint."

Honor shrugged and Luna stood speechless as they made their way onto the flight.

. . .

Ashton rushed through the airport, dodging the other travelers around her as she made her way to her gate. "Please be delayed, please be delayed," she whispered. She knew if she didn't make it to New York, she would only be proving Sutton right. Her sisters already thought she was unreliable. She would never live this down. Her thigh-high stiletto boots clicked against the tiled floor as she approached gate D12.

"Wait! Wait! My sisters are on that plane!" she screamed as the gate worker went to close the door.

"I'm sorry, the boarding door to the aircraft is closed," the woman said.

"But it hasn't taken off yet. I'm right here. Please don't let this plane take off without me on it," Ashton said, pleading because the last thing she wanted was to be at odds with Sutton again.

"Once the aircraft has been sealed, we can't open it. It's above my pay grade, ma'am."

"Don't 'ma'am' me," Ashton said, rolling her eyes. "When is the next flight out to New York?"

"Not until the morning," the woman said. She typed on the keyboard of the computer that sat in front of her. "All of our remaining flights are in a sold-out situation. We have a flight that departs at six fifteen A.M."

"But nothing tonight? I won't need to be there by then. I have a family emergency. I need to be in Manhattan tonight."

"Ma'am—"

"Bitch, I'm twenty-one! If you say 'ma'am' one more time . . ." Ashton swept her hair out of her face in frustration as she snatched her plane ticket from the counter. When she turned, she bumped right into the man behind her.

"You'd get more bees with honey, I'd think. The black girl thing with the attitude and the loud shit is a little overdone. You need a new act, baby." The man didn't even glance up from his phone. A white boy with blond hair swept over, tattoos covering his neck and hands. The diamond necklace he wore rested on his crisp white button-down shirt. He was neat—not businessman neat, but rock star neat, like he had been tailored specifically for an event but was a little uncomfortable in the fitted slacks and thousand-dollar shoes. It took seconds for her to take all of him in. He was handsome, striking even, with model looks wrapped in the shell of a bad boy.

"And the 'white boy trying to be down' thing is lame as fuck. Mind your business with your appropriating ass." The entourage that flocked the man all took pause, like someone had scratched a record. They waited for him to react but all he did was caress his unkempt beard.

"You want to let me by?" she asked.

He snickered. "Sure thing, angry black woman." The tension melted as she passed.

"Thanks, privileged white man," she shot back. Ashton found her way to the bar and set down her bag in the chair beside her, sighing in exasperation. She dug through her things until she retrieved her phone's charger and then searched for outlet. She already knew her sisters were going crazy wondering where she was. When her phone finally powered on, she had six missed text messages. She could tell from Sutton's tone that she was pissed. There was no point in responding. Her sisters were in flight.

"I just need to get there," she mumbled. She opened her browser and began searching for flights. The sound of laughter filtered into the restaurant and Ashton looked up as the white boy walked inside with his entourage behind him. The gushing the four women were doing was so over the top that Ashton rolled her eyes as she turned her swivel chair back to the bar. She didn't miss the guy who accompanied the group, however. The mountain of testosterone was the color of tree bark and his presence seemed to shade the room. She felt a chill run down her spine. Some men just exuded power. The white boy looked like money, but the handsome gentleman who swaggered in behind him, scrolling through his phone without acknowledging those around him, looked like the boss. If Ashton's heart weren't wrapped up in the past, she would want to fuck him. He was just that type of man. The kind you knew could take your panties off as soon as he entered a room. The ping of her cell phone pulled her attention. Honor had connected to Wi-Fi, and the blue iMessage came through as soon as they reached cruising altitude.

Honor

I don't know how you let yourself miss this flight, but you better get to NYC. I'm not trying to hear Sutty's mouth this entire trip. Don't flake Ash.

Before she could type a response, the bartender walked over with a drink in hand. She set down a napkin before placing the glass on top.

"I didn't order this," Ashton said.

"From the cute white guy in the corner," the woman said. Ashton smirked. She didn't even turn to acknowledge him. She knew he wanted attention. Just by the number of women around him, she could tell he was used to commanding it.

Probably some kind of trust-fund brat, Ashton thought. There was nothing worse than an entitled man who wasn't used to working for anything. It took more than an apology drink to spark her interest.

Just as she expected, he came right over, placing one hand on the bar top and the other on the back of her chair, turning it so she faced him.

"Why you look so mean?" he asked.

"*Oh my God,*" she sighed to herself, pinching the bridge of her nose and then rolling eyes in frustration up at him. She chuckled. "Which of your black friends taught you that line, homeboy?"

He laughed. "You're funny. Stranded, but you are funny. Maybe you can set up in the corner and do a bit since you'll be here for a while."

"Ha ha," she said. "You see I'm having the worst day ever. Why don't you just leave me alone?"

He shrugged. "Fine. I got a jet waiting to take you to New York, but cool, stay here with your mean ass," he said.

He took one step back toward his seat before Ashton stopped him.

"And what exactly do you expect me to give you for the ride?" she asked.

He rustled his hair and his brow wrinkled as his eyes sparkled in amusement. "Who knows? Maybe you'll give me a ride one day."

Ashton laughed. "Now that's a line, white boy!"

He nodded. "Yeah? You like that one?"

They shared a laugh and he held out his hand. "I'm August," he introduced himself.

"Ashton." She shook his hand, wishing she could have given him an alias. There was no boarding a flight without giving the pilot a manifest. She had no choice but to give him her government name if she wanted to make it to New York.

"Ashton? You sure? That attitude is giving me more Keisha vibes," he stated.

Ashton hollered in laughter. "That's so racist!"

"No more racist than you calling me white boy," he shot back. "Enjoy your drink, beautiful. Wheels up in thirty."

Ashton turned toward the bar. "White boy got money and game," she whispered to herself, halfway impressed. She peered over her shoulder at the group, taking one more glance as she wondered who fate had placed in her lap.

• • •

Sutton's car pulled up to the five-star hotel and she looked up at the skyscraper of a hotel, stepping out onto the filthy streets. Luxury heels on pissy pavement was such an oxy-moron. She hated the big city. New York's pretentious aura clouded the air. She had been there many times and there was just something about the place that turned her sour. The Southern belle was used to a certain amount of hospitality. The city was full of culture but lacked the charm she was used to.

She looked back at the two additional cars that were pulling up behind hers. While the sisters always rode apart, this time, it was due to the excessive amount of luggage they carried.

Dripping in designer so subtle it could have easily come from the swap meet, Honor and Luna emerged from their cars. High fashion and diamonds draped their bodies. It was clear that these weren't groupies breezing into town. They were about their business, ready to mingle with the elite.

"Do we have access to the Draft?" Luna asked as the hotel's automatic glass doors opened to let them inside.

"No, but we have access to the after-party," Honor said. "I called in some favors. We're on the list."

They bypassed the front desk and approached the con-cierge. Keys were already waiting to four executive suites on the top floor with city views. Nothing but the best.

"Call Ash and see where the hell she is," Sutton said as she headed toward the elevator. "I'm going to get some sleep. We'll meet for dinner and then head out to the party together. Let's say seven thirty?"

"Yes, ma'am," Honor said, rolling her eyes. "You're such an old lady. I want to go shop!"

"You do that. I'm going to my room, ordering room service, and taking a nap. And I ain't old, a bitch is in her prime," Sutton shot back, snickering as she kissed her sisters goodbye.

Sutton hadn't come to New York to spend money. She had come to make it and she wouldn't be easily distracted. She didn't want to purchase brand names; she wanted her name to become the brand name. Sutton LaCroix was determined to build their company and become the most respected consulting firm in the country. She was well on her way, but she was still a small firm, and they were still stretching their wings into new sectors. She didn't just want to be known for fixing scandals and handling PR nightmares, she wanted to touch tech and natural resources, specifically oil, and August Sinclair and his family's fortune was her way in.

. . .

"I have never met a girl who hops a free ride and then acts like I'm invading her space." August chuckled as he lifted a bottle of champagne to his lips and waltzed to the seat across from Ashton's.

She rolled her eyes. "I haven't said one word," Ashton replied.

"That's my point. You aren't even pretending to be polite," August snickered.

"What do you want me to do? Be like your little friends up there?" Ashton asked. "They're so easy to impress. I've been on a private jet before. I appreciate the ride, thanks," she said.

August's bent brow of curiosity irritated Ashton. "What are you looking at? That's about all I got for you," she said.

He shook his head, smiling. "I like to go after the tough nuts," he said. "The harder they are to crack the better they taste," he said before standing and making his way back to the front of the plane.

I swear I should rob him, she thought. August was lucky he was already marked by her sisters, because if it were up to her, she would humble his ass. Leave him leaking somewhere and run his entire trust fund because she knew his money was given, not hard earned. He spent it too frivolously. He was young, rich, and entitled. His arrogance was both a turn-on and turnoff. She could understand how he had pulled the beautiful women at his side.

She stood and headed toward the restroom, but the sight of a room at the back of the plane pulled her farther. She peeked through the slit of the semi-open door and a beauty of a man stood inside. He removed his shirt, revealing an athlete's body beneath. She wondered how it was possible for a man to hang a suit so well. The build beneath was flawless.

He lifted his eyes toward the door and Ashton's breath hitched as he pulled it open.

"Sorry, I was looking for the bathroom," she said.

"This one's private. August's company utilizes the one up front," he said.

"I didn't mean to pry," she replied.

"I think you meant to do exactly that," he said, then shut the door in her face, stunning Ashton. She scoffed in disbelief. She had never met a man who wasn't putty in her hands. She was beautiful and young. She hadn't detected a hint of lust in this man's eyes, however, and that was odd. It was the first time in her entire life she hadn't felt like her looks gave her an advantage. She wondered why he was secluded in the back of the jet while August practically had an orgy going on with beautiful women up front. The level of discipline intrigued her. Most men would indulge when tempted with pussy. This man blocked it out.

"You're the one we need to figure out," she whispered to herself. She hurried back to her seat and grabbed a bottle of champagne from the ice bucket near her. She poured herself a drink and sat back as the wheels in her mind turned in overdrive. She knew when she was looking at the boss and August wasn't it. She couldn't wait to get to New York so she could fill in her sisters on this new mystery man she had discovered. There was more to him than met the eye and Ashton had a feeling they had their sights on the wrong target. It was time to develop a plan B.

CHAPTER 6

"You're out," Sutton said. She didn't even give Ashton the courtesy of looking at her as she sat, posture perfect, dainty hands gripping the fork and steak knife that were annihilating the cut of Wagyu beef on her plate.

"You're so unreasonable, Sutty! So I missed my flight. You act like that's the end of the world. You and I need to get something straight. I'm the youngest, but I'm not a baby anymore. I don't need you holding my hand or playing it safe with me. I handle my business just like the three of you, so take off the training wheels," Ashton said.

"Handling your business means being prompt. You're burnt, Ash. You hopped on the nigga's private jet. You can't join the mile-high club and pop champagne, then approach him on some legit business. He will never take you serious."

"Mile high? That's what you think?" Ashton asked.

"I mean, you did pop pussy for the geek a few days ago, Ash, it ain't far-fetched," Honor said.

Luna snickered as Ashton rolled her eyes. "Was the dick good at least?"

"Trash, just like these rules y'all putting on me," Ash answered, perturbed.

"You'll just sit this one out," Honor said. "Let us approach it the right way before he sees your face again. Even if you didn't fuck him, you think he's going to let you manage his company and you couldn't even manage your own travel arrangements without fucking up?"

"Fine," Ashton said, finally picking up her silverware to eat. She snapped the linen napkin open and placed it in her lap. She was livid. They were treating her like an amateur. They had no idea how much work she had put in on the streets of Miami, but she knew in their eyes she would always be little Ash. To her, she was the fuckup, the hothead, the one who had brought the family tumbling down. They held some resentments about the incarceration of their father and because she knew it was her fault, she let them have this one.

"I'll keep my distance from this one until it's set in stone, but FYI, we're focused on the wrong man. August Sinclair might be the prince of Daddy's company, but the nigga I saw on the jet with him today, he's the next king. I could feel it just by being around him."

"I'm not worried about the right-hand man. I want the son of the white billionaire, the oil tycoon from Texas," Sutton said. "August is the eldest son; he's the one with the power. He is a legacy. Nobody else matters but him. So, whoever you saw on the jet is not our target. Forget about him and focus."

"You didn't see their dynamic, Sutty. August may be filthy rich, but he ain't the one calling the shots."

Sutton was slow to respond, and Ashton shook her head. She hated when Sutton acted like no one else was in the room. Sutton only moved when she was ready, only spoke after carefully considering what she wanted to say. She was calculating.

"Tell me about him," Sutton said, finally biting. If she knew nothing else, she knew Ashton knew how to spot the boss.

"Whoever he is, he's official. Not being arrogant or anything, but he didn't even look in my direction," Ashton said.

"That's not arrogant at all, baby sis," Luna said sarcastically, laughing.

"Hey, that's hard for a man to do! Hell, it's hard for some women to do," Honor added.

"I'm serious, y'all. It was hella women on their jet and I mean they were there for his entertainment and he had nothing for them. He stayed to himself, barely spoke. Was rude, in fact. For four hours, he was invisible to the bullshit. He opted out. I don't think I've ever seen a man with that much self-control," Ashton said.

"You were raised by a man with that type of self-control," Luna said. "What's his name? I can look up his net worth."

"I don't know," Ashton admitted.

"Where are they staying? If we have that information, we can skip the party altogether. A little coincidental meet-cute will go over better than a conversation in a crowded club."

"I don't know," Ashton said again.

"You were on a jet for hours with this man and you didn't get any information we could use?" Honor asked. "You're slipping, Ash."

"He didn't socialize at all. I'm telling you. This nigga's

different. When I know, I know, and this is the lick of a life-time. He's loaded. The jet we flew in on wasn't some rented aircraft with some random pilot. It was his. Not August's. A brother in a ten-thousand-dollar suit and brown skin owned it. The pilot knew him; the flight attendant was familiar with him."

"We'll worry about the mystery man later. Let's talk about August Sinclair," Sutton said, growing impatient.

"He's worth . . ." Luna began to roll down the statistics on the Sinclair family, but Sutton was already in the know.

"Billions. I'm aware," Sutton interrupted. "August Sinclair is worth two point four billion dollars and that's not counting the valuation of the company. I don't do anything blindly. I've done my homework. Get dressed. We've got a Draft party to go to."

"Me too?" Ashton asked.

"How else am I supposed to know who the king is?" Sutton asked, winking at her sister and showing a bit of leniency because they all knew Sutton had a radar for made men. Even without Ashton's help, she would have sniffed her target out of the crowd.

"About time you took the stick out your ass," Honor said. "Now, can I have a dope-ass girls' night with my sisters?"

Sutton nodded, smirking a bit. She never smiled. She was such a tough girl, but they all knew that she was happy about the reunion. Tough love was the only kind of love she knew how to give, but it felt miraculous all the same. They finished their dinner and stopped into their suites to freshen up before heading out on the town.

The LaCroix sisters stepped out the Mandarin Oriental looking like money. They were so glamorous that people spoke in hushed tones, speculating about their identities as they made their way to the awaiting cars outside.

"Relax, Sutty," Honor said as she reached for the bucket that housed the champagne.

"I'm relaxed," Sutton said.

"No, you're not, you're thinking of every single way this can go wrong. Tonight should be fun. We're headed to a party full of millionaires and we're going to be the prettiest bitches in the room. Ain't no way we're walking out without a bag," Honor said as she slipped into her waiting car.

Again with the separate cars because even though they anticipated a night full of fun, they took precautions, nonetheless. Multiple exit strategies.

They pulled up to Soho House and this time, they didn't mind the camera flashes as paparazzi called out to them. A little red-carpet slay for *Page Six* was necessary. It created good publicity for their firm, using their good looks as the carrot they dangled in front of potential clients. Men were the easy ones. Just the potential to fuck one of the LaCroix sisters brought them through the door. The sisters were exquisite. It wasn't until they opened their mouths that people realized they were the real deal. Intelligent and savvy, they were brilliant negotiators and exceptional at all things business.

Sutton gave a look over her shoulder as she posed one last time before walking inside the exclusive club.

Chatter filled the air as music played in the background. It was a gold digger's dream to be in a room filled with so many connections. Every major sporting league was in attendance, as well as entertainers. Sutton thanked God she and her sisters weren't easily impressed.

Even some of the most successful women ended up tricking

when this much money was in one room. They reduced themselves for attention. Sutton saw it happening already all around the room and the night had just begun. It was a contest of clout. Who wore the least amount of clothes? Whose weave was the longest? Whose ass was the fattest? It was a silicone and pussy contest. Classless was in style, but Sutton knew better. She and her sisters were timeless.

Without any effort at all they pulled the eyes of every man they passed. Sutton didn't even smile as she walked by the crowd. Friendliness was an invitation for communication. She had zero kick it for these men. She didn't need their compliments or their time. She was there for one reason alone, to scope out August Sinclair, and as she looked around the room, she wondered how she would make an intentional meeting appear incidental.

• • •

"It must be a hell of a feeling having two of the top ten picks on your roster. Congrats, my man. That's big business. Black-owned sports agency competing with the big boys."

West nodded at the two-time Pro-Bowl quarterback and lifted his crystal tumbler in acknowledgment. "It's just a good day. Makes it seem like none of the bad ones came before it, but trust a lot of work went into building this night," West stated.

"A lot of play too," the quarterback said as a random woman slid into his lap. His hands immediately rounded to the woman's behind. "A lot of play, indeed. Best perks of the job."

West smirked, but he was unamused as another one of

the groupies in the suite tried to enter his space. "I'm good," he said.

"Big bro always so serious!" August shouted, holding his arms out while gripping a bottle of champagne in both hands. "We've got to celebrate! You have these owners eating out of the palm of your hand. West Coast is really taking off. I remember when that used to be you out there on the field."

"That was before I knew the real flip was in the skybox, not on the field. NCAA made millions off my jersey sales and I didn't see one dime," West complained. "Tearing my ACL ended my career, but it made me wise up."

"You know the game. You understand the player's side of things, West. It's why I'll never switch representation. Congrats on the new blood," the quarterback said.

West nodded, raising his glass to tap the bottle August held up and the glass of his client before taking a sip.

"If you gentlemen will excuse me," he said.

West eased through the crowd and slipped out the door to the private room, mixing in with the chaos of the nightclub. This wasn't really his scene. He was far removed from bottle service and random women in nightclubs, but he knew this celebration was hard earned. His sports agency might be his second priority, but he wasn't blind to the fact that the other men in the room had awaited this moment their entire lives. It was a night to commemorate. He took the metal stairs up to the second floor and slipped out onto the rooftop. He was grateful to the high winds that kept everyone else inside. He just wanted to take a moment to himself and celebrate his way. A good cigar would mark the occasion and a little solitude would allow him time to process the night's wins.

• • •

Sutton looked around the room of athletes. They were young, eager, and waiting for her to spend some of the multimillion-dollar checks they had just received. She watched the young women in the room attempt to make a good impression on the young stars, and she shook her head because they had it all wrong. Their game was backward. Instead of Sutton asking for them to spend money on her, she would make them need to step it with her. Gold digging was retro; the new hustle was to be useful to a man. To be an asset. Men treated women like cars, trading them in to move on to the next ride every so often. Sutton didn't want to be a toy to a man, whether personal or professional. She was the license they carried that allowed them to purchase their toys at all. She helped secure the bag and then protected it at all costs; they didn't need to know she was also the one making them feel like their careers were at stake.

"Here! Have a drink!" Luna shouted over the music, passing Sutton her martini glass. "You look uncomfortable!"

"Just not my thing! I prefer boardrooms to bars!" Sutton shouted back. The music was so loud a normal conversation was impossible.

"This is their boardroom! Athletes do business over bitches and bottles!" Honor shouted across the table.

"Facts!" Luna added, laughing.

"These ballplayers are fun and games, where are the big fish?" Luna asked.

"Soho House has so many private rooms. August Sinclair could be anywhere," Ashton answered.

Sutton was so uptight that she felt like her awkwardness

was visible. Thighs clenched tight, hands folded in her lap, and body rigid, her entire demeanor screamed she was out of her element. She was beautiful, but the knitted brow and tight-lipped scowl was a natural deterrent for any man in the club who even thought to look her way. She knew her sisters were in their element, but Sutton just couldn't get into the vibe. It was too hot, too loud, and too social. She just wanted to retreat to her hotel suite, finish off her bottle of red, and get into the September issues of *Vogue* and *Black Enterprise* she had waiting in her bag. This crowd made her uncomfortable and she couldn't hide it. When a guy she recognized as a wide receiver for the Buffalo Bills leaned over their booth to whisper in Honor's ear, Sutton knew it was time for a bathroom break. The LaCroix sisters attracted men wherever they went, and she knew they were about to turn their section into the hot spot of the night. Sutton grabbed her drink and stood from the table.

"Where are you going?" Ashton screamed over the music.

"I need to take a call. Don't worry about me. Have fun. Keep your eyes open," Sutton reminded them as she stepped away from the table. The line to the bathroom was irritatingly long so she bypassed it, going up the stairs behind it. She didn't know where they led until she burst out of the steel door. The air hit her, and Sutton sucked it in gratefully.

"Hey catch that—!"

Before the man could finish his sentence, the door closed, echoing in the night.

Sutton pulled on the door. Locked.

"Shit," she muttered. She pulled again, this time harder.

"It's locked," the man behind her said.

Sutton blew out a sharp breath. She grew irritated by the

simplest things. Being locked on a rooftop with a strange man was not on the night's agenda.

She pulled out her cell phone and attempted to dial.

"Too many buildings. No service," he said.

She sucked her teeth. "Great," she responded. For the first time she looked in his direction.

Wow, she thought, taken aback. It was the second time she had seen him. It was hard to misplace a face like his. He was brooding and handsome, standing in the night's shadows as cigar smoke corrupted the air around him.

"I don't believe in coincidences, so you must be following me," she said.

A lighthearted chuckle fell from his lips.

"You're saying seeing you at Lathan Naples's event and here all within a few days is all by chance?" she asked.

"Important people often seem to fill the same room, Ms. LaCroix," he answered.

"How do you know me?" she asked.

"I'm a black man in business. I like to keep up with other black people making waves in business. I've seen the write-ups. You're doing your thing."

"My thing? Is that what I'm doing?" she asked.

"Apparently, that's all you're doing. You're wound up real tight, baby."

Sutton scoffed, shaking her head as she turned back to the door and knocked. "Hey! Open up!"

"No one can hear you," he stated.

"Ugh!" Sutton groaned. "This is not my night. I knew I should have stayed in. Rowdy-ass crowd and now this."

"It's that bad?" he asked.

"I'm stuck on a rooftop with a stalker. I'd say it's terrible," she said.

He smiled but didn't reply as he continued his smoke. He was enjoying it. She could tell by the way he hummed a bit when he inhaled.

"If I hadn't been trying to escape the bottle popping contest in there, I would have never come up here," Sutton answered sarcastically.

"It's just a bunch of niggas with new money," West answered as he looked at the exhibit in front of him. "The check ain't even cleared and they've already blown hundreds of thousands on bullshit." He shook his head and rubbed both hands down his head.

"Can't expect the conditions of someone's mind to change just because their status does. A day ago, they were struggling college students," she said.

His eyes froze on her, not long, but long enough to recognize her words had affected him.

"Maybe," he answered. "Or maybe they're just stupid as fuck."

She scoffed, then laughed. "Or that," she said. "I didn't mean to interrupt. I just needed some air. I don't remember hating noise this much. When I was twenty years old, I would be with all the shits. Guess I'm getting old. I'm normally in bed at this time of night."

"Lucky bed."

She pulled her neck back, stunned. His forwardness had taken her by surprise. He smirked, licking full lips before focusing his brooding stare back on the skyline.

The way he continued to smoke the diminishing cigar as

if he hadn't said a word made her peer at him in wonder. He was hard to read, and she was almost sure that was intentional. His suit was tailored and not just a brand name pulled off a rack at Neiman's. It was bespoke, one of one, designed personally for him. The cigar he smoked was Cuban, authentic, and hand rolled. She picked the scent right out of the air as he blew the smoke out into the night. Tattoos peeked above the collar of his shirt and up the back of his neck and the intensity of his presence . . . That alone—along with the aura, the stature—screamed his authority without him having to speak one word.

She smiled stubbornly, looking away because she shouldn't be this flattered. Her cheeks flushed as he bit his bottom lip and then ran his tongue across it. Sutton didn't know if he was moving slowly or if time had stood still, but the nigga was a walking fantasy. Powerful and paid; subtle yet dripping in luxury. He wore his crown well. She had to admit that much.

"I never met a pretty girl who complained about being in a room full of money," he said.

"Money doesn't buy access to me. If it did, nobody in this building would be able to afford my vig," she said.

"You sure about that?" he asked, turning to face her.

"Positive," she said.

"Everybody has a price," he countered. "It's the first thing I learned in business. Niggas on the block, men in suits sitting across the boardroom, beautiful women on rooftops . . . even if it's expensive, there's a price."

"Not really, but okay," she answered, not at all affected by his arrogance. Men with money had the hugest egos, but he wasn't boasting, just speaking from experience. His affluence had made rules bendable. Right and wrong were an illusion put on those who couldn't afford to change the definition. Sutton was familiar with the way the world made exceptions for men like him.

"A hundred thousand," he said.

Sutton laughed, shaking her head. "I spend that in Hermès."

He was amused. His eyes glistened and he scoffed playfully. Sutton was no average woman. Everything about her was an elevated experience very few men could say they had ever indulged. With just the time they had spent talking, this man had already been given more than most.

"What?" she asked.

"Not many women stand by their word. They say it to say it, to dismiss feeling cheap, to put up a façade of respectability," he answered.

"The type to say, 'I don't normally do this,' knowing all along they're going to do the shit?" Sutton asked, smiling.

"That exact type," he confirmed.

"Yeah, wrong girl," she said. "Sorry to disappoint."

"The opposite, actually. It's low-key refreshing," he answered. He sat on the edge of the cement ledge and peered at her curiously, taking one last puff of his cigar before snuffing it out and placing it inside his inner jacket pocket.

"So business is your thing? That's surprising," he said.

She frowned. "How so?" she asked.

"The room full of wasted potential in there should explain why I'm surprised. A girl like you—"

"A woman," she interrupted, correcting him.

He paused for a beat, taking the time to look her up and

down before settling on her eyes. "Indeed," he agreed. "My mistake. Women who look like you don't normally do what they don't have to do."

"So attractive women lack work ethic?" she asked. "That's not chauvinist at all."

He smirked at her sarcasm. "They work, they just work niggas, not jobs," he answered. "Crazy part is they don't even know they're the one with the leverage. Women can be bought; it's their greatest flaw."

"Not all women," she fired back proudly. "There are some women men just could never afford. The money might be right; but in order for a man to really be rich, to really be able to afford to have his way, he'd have to have finesse. He'd have to be so used to money that he never even mentioned it; that he no longer saw the purpose of it."

"Where are you from?" he asked, curious as to where her ideologies originated from.

"Miami." Sutton bit her tongue after the truth slipped from her mouth. It snuck out too quickly to chase it back. He didn't need to know background information. It made her traceable. It was his aura. It demanded the truth and nothing else. His authority was passive, but present, and Sutton was intrigued.

"Sutton LaCroix from Miami," he said, mulling it over, going inside his head, making assumptions about who she was. She was sure all of his assumptions were wrong.

A random couple pushed open the steel door, bursting out into the night.

"Hey, my man! Hold that door! It locks behind you," he said. He then turned his attention back to Sutton.

"You can't be bought. I believe that," he said, nodding.

"So why don't you give it to a nigga for free?" He rose and Sutton watched him walk back into the party.

He left behind the scent of his cologne, a key card to his hotel room, and a business card.

WEST SIDE MANAGEMENT
WEST S. AUSTIN
CEO

She picked it up, taken aback. No man had ever been so forward with her and oddly it hollowed her gut. It had been a long time since a man had given her that feeling. That giddy, sick intrigue that made her heart quicken.

She picked up the key. *Four Seasons.*

She placed the key back where she had gotten it from and went to find her sisters. *Arrogant ass,* she thought.

The party was going strong inside and she quickly found them at a table of football veterans. All the groupies in the building had their sights on the newly inducted NFL stars. The LaCroix sisters knew it was the established players who had the biggest salaries and they weren't looking to fill their beds. Events like this were for networking. She was certain they would walk out with a slew of potential clients.

She walked over to the booth and leaned down to whisper in Honor's ear.

"I'm going to head out. Y'all be safe and keep Ash on a leash. One of these niggas show a little weakness, and he'll wake up with his bank account on empty messing with her."

Honor laughed. "I got it. You sure you don't want to stay?"

Sutton shook her head and blew her other two sisters kisses before heading for the exit. Her car was waiting curbside as instructed and she slid inside, feeling relief as soon as she was behind the dark tint.

"Back to the hotel, Ms. LaCroix?"

• • •

"There's our boy," Ashton said as she watched August step out onto the second-floor balcony. He overlooked the main floor as women flocked behind him. Ashton recognized two all-star players beside him, but somehow the white boy was the center of attention. People liked him. His charisma mixed with unlimited pockets made him the life of every party.

"Talking business in a nightclub is a sure way to ruin a deal before we even get started," Gadget said. "Now that we've laid eyes on him, let's find out where he's staying." Gadget pulled a small GPS tracker from her makeup compact. She opened her palm to show the small device to her sisters. It looked like a random button.

"We slide this in his jacket pocket, and we'll be able to see where he's staying without having to follow him—down to the room number. We'll send a girl to him, underaged of course, and when he realizes he's had sex with a minor, we'll have him exactly where we want him."

"Who's up?" Ashton asked.

Honor slid out of the booth, taking the button into her hand, and crossed the room.

It took her ten minutes just to get to August. Every few steps Honor took, a new man stopped her. She was offered six drinks and a marriage proposal; that last one she found charming, but she graciously declined it as she made her way to August.

"Excuse me, can I get by you?" she asked as she waited for him to turn her way.

When he did, August looked down at her then lifted hands, taking a step back to let her by.

"You're seriously beautiful," August said, looking down at her. Honor turned to let her body rub against him. She looked him square in the eyes, sliding her hand inside his pocket. She rubbed his dick and to her surprise she was satisfied as it reacted in her hand. Neither cared that there was a section full of people around them.

"You don't seem like the type," he said. "But I'm not complaining."

Honor removed her hand but left the button inside his pocket. "I'm not," she replied. "I don't fuck with white boys." She walked off, leaving his mind blown as she headed out the club. She sent a text to her sisters telling them her part was done and she was headed back to the hotel and then climbed into her black SUV, letting her driver carry her back to her hotel.

• • •

"It's time to go, sis. We're out," Gadget stated as she gathered her belongings.

"I've got to pee. You can head out. I'm five minutes behind you."

Gadget nodded, kissed Ashton's cheek, and then the sisters went their separate ways. Ashton headed for the restroom, suddenly feeling flushed and hot as nausea pushed vomit up from the back of her throat. She practically ran through the club, only to find the ladies' room had a line a mile long. She ventured farther down the hallway, searching for a second bathroom. She opened the door at the end to find an office. She entered, closing it behind her, and sighed in relief when she saw the light illuminating from the attached bathroom. She rushed to the private bathroom and tossed up her dinner in chunks. She panted, feeling dizzy as she gripped the countertop. Turning on the water, she rinsed her mouth and then looked in the mirror. She was so disoriented. She turned to exit, but the commotion of a tussle froze her. Ashton pulled the bathroom door, shutting it, only leaving a sliver of space for her to see through.

"Empty the motherfucking safe."

Ashton's eyes widened as she watched three masked men walk into the office. They shut the door behind them, flipping the lock, and then one man walked the manager behind his desk.

"We don't keep cash on hand," the manager said, his hands raised and trembling.

"You tell me one more lie and it'll be your last. You keep celebrity jewels and cash in the safe. Open it!"

The manager fumbled as he bent down, pressing a button beneath his desk. The back wall of the room slid open. A hidden safe stood behind it.

"Let's go! I ain't got all day."

The man tapped the gun to the back of the manager's head until the safe was popped open. The manager made the mistake of tussling with one of the men, grabbing his ski mask and exposing his face. A silenced bullet quickly followed. The manager's body dropped instantly. Ashton's hand shot to her mouth and she turned away from the door, her heart beating out of her chest. She had no way to protect herself if they found her. The best she could do was stay quiet. Ashton squeezed her eyes tight.

"Man, empty the safe and fold this motherfucka inside, mane."

The safe was big enough and Ashton felt bad for whoever came along to open it next.

Ashton was home free until the ringing of her phone erupted through the room.

She fumbled to silence it, but it was too late.

"What the fuck was that? Check the bathroom, mane!"

The door was pushed open and Ashton lifted her hands in defense. "I swear I won't say shit. Not one word," Ashton pleaded.

"Bitch, get'cho ass out here!" the man said. Ashton bucked and kneed him between his legs before grabbing the toilet tank cover and swinging it so hard he fell back into the sink.

"What the fuck, nigga? You can't handle this bitch?" another one shouted. Ashton tossed the toilet cover at the burglar but he dodged it.

"Bitch, I'll blow your head off," he said through gritted teeth and aimed the gun in her direction. He snatched her out of the bathroom and put a gun in her back. "If you scream, I'll blow your pretty ass to hell. Walk."

He jammed the gun into her lower back so hard that the blow took her breath away. She looked down the hallway toward the commotion of the party. No one noticed as she was led out the back door. Red taillights awaited them from a black BMW parked in the darkened alley.

"Wait! Where are you taking me? Please, I won't say shit," she begged. "Just let me go. I have money. I'll give you whatever you want."

She had been trained by Miamor, but up against three men she was useless, especially empty-handed. The man grabbed her by the back of her neck and forced her into the trunk of the car.

She stared up at the man, peering into onyx eyes. They were all she could see through the ski mask he wore.

"If you hurt me, my family will haunt you for a thousand years," she said. She was dead serious. Her Haitian roots were strong. The LaCroix family was known for their ability to seek revenge. They had ruined the Diamond legacy; not with the war, but with the sacrificial ceremony that had been placed over their family after her uncle Matee was killed. If anything happened to Ashton, her people were crossing the Atlantic in boats and they wouldn't be coming in chains.

He scoffed and froze on her for a beat before slamming the trunk and cloaking her in darkness.

• • •

West loosened his tie as he lifted the crystal tumbler to his full lips. He had never been one for crowds, but it was necessary in his industries. From oil to his sports agency, his attendance was mandatory, but he didn't prefer it. The limelight. Somehow it preferred him. His good looks attracted the blogs, his hood instincts to say less intrigued the grapevine. They knew nothing personal about him, so the media tended to flock to him whenever he came around. He didn't mind the business inquires, but the personal ones felt intrusive. This five-star hotel room and the good whiskey in his glass made for a perfect night of solace.

He unbuttoned his shirt and shrugged out of it, leaving

it at his feet because he had a thing about white shirts. He never wore them more than once. It was in direct contrast to his upbringing when circumstances had forced him to wear the same shirt for days because one was all he had. He didn't think about those days often.

The knock at his door pulled his eyes to it and he crossed the room. He pulled it open and just like she had hours before, she took his breath away.

"So, I'm going to skip the part about 'I really never do this' because you won't believe it, anyway. The truth is it's been a long time since I've had some dick and you look like you got the type of dick to make me lose my mind a little, so here I am, acting like I have no home training."

The fact that she didn't flinch made him want her in ways she could never imagine.

He stood there, staring at her.

"Are you going to invite me in?" she asked, irritation vexing her.

"I need you to understand what I'm about to do to you," he said.

"I'm a grown woman, I'm pretty sure—"

"You're not sure and I want you to be sure before you come inside." He sounded like he was issuing a warning and the serious glower on his face told her she just might want to take heed. He had the disposition like they were negotiating a contract, not pussy, and her instincts to flee erupted. Sutton was too bullheaded to back down, despite her screaming intuition begging her to. She stepped across the threshold and around him, taking his glass out of his hand and sipping the hard liquor as she entered the suite.

"Nice view," she admired.

"It's brick and man-made lights; that's not a view," West countered.

Sutton turned to him in shock. "What would be considered a view?"

"The Swiss Alps from the Jacuzzi tub in the penthouse suite at hotel Megève," he answered.

She nodded, impressed. "I'll have to get there one day. I've never been partial to snow."

"I've never been partial to small talk," he shot back. "There's a nondisclosure I'll need signed."

She scoffed. "Excuse me?"

"A letter of consent," he said. He didn't even give her the courtesy of looking in her direction. He retrieved his phone from his pocket and his fingers danced on the screen. When she heard the chime of her phone from her handbag she pulled it out in disbelief. A DocuSign file had been Air-Dropped to her.

"You're kidding, right?" she asked.

"Not at all," he replied.

West had no time or room for games. A man of his caliber and with his net worth had to protect himself. He didn't want there to be any gray area. She was either with it or she could leave. He had a phone full of willing participants if she chose the latter.

"Just protecting us both," he said. "No offense, but I met you at an industry party. You sign and I'll make sure you enjoy the rest of your night. You don't sign and I can call you a car, no hard feelings."

She peered at him curiously, clearly weighing her options. Sliding her finger across the phone screen she signed the electronic agreement. She typed on her screen. "Since we're being cautious," she said.

His phone buzzed and he chuckled as he opened her message.

"My status and my last physical exam," she said. "I'll need yours if you think you're even going to breathe in my direction."

This felt like more of a business deal, like they were two sharks on two different sides of the table, negotiating the terms of engagement. To the average woman it would have been a turnoff, but Sutton lived for shit like this, for niggas just like this. Bossed up and cocky. Rich and in control. Smart and prepared. The audacity of this man. The frankness. The presumption. It was like he'd known she was going to end up in his bed the moment she stepped foot on that rooftop.

Within moments, the document was at her fingertips. As she looked over the email, he approached her, removing the phone from her hands and tossing it on the bed.

"Now we gon keep playing or you gon let me have my way with it?" West asked.

He grabbed her face with one hand, pinching her jaws in, and smeared her lipstick with his thumb. She was beautiful but her body was rigid, her neck sank like she was holding her breath.

"How long has it been?" he asked.

She pulled her neck back, stunned.

"You're uncomfortable with touch," he said, reading her mind. "A woman who's getting fucked on the regular ain't this stiff."

His lips were on her shoulder and moving up her neck.

She quivered as he kept talking. "You react to me like you're dying to cum, desperate for it. I'ma take my time with it."

Her ears, her neck, her chin—she pulled back before he could get to her lips.

"I don't kiss," she whispered, slightly panicking as she placed a guard up, putting her hands on his chest to stop him.

"Tonight, you do everything," he said, taking her lips anyway, disregarding her rules. His territory. House rules applied. She wanted to protest but somehow, for the first time ever in her life, she gave in to someone else setting the tone. She hadn't kissed a man ever. Kissing disgusted her. She remembered being kissed as a kid in the most inappropriate ways, by the most inappropriate of men. A young girl, tainted, and misused before she even knew how good kisses could be. She hadn't kissed a man since, until now. Her body was rigid, but his strong hands took control, one rounding her body and gripping her ass, pulling her into him. She was like a rag doll in his grasp because her limbs felt like noodles. He made her weak. His free hand caressed the side of her face as he devoured her.

Sutton was breathless. Every place he touched came alive and her face wrinkled in pleasure as he pulled her lips and tongue into his mouth, sucking on her like he had been craving her all day. She hadn't ever felt this aroused. Her panties dewed and her breath hitched as he circled her body, breathing on the back of her neck, pressing into her body, hard dick against her soft ass.

He exposed her slowly, pulling her zipper down and peeling her out of her skintight dress until it lay defeated at her feet.

"Relax," he said as he reached around her body, finding

her clit and trapping it between coarse fingers as he rubbed. He lowered to his knees and opened her from behind, lifting one thigh in his hand until her foot rested on the couch. Her forehead pinched and she drew in air as he pulled her clit in between soft lips.

"Oh my God," she moaned. She hadn't even meant to be so vocal. He could tell the words had escaped to her dismay; but once freed, her pleasure was hard to chase down. He dove deeper, nose first, moving his head side to side as he sucked, then lapped at her womanhood with no mercy. He loved pussy—good pussy preferably—and it had been a long time since he had selected a cut this fine. She was freshly waxed and surprisingly tight as he pushed two fingers into her depths. Her back arched as he pumped his hand slowly.

Sutton placed her knees on the couch and reached between her legs, gripping a dick so massive she wondered if she could take it. Still, she guided him toward her wetness. She was nobody's virgin, but she wasn't getting knocked down on the regular either. His size alone leveled her, sending her belly into the couch before instinct told her to press pause. That one stroke knocked all common sense from her brain. Toxic dick. That was what this was. The type to make you have a baby just to provide receipts that you took that dick for a stroll a time or two.

"Wait!" She scrambled and turned around, flustered as she mustered every ounce of willpower she had to stop him because, damn, she didn't really want to stop him at all, and the lack of self-control was a problem. He rubbed the sides of his mouth, taking a step back as she reached for her handbag. Sutton was undone. She couldn't stop her eyes from lifting to the mountain of a man in front of her. He was so fucking solid—sturdy thighs, definition everywhere—and his hands, God his hands were huge, and he was skilled in using them. She wondered if the hand he was using to rub his beard smelled like her. There was something erotic about leaving her scent there. Her mark. She fumbled with the bag, pulling out everything except what she was looking for. Lipstick, compact, tampons, because with three sisters someone was always starting a surprise period, until finally . . . a condom. She sighed in relief because she didn't know if she would have the strength to walk away if she hadn't located it.

She held it up and he smirked.

"Precautions," she said.

"Precautions," he confirmed.

Sutton was almost intimidated by his prowess. He pulled out his phone and pressed a button on his phone. Music streamed out of the Bluetooth speaker.

I likeee when you're stressed, but I like it when you take your stress out on meeee . . .

"For when you scream," he said. Her neck snapped back, shocked at his assumption that she would scream as dvsn filled the room. The soulful music would undoubtedly mask any sounds of pleasure that escaped her.

He didn't give it a second thought as he backed her up to the bed and then strapped up. Her back hit the cool sheets and he hovered over her, covering her lips with his before she could catch her breath. The taste of tobacco and liquor was masculine and overwhelming and oddly enticing as she did something she never did: kissed him back. It was like the taste of him intoxicated her. Biceps bulged around her head as he balanced on balled fists over her body. The nigga didn't even knock before entering. He just unlocked her doors and barged in like he owned the shit. Sutton's back arched so high off the bed that he picked her up.

With one arm wrapped around her back and the other around her throat, his dick was somewhere near China because he was digging through her earth for sure. The bed only gave him more room to explore her wet and he splashed in that shit relentlessly.

She reached out for help, gripping sheets above her head. His hand followed hers, grabbing her hand and intertwining their fingers as he stroked her from behind.

Sutton threw ass back at him like a star pitcher in the bottom of the ninth who was dealing with loaded bases. She wanted to scream his name, praise him, slap him, fight his ass for hitting it so good, but instead she bit down on her lip as he made up for every inch of mediocre dick she had ever endured in her life. She had never met a man who knew exactly what to do, where to touch, and how hard to beat it. Nothing about him was gentle; he didn't know her well enough to make love. A whole lot of fucking was going down in the penthouse of the Four Seasons and she couldn't help but wonder how he would handle a woman he held some affection for.

West gripped her waist with both hands and pulled her back onto him, no running. "Damn."

The word only boosted her ego. Hearing his enjoyment, her nectar fueling his pleasure, made it even better.

"Agh!" she cried. Her fingers opened and then closed again, pulling the sheets from the mattress. West came up on one foot. Too deep. He was submerged and when he bit the side of her neck, she lifted her chin to the ceiling . . . praise this nigga.

Bitchhhhh.

It was what she would tell her sisters later.

It was so fucking good. He slapped her ass, gripping it, and then licked the back of her neck. His tongue trailed down the center of her back, making her weak. That tongue was glorious, an extrovert as it made friends with the crack of her, then traveled to her most sensitive spot.

"Turn over," he ordered.

She rolled over on her back, covering her eyes as he pulled the scream from her depths.

"Nigga!"

He chuckled but he didn't miss a bite, eating her up, finishing his plate, cleaning it, because it was ungrateful to leave even a morsel of a delicacy untasted.

She came so hard her body shuddered, and he kissed his way up the front of her, appreciating toned abs and tasting dark nipples before letting her enjoy her own flavor on his tongue. For a girl who didn't kiss, she couldn't stop kissing him. She moaned as he filled her again, hitting circles in her shit like he was doing donuts on a hot summer day. Hood shit. Hood nigga. He was too cocky to be anything other than that. The suit had fooled her.

"Shit ain't free," he said in her ear. "You charging this shit to a nigga soul." Her eyes popped open. "Your mean ass."

He sexed her into exhaustion. By the time he was done, she had lost count of her orgasms.

He didn't even lie down afterward. He climbed from the bed, taking the condom straight to the bathroom and flushing it down the toilet. When he returned, she was barely awake and the predicament he found himself in was one he had never allowed before: a woman in his room overnight.

He finessed his beard as he stood over her. She was too stunning to disturb, so instead he dressed himself. He was halfway to the door when he stopped, reaching for the checkbook he kept in his inner jacket pocket. He pulled out a ballpoint Cartier pen and wrote out a check.

$25,000

On the memo line he wrote: *It's too good to be free.*

He set it on the nightstand and then made his way out of the room. It wasn't his first one-night stand and he was sure it wouldn't be his last, but it for damn sure was his best, one he wouldn't soon forget.

• • •

Sire sat passenger side in the car. He finessed his lips as he peered out of the window. The city of New York passed them by.

"Man, that bitch won't shut up. I'ma put something in her mouth, shut her pretty ass up for good."

Sire looked at the driver. "Why don't you shut the fuck up and nurse that black eye shawty gave you," he said. "What the fuck did I tell you niggas? We go in through the back, get the money, keep it quiet, make a clean exit. We dumped a body in that club and got one in the trunk. This shit is messy."

"We good, bruh. Cameras was disabled and all. Get rid of this bitch and bust this bag down with August and we good. Get out of this stanking-ass city, mane. H-Town ain't never seemed better, you feel me?" Wasan said as he rifled through the night's take.

"Bitch had a fat ass though, didn't she?" the driver chuckled.

"Be quiet and drive," Sire ordered.

The sound of the screams coming from the trunk gave Sire an instant headache. He was in a whole different state, moving around a concrete jungle that was unfamiliar. Any single little misstep would land him under the jail. These fuckups were intolerable.

They pulled into the alleyway that led to the vacant restaurant.

"Get her out, put her in the freezer," Sire ordered. "And find out where the fuck August at!"

They popped the trunk and dragged Ashton inside, kicking and still screaming.

"Aye, Wa, what the lick be like?" Sire asked.

"Six hunnid Gs and still counting my nigga," Wasan said.

"And the deed?" Sire asked.

"Right here," Wasan answered, handing over the paper.

August entered the building; the sound of his thousand-dollar loafers slapping the floor echoed through the empty two-story structure.

"Broooo! Did you get it?" August asked as he came out of his suit jacket, tossing it on an old wooden chair as he crossed the room. August had been the one to lay out the opportunity for the lick. An influential real estate tycoon had held the deed to a Sinclair boat slip at a New York marina. Senior had lost it in a poker match years ago and had never been able to get it back. It was kept at the safe at Soho House and August was willing to do anything to get it back. By any means necessary. When Sire had brought it to August's attention that many celebs use Soho House's safe for jewelry and large amounts of cash, it was a no-brainer to rob it during one of the social house's most packed nights. The Draft had brought all the heavy hitters to town, so the take had been large. It had been eventful, indeed, but the extracurricular he had picked up during the robbery had elevated the stakes.

"I got more than what I came for. The fucking club manager is leaking in the safe," Sire said as he handed over the document.

"What the fuck? I said keep it clean!" August shouted.

"That's not the best part," Sire said. "Look at this shit, man. What you want me to do with this?" Sire pulled open the meat freezer and Ashton sat in the bottom right corner, shivering violently. Her back was to the wall and her eyes were on the door. She stood to her feet as soon as the door had opened.

"What the fuck are you doing, Sire? I know her."

"August?" Ashton said, frowning. "August, I swear I won't say anything."

"How do you want to handle this? I'm open to all suggestions, but just make sure whatever warranties you take covers a nigga. If you want to be civilized and let shawty go, I can do that too. Money can buy her silence. It's all the same. Either way, I'm back to H-Town tonight."

August looked at Sire's two goons and then down at Ashton.

"I didn't tell you to kill a high-profile club owner or take a hostage! This wasn't the plan!" August shouted. "This is your mistake. You fix it. Your money has been wired into the Cayman account."

August looked at Ashton once more and then stepped closer to Sire.

"Do what you have to do," he whispered.

He walked out without ever looking back.

Sire turned to Ashton.

"You don't have to do this," Ashton said.

Sire closed the freezer door and turned to Wasan and his goon. "Wrap this shit up. Make it quick and painless, then clean it up. I'll meet y'all at the clear port in three hours."

Sire looked through the square glass window into the freezer. His guilt pulled at him. He had no problem putting his murder game down, but he had never been the type to touch women and children. Ashton had been in the wrong place at the wrong time and it would cost her everything. She looked up at him and her stare captured him. To his surprise, she wasn't afraid.

She's pissed, he thought. It was an odd emotion for a woman in Ashton's predicament. It was as if she had the power.

He wanted to let her go, but he couldn't. He had never let a threat walk and today wouldn't be the day. *God forgive me,* he thought as he turned away from the freezer, leaving her to face an undeserving fate.

• • •

"Maid service!"

The sound of the electronic key opening the door was the only thing that aroused Sutton from her slumber. She hadn't slept like that in months; even with her prescription sleeping pills, she found it hard to rest her mind. Disoriented, she sat up. Her body hummed, her pussy swollen as she scrambled out of the bed.

"I need a minute!" she called back.

"Ma'am, the manager is here, we need the room, it's two hours past checkout," the maid called back. Sutton wrapped her body in the white sheet and hurried to her handbag. She pulled out her wallet, fumbling to retrieve one of her credit cards. She cracked the room door and slid it to the man.

"Just charge another night," she snapped. "I'll stop by the front desk to give you my ID and to sign for it."

She shut the door before the man could respond. Looking around the empty room, she didn't quite know how to feel. She had never intended to stay the night but even if she had, she wanted to be the one to wake up and leave first. No signs West was ever there remained. If her body wasn't humming from the aftershocks of the quaking sex he had put on her, she would wonder if she had dreamt the entire thing. She sat on the edge of the bed and her eyes landed on the check on the nightstand.

"This motherfucker," Sutton scoffed. She picked it up and shook her head. "He got me fucked up." She ripped it in half before heading to the shower. If he hadn't been on her radar before, he was definitely on it now, and Sutton would be the one with the last laugh.

CHAPTER 7

"Have you heard from Ash?" Gadget asked.

"Wasn't she with you? When I left Soho House, y'all were supposed to be right behind me!" Honor exclaimed.

Luna's brow furrowed as she dialed Ash's number one more time. "I mean, we were. She went back in to use the bathroom. I left before her, but she was on her way out."

"But you don't know if she actually made it back to the hotel?" Honor shouted. "Bitch, you know the rules. Door to door!"

"She was right behind me! It shouldn't have taken her long to use the restroom. She was supposed to come right out. She had to make it back here! She's probably just hungover," Luna defended. She stalked over to the front desk. "Excuse me, can I get the key to Ashton LaCroix's suite? We're her sisters and she isn't answering her phone. We just need to do a wellness check."

"Let me get my manager," the woman replied, retreating to the office in the back.

Honor hadn't thought twice about retreating to her room last night; but now that Ashton was MIA, regret lived in her bones.

"And where the hell is Sutty?" Luna asked. "Have you heard from her?"

"She's on her way back to the hotel. Said she had an early meeting." Honor's intuition was telling her something was wrong. She knew Ashton was the youngest, but Ash was trained. Ash knew the rules. Ash knew how to move accordingly. So if their little sister was unreachable, it was because something was awry.

"What kind of meeting did she have on a Sunday morning?" Luna questioned.

The clerk returned. "I can't give you the key, but I can escort you up," she explained.

"Let's wait for Sutty. She's five minutes away," Luna said. Honor was too anxious to stand still. She made her way through the lobby and paced the front of the hotel, avoiding the busy pedestrians as her mind worked in overdrive. Anxiety was a motherfucker. All the possibilities played in her head. When Sutton hopped out of the back of a yellow cab, Honor frowned.

"A meeting in last night's dress?" she asked. "Sounds like a dick appointment to me."

"Sounds like you need to find you some business," Sutton fired back. "Why are you policing the entrance to the hotel? And why is Luna blowing me up every five minutes? What's wrong?"

"It's Ash. We can't reach her," Honor said. "We have the key to her room. We're about to go up to do a wellness check. Something feels off."

Sutton stopped walking and her eyes widened, fear lacing them, causing them to prickle. She could feel the sting of worry. She blinked the emotions away, but her stomach knotted. The last time something felt off, they lost their father and Ashton to prison.

"Call her," Sutton said.

"We have."

"Again, Honor, call her again," Sutton ordered.

Sutton pushed into the hotel and hugged Luna.

"We're ready to go up," Sutton told the hotel clerk.

The ride up was long, silent, as the steel box carried them up thirty-five floors.

"What if—?"

"Nope," Sutton interrupted. "We're not doing that. Just be quiet."

The girls spilled out into the hallway, following the hotel worker to the door. The chirp of the electronic lock made Honor's heart skip a beat and she paused at the threshold.

"I'm going to stay out here," Honor said.

Luna looked back in concern.

"If something's wrong, I don't want to see it," Honor said.

Honor watched her sisters enter the suite and she braced herself for the worst.

"The bed is made. She didn't sleep here last night," Sutton said. "Did you check her locations?"

"Her locations aren't on," Luna replied.

"Where the hell is our sister?" Honor asked.

• • •

Ashton could hear her phone ringing in her bag and the sound pulled her back from the light she was walking toward.

She could barely breathe. She felt like she was choking as she lay on the cold cement floor of that abandoned building. Her entire body hurt. She was clinging to life. Her body was beaten so badly that every breath she took felt like it would be her last. August's men had left her for dead, but not before having their fun. Rape and murder. That had been their plan, only Ashton didn't die. A part of her wished she had.

Again, her phone rang. Ashton groaned as she tried her hardest to move. There was blood in her line of sight, and she couldn't even pick her weight up off the floor. She lay there, trembling violently in a pool of her blood.

She couldn't move her head, it felt like bones were broken. Her body, in addition to her spirit, was shattered.

She reached one hand out, inching bloody fingers across dirty concrete toward her phone. Her nails were broken from fighting the men off. She could see it, but it felt so far away. It was just out of arm's reach. The ringing stopped and Ashton sobbed. It felt like a lifeboat was retreating to shore, leaving her out to sea to die.

Ashton's instincts clicked in suddenly and she turned her head, enduring blinding pain to let blood drain from her mouth. Though she could barely get her jaw to move, she croaked out, "Hey Siri!"

Her voice was too low for the phone to pick it up and she cried.

"God, please," she whispered and tried again, louder this time. "Hey Siri!"

"Hmm?" the automated voice answered.

Relief flooded her. "Turn on my locations and call Gadget."

"Your locations are now on. Calling Gadget."

Ashton sobbed as she waited a few seconds for Siri to

place the call. Even if they didn't make it in time, just knowing her sisters were on the other line brought her comfort. If
she died, she wouldn't die alone.

After a minute, she spoke as loud as she could. "Gadget—" More blood came up, choking her. She couldn't
breathe. She could barely push words out. "Help me."

"Ash!"

She heard her sister screaming her name through the
phone, but she didn't have the energy to keep her eyes open.
Everything went black.

• • •

"Ashton!" Luna shouted. "Ashton!"

"Track that location now, Gadget. I don't care what you
have to hack into. She's hurt," Sutton ordered. Honor sat on
the edge of the bed. Her legs barely even worked.

They walked out of Ashton's room, following Gadget
back to hers.

"I can hack into the phone company's database and see
which cell tower her phone is pinging off of," Gadget said, her
voice shaking, matching her trembling fingers as she flipped
open her laptop. "This is a federal crime, Sutty. If I'm caught—"

"Make sure you're not," Sutton interrupted.

Gadget traced the call and squinted in confusion. "Wait a
minute—" she whispered. She opened an additional screen.
"The tracker we placed on August Sinclair is at this location
too. He's there." She googled the address, pulling up the
street view of the building.

"Something is wrong. We've got to go," Gadget said,
urgently. There was no reason for Ashton to be in an abandoned building. Her mind automatically assumed the

worst. She slammed her laptop shut and picked up her phone, calling 911.

"You're calling the police?" Honor asked.

"It's an abandoned building. Somebody hurt her and left her where nobody would look. She's in trouble."

• • •

"Ashton!" Honor shouted as she banged on the front door of the restaurant. "It's chained! Where are the police!"

"Down the alley! There has to be a back door," Luna said, leading the way. Sure enough, it was slightly ajar. Sutton barged in first. The boarded windows made the inside dark. They moved through the restaurant searching desperately. Honor felt sick to her stomach as she followed closely behind.

"Ashton!" she shouted once they reached the kitchen.

"Sutton, I think this is blood," Luna gasped as she came to the freezer door. Honor shook her head. She was sick with worry.

"I can't go in there. I'll stay out here," she said, turning around, eyes burning with tears.

Luna pulled open the commercial freezer.

"Oh my God!" Sutton whispered. Honor heard it in Sutton's tone of voice. Confirmation. Their sister was inside.

"Ashton!" Sutton shouted. "Honor, get in here now!"

Honor's feet felt like they were weighted, like someone had tied bricks to them and tossed her in the ocean. When she stepped inside the freezer, tears filled her eyes. Ashton lay on the floor, beaten and bloodied, a pool of blood staining the floor beneath her. Her panties were ripped and dangling from one foot. She looked like a mass of blood and hair on the floor.

"Is she breathing?" Honor asked, frantic as she came to her knees in front of Ashton's body.

"Baby, wake up! Ashton!" Sutton shouted as she pulled Ashton's body into her lap, covering herself in red. Ashton's face was swollen and red bruises marked up her skin. Her nails were broken, like she had fought someone off, and the handprints around her neck showed that she had been choked. Ashton looked lifeless. Perhaps she was. Perhaps they were too late to save her. Honor's heart ached. How could someone do this to their baby sister?

"How did this happen! I left her with you two!" Sutton shouted.

"I don't know! She was fine when I left the club!" Luna defended.

"We should have never left separately," Honor said, shaking her head in regret.

The room suddenly became crowded as paramedics rushed in.

"She's not waking up!" Sutton cried.

EMT workers pushed the sisters out of the way as they began to work on Ashton.

"Wake up, wake up, wake up," Honor whispered.

Ashton was whisked out of the room on a stretcher and Sutton was right behind her. "Meet me at the hospital!" It was the last thing she said before hopping in the back of the ambulance.

Honor and Luna clung to one another as they watched it drive away.

. . .

The hospital was freezing. Sutton's clothes were damp from the blood and she shivered as she paced the halls while screaming into the phone.

"He did this to her," Sutton whispered.

"Who?" Honor asked. "August Sinclair?"

Luna lifted the jacket she had taken from the restaurant. She dug through the pockets until she found her button tracker.

"I put it in his pants pocket," Honor said.

"Maybe he moved it. Either way, it's his. He was there. He did this shit to her," Sutton said, already browsing August's social media. "It's his," she confirmed.

"It's not their fault, Sutty," Luna said. "I can just hack into their security system to get the footage."

Sutton turned to walk away but she couldn't hold her judgement a moment longer. "I left her with you two! We don't leave a man behind."

"Fall back, Sutty, you're going way too hard," Luna said. They all knew Sutton's way of masking fear was by piling anger on top of it. She didn't mean to take things out on them, but she had nowhere else to redirect this feeling. The pit in her stomach was bottomless and she was free-falling.

The doctor entered the waiting room, interrupting the quarrel.

"How is she?" Luna asked.

"She's conscious but under heavy sedation, so she's a bit out of it," the doctor revealed. "She has three broken ribs and a ruptured spleen; lacerations to the face, neck, and groin. There was also evidence of rape, which resulted in miscarriage of the fetus."

Honor gasped. "She was pregnant?"

It was against their rules, but Ashton had always been a rule breaker. She was the sister who went against the grain, the youngest, yet somehow the most rebellious. Babies made them vulnerable. They complicated things, making it hard to move around, making it impossible to evade trouble if it came their way. Babies planted roots and they had always been taught to be the leaves on the trees, not the root in the ground; that way whenever the winds of life came along, they could blow along with them.

"He beat a baby out of her?" Sutton asked, lips trembling and eyes prickling.

"The police will have some questions for your sister when she's feeling up to it. They'll want to conduct a physical examination and rape kit," the doctor said. "We haven't washed her for this very reason. We could get rid of important evidence."

"Can we see her?" Honor couldn't contain her urgency and Sutton felt a streak of guilt because she knew Honor would never purposefully leave Ashton in a dangerous situation. She grabbed Honor's hand, brought it to her lips, and then patted it for reassurance.

"Yes, this way."

Sutton's phone buzzed and she stopped walking. "I'll be in. Give me a minute." As soon as her sisters were out of sight, Sutton broke down. She covered her mouth, crying so hard a nurse stopped to assist.

"Are you okay, miss?"

Sutton quickly sniffed away her emotion, wiping her tears as she nodded. "I'm fine, thank you."

August Sinclair had hurt her baby sister and Sutton felt responsible for the offense and the resolution.

I was sleeping with some nigga I don't even know while my sister was in trouble.

"Oh, I'm going to ruin this motherfucka!" Sutton hissed,

nostrils flaring as her temper blazed. She was so angry she couldn't steady her heart as she stepped inside Ashton's room.

"Sutty, I'm so sorry," Ashton cried. Her eyes were barely open and the first thing she did was apologize. It only made Sutton feel worse. "I didn't know I was pregnant. I didn't know . . ."

"Shhh." Sutton didn't even have it in her to be the disciplinarian. She was just happy her sister was alive, grateful to hear her voice.

"It's okay, baby. I'm just glad you're okay. You scared the shit out of me. Don't do that to me, Ash. Who's going to get on my nerves if something happens to you? Huh?" Sutton flicked a tear off her nose and then caressed her sister's forehead. They shared a laugh only for Ashton to grimace in pain.

"Don't worry about anything. I'm going to take care of it. I'm going to make everything better."

"You sound like Mommy, Sutty," Ashton whispered. She was groggy and Sutton's back straightened in discomfort. They didn't mention their mother. She had died so long ago, it barely hurt anymore. They almost forgot she'd existed, but moments like these reminded them that she had.

"Get some rest. You're tired," Sutton said, smoothing Ashton's messy hair before turning to walk out of the room.

"Sutty, you okay?" Luna asked.

"I'm fine. Stay with her, Gadget," Sutton answered, voice trembling as she walked out of the room.

• • •

Sutton bumped right into the police as she exited. She tensed when she saw them, a byproduct of growing up in Little Haiti where Miami PD were more foe than friend.

"We're sorry to intrude, but we really need to speak with Ashton LaCroix."

Sutton turned on her heels, deciding to stay and support her sister through their questioning process instead.

"We need to perform a rape kit, Ashton. Is that okay?" a female detective asked.

"Yeah, let's get it over with," Ashton said. "I don't need anyone else in the room."

"Ash, we just want to support you," Honor said.

"I just need a minute," Ashton said, lip trembling as she snapped her eyes shut.

The girls turned to leave but Ashton's voice stopped them. "Sutty, can you stay?" Ashton asked.

Sutton nodded and the others waited in the hall. She held Ashton's hand as the detective and doctor swabbed every inch of Ashton's body. Ashton shook violently; even her teeth chattered.

"Are you cold?" Sutton asked.

"I'm scared," Ashton admitted.

Sutton was devastated. She hated that her sister had to experience this. "Just look at me, okay?" Sutton instructed. "So you want to tell me about the guy?" Sutton was reaching for a distraction. A conversation to take Ashton's mind off the intrusive exam taking place.

"There's no guy," Ashton whispered.

"Of course, there's a guy," Sutton responded. "There was a baby so there has to be a guy. A really special guy because we don't do babies. So if you slept with a nigga without protection, you must love him."

Ashton's eyes filled with tears and one slid down her face. Sutton wiped it away, sniffing away her own as Ashton grimaced from the swab the doctor was using between her thighs.

"Is he fine? I know he's fine, Ash," Sutton said, snickering as she kissed her sister's fingers. Ashton was holding her hand so tightly. Her baby sister was afraid, and Sutton's heart ached because Ashton was one of the toughest women she knew; she didn't fear anything. Ashton smiled but didn't open her eyes. More tears. A tighter grip. Sutton squeezed back.

Ashton nodded. "He was perfect, Sutty."

"Well, where is this man?" Sutton asked. She wanted to keep Ashton talking, keep distracting her.

"He's in Miami," Ashton said. Her face broke and her tears worsened. "I lied to him, Sutty. I took everything from him. Ruined his career, took his money, and I came home."

"Why would you do that, Ash?" Sutton asked.

"He's Carter Jones's son," Ashton revealed.

Sutton didn't even realize she had released her sister's hand until Ashton opened her eyes.

She had to bite her tongue to stop herself from reacting. She felt fury fill her body, turning her rigid. Of all the men in the world, why Ashton would choose to fall in love with one who was a direct relation to the Diamonds was beyond Sutton.

"I messed up, Sutty. So bad," Ashton admitted.

"Just let them do their jobs, Ash," Sutton said. "We'll talk about it later."

"I'm so sorry," Ashton whispered.

Sutton didn't respond.

This conversation wasn't to be had with witnesses. Carter Jones and the Miami Cartel had a sordid history with their family. They had been to war with her uncle Matee. Her cousins and uncles had died on the streets of Little Haiti at the hands of the Diamond family. Ashton knew the history. How had she fallen in love with the enemy?

Once all the samples were taken, Ashton sat up and gripped the hospital gown.

"We know who did this to her. It was August Sinclair," Sutton said.

"August Sinclair of Sinclair Enterprises?" one of the detectives asked.

"Does his title matter?" Sutton asked. "That son of a bitch did this to my sister. I want him arrested. I want the perp walk and the whole nine," Sutton said passionately, stabbing her finger in the direction of the officers.

The pause that followed was filled with skepticism.

"Does that change anything? Look at my sister! He did this to her! Do your jobs and arrest him!"

The detective sucked in a deep breath and glanced at his partner before looking at Ashton. "Is that who did this to you? Would you be able to identify him in a lineup and point him out on a witness stand in a court of law?"

Ashton tried to jog her memory. She had sustained so much trauma, endured so much pain, that she couldn't even recall. The last thing she remembered was being snatched out the back entrance of the nightclub. Everything after that moment was a blur. All she remembered was pain. She was so foggy.

"I don't know. I can't really remember. I don't know," Ashton said. "He was there, but . . ."

The doctor who had been standing aside silently interjected. "It isn't uncommon for rape victims who experience this type of trauma to have memory lapses. She's been sedated and given heavy medication. Now isn't the best time to ask her this."

The detective handed Sutton his card. "There are steps to an investigation. We'll be in touch with what those next steps will be," the man said.

Sutton took the card, but she knew when she was being brushed off. "Steps?" she said. "He committed a crime!"

"If that's true, we'll get him," the detective responded.

"If it's true!" Sutton shouted.

"Sutty," Ashton interrupted. "Just let them leave. Black girl accusing a rich white boy of rape. They don't see a victim in sight. They're all on the same team."

"Ma'am, that's not—"

"Get out my room," Ashton said.

The detective retreated with empty promises in tow and Sutton wrapped Ashton in her arms, letting her little sister cry on her shoulder.

"I'm going to take care of it, Ash. That's my word."

. . .

Sutton sat in the shadows of her office. She was grateful for the darkness. The migraine that plagued her retreated a little in the blackness of the room. She shouldn't even be here this late, but her mind wouldn't rest.

The knock at the door was followed by a low creak as Luna pushed into the room.

"Burning the midnight oil?" she asked.

"I couldn't sleep so here I am. What are you doing here?" Sutton replied.

"Same."

Luna took a seat and Sutton sighed. "Ashton could have

died. All I can think about is ruining that smug, entitled son of a bitch."

"He's a trust-fund brat with generational money, Sutty. Getting back at a man like that . . ."

"Means we take it all. Strip him of everything. His last name, his money, his power. This one is personal."

"You know we don't move like that. It's never personal. It's always business. When you start letting emotion steer you, you make mistakes. This isn't what we're about," Luna said.

"It is now," Sutton insisted. "We just got her back. I wasn't even sure that I was happy about her being back, but seeing her in that tub, all beat up . . ." Sutton shook her head and picked up her wineglass, tilting it to her lips. She scoffed. "I called the police to see if there had been any updates, any arrests, and they haven't even questioned him. It's personal, Gadget."

"What's our way in?" Luna asked.

Sutton pulled out her phone, typed onto the screen, and then slid it across the desk.

"An oil rig?" Luna frowned. "How does this factor in?"

"You remember the BP oil spill in 2010?" Sutton asked.

"Yeah, it was all over the news," Luna responded. "I'm not following you though, Sutty. That was an accident."

Sutton sat back in her chair and gripped the armrests. "This one won't be. We're going to blow their rig. The stock market will plummet, their stock will suffer, and then I'm going to make them pay us to fix it. Only I won't fix it. Once they hire our firm, we'll have enough access to destroy their entire company from the inside out."

"How the hell are we supposed to pull off an explosion on an oil rig that sits in the middle of the ocean?" Luna hissed, voice low because they were crossing lines of morality, lines of legality. Even the conversation could land them under the jail.

"Let me handle that part," Sutton responded.

Luna stood and headed toward the door. "You need to get some sleep, Sutty. We all do. This is not us. This is criminal. Felonies. Maybe after you rest, you'll be thinking straight. I'll call you in the morning."

Sutton waited until her office door closed before clicking the keys to her open laptop. She pulled up the article she had been reading.

Navy SEAL Dishonorably Discharged

Sutton sipped her wine as she stared at the man on her screen. Her mental wheels turned and she considered stopping herself before she took things too far. Sutton was a bull, however, and once she settled on an idea, she had to follow through. She was like a dog with a bone.

She ran his name through the state database. She wasn't a computer whiz like Gadget, but she knew how to look a nigga up. Black women became more inquisitive than the FBI when they needed to be. Sutton looked up the address of the naval officer, writing it down on a piece of paper before closing her laptop in haste. She snatched her jacket off the back of her chair and rushed out of the office.

• • •

Ashton grimaced as she rolled out of bed. Her entire body ached. Her soul hurt more. She hadn't even known she was pregnant. By him. Carter Jones II, world-famous boxer, son of the Cartel. The love of her life. Running from him seemed impossible. Just when she had thought she could evade his memory, the discovery of a baby they had made reminded her of how much she loved him. She couldn't even call him to tell him what they had created because he would undoubtedly have her killed. Even if he could somehow get over her treachery, his mother, Miamor, surely would not.

She stood to her feet and slowly made her way to the closet. The box in the bottom contained a burner phone, a hundred thousand dollars cash, and a gun. Her emergency stash. She powered on the phone and dialed CJ's number. She had erased his contact from her normal iPhone, but the numbers were etched on her heart. Her finger lingered over the call button, and before she lost her nerve, she pressed it.

"Hello?"

The baritone of his voice snatched the bottom out of her stomach, and she closed her eyes.

"Yo, who is this?" CJ asked. There was commotion around him, but Ashton blocked it all out, concentrating on his breathing. This call was already too long. There was an awkward silence, then recognition as she heard him move away from the crowd. "Yo, you got a lot of fucking balls to call me right now," he said. "You know how much money I got on your head? And you dial my line like it's nothing, like you ain't a snake out here?"

The overwhelming urge to defend herself brewed inside her, but she didn't say one word. She would neither confirm nor deny she was on the phone. It would be stupid to speak; it was already reckless to call in the first place, but she had just lost his baby. She just wanted to hear his voice.

"I fucked with you. I don't trust nobody, but I trusted

you and you drug a nigga soul through the mud. For what? Some paper? I had that for you all day. You would have been better off asking. Instead, you was on some foul shit. A nigga treated you good and you were out here like a bird, moving wrong for some fucking money?"

Ashton's lip trembled. She couldn't even defend herself. She was too afraid to let him know it was her. Although, she knew that he knew exactly who he was speaking to. "I ain't got to tell you to stay out of Miami. You're a smart girl. You know what's waiting for you here. I can't save you, Ash. It's beyond me now. The order already been called in. You should have stayed down. It could have been a hell of a life, baby. You take care of yourself," he said. He paused and her breath caught in her throat. Her heart thundered and she felt sick. She had messed up a lot of things in her life, but this had to be the worst. A part of her wished his baby still grew inside her because then he would have to forgive. He would have to let her explain. Without that connection, she was nothing to him. She could hear the contempt through the phone.

She had known the moment she decided to burn that bridge that no one would send a lifeboat. A failed pregnancy didn't change that. She would have to nurse these wounds alone.

"You fucked me up," he said, his tone relenting slightly as he allowed himself to feel something other than disgust for her. "If it's you, just hit a button."

Ashton felt the tear slide down her face as she pressed the number 1.

She heard him scoff. "You be good out there in the world, Ash."

The disconnection tore her heart in half, but she knew she

had to let go. She wouldn't call him again. She couldn't. He wouldn't let many more attempts slide without finding her location. She removed the SIM card from the burner phone and went to the bathroom. She tossed it in the toilet along with her dreams of love and happiness. She had made her bed, now she had to lie in it.

. . .

Sutton sat in front of the one-story house, listening to the barking of the German Shepherd that guarded the perimeter of the fence. She had been there for some time. She hoped the longer she stayed inside her car, the more she would come to her senses, but she hadn't. Trespassing against her was one thing, but doing harm to any of her sisters was out of bounds.

She exited her car and approached the house, ignoring the barking dog as she fearlessly opened the gate. It lunged and barked wildly, but Sutton simply bent and lowered her hand, summoning the dog to her. Dogs were pack animals. They always acknowledged a leader and Sutton exuded leadership in every way.

"Good girl," she whispered, petting the intimidating beast as it sniffed her other hand. The dog eventually licked it as she rubbed its thick coat with her free hand. "You're beautiful."

She heard the creak of the front screen door as it was pushed open and she looked up to find a pair of coal eyes staring at her. In one hand he gripped a long-barrel shotgun; in the other he held a bottle of Budweiser beer.

"Guard dog, my ass," he said. "Com'ere girl!" On command, the dog retreated to its owner's side, settling on the porch next to the man's feet. "Who are you?"

Sutton stood. "My name's Sutton LaCroix," she announced.

"Sutton LaCroix, you want to tell me why you're on my
property before I shoot you?" he asked.

"I have a job. It requires discretion and I believe it's
something only you can do. I've read about your struggles
recently. The discharge from the Navy. I think you can see a
good opportunity when it comes your way and you can put
emotions to the side for business. I could be wrong, but you
tell me," Sutton said.

The man eyed her skeptically and took a swig of his beer.
"I can't help you," he said.

"I know," Sutton responded. "I'll be helping you. Ex–war
hero turned public enemy number one. You need to change
the narrative. You need the people back on your side."

"And you're gonna help me?" he asked. "Little pretty lady
like you is gonna fight the world just for me? Why would
you do that?"

"Because you're going to do something for me in return,"
Sutton said. "You were the most decorated diver in the Na-
vy's history. I need that skill for something important, and
I'm willing to pay for it."

"How much?" he asked.

"A quarter million dollars," Sutton said.

The man emptied the beer bottle into his mouth and
tossed it into his yard. "Come in," he said. He turned and
entered his house, whistling for his dog to follow behind him.
Sutton smirked as she followed behind him. Finding someone who was qualified to dive beneath the Sinclair's oil rig
was the biggest challenge. She was a master negotiator; she
wasn't concerned about him declining the offer, but finding

someone with the know-how and skill to pull it off success-
fully was the biggest challenge.

She stepped into his home and her heart sank as she took
in the conditions around her. The house was old, barely
standing, and old furniture crowded the inside. A bucket
of dirty water sat in the corner catching water from a leaky,
exposed pipe that protruded from the ceiling. Empty beer
bottles and filth were everywhere.

"Take a seat," the man said. He cleared old newspapers
from the tattered couch to make a space for her. Sutton reluctantly sat.

"What I got to do?" the man asked.

"I need you to blow an oil rig," she said, voice low.

"I'll need my money up front," the man said. "And it'll
take a team. One diver can't blow a whole rig. Those things
are small cities. My men will have to be paid."

"Money isn't a problem. How many men?" she asked.

"Four."

"I'll need names and addresses. I need to know who I'm
in business with," she said. "I can pay you half now, half after
the job is complete. A quarter for you and fifty thousand for
each of your men."

"Consider it done."

CHAPTER 8

"What's this I hear about a strike?" August Sinclair Sr. walked into West's office. He was an aged version of his son. Distinguished, wealthy, and powerful, his presence filled the room as he entered like he owned the place. In fact, he did. He was responsible for building Sinclair Enterprises from the ground up. Every piece of wood, every nail, every door handle was property of this visionary oil tycoon. He was the only person in the entire building who didn't need to knock. Known to everyone he loved as Senior, he was the head of the Sinclair family and a mentor to both his sons. West might not be blood born, but he was of equal importance to the Sinclairs.

"The workers on the Galveston rig have walked out," West answered, standing to embrace the man in front of him.

"Your mother asked me to bring you this," Senior said, placing a pie on his desk.

"She's the best." West chuckled as he rounded his desk and sat in his executive chair. "Every Friday night, win or lose, I came home to this blackberry pie."

"You're her son," Senior said. "Our family changed the moment we met you, Westin. I'm very proud of you. We all are."

West remembered the days when he was sleeping in a beat-up, old-school car. He would never forget the day Mrs. Sinclair pulled him into her office and asked him if he were homeless. He had been in the sixth grade; and from that day forward, she took him home so he would have a warm bed to sleep in. She went from principal to his foster mom; and before he entered high school, the Sinclairs had adopted him officially. He had clicked instantly with August, and their friendship had transformed into brotherhood. Overnight, West had become a part of the upper class. The Sinclair family had changed his life, and he had planned to pay them back when he made it to the NFL. He had been a star on the field; but in his second year of college, he'd ruined his knee, ending his career before it'd even begun. Since oil was the Sinclair family business, he fell into place and soaked up the knowledge Senior had to offer.

"I appreciate you, old man," West said. "I'll never be able to say it enough."

"You don't need to say it at all, son," Senior said. "Now, tell me about this strike. Have you spoken to the head of the union?"

"I've requested a list of their concerns. This is bad. The longer we let this linger, the more money we lose. We're bleeding profit by the minute. Every single second that the rig is down, it's costing us. My instincts tell me to be very flexible. Also to keep it out of the press."

"We'll bend as much as we can. These workers give their lives to the rig. It's their home. They spend months on end on that boat. I want the conditions as comfortable as possible. Whatever they want, let's try to meet them halfway," Senior said.

"You're the king they love," West said.

"And you're the one they fear," Senior replied. He reached for West's brandy-filled decanter and poured two glasses. "You're what I always wanted out of a son. All of this will be yours one day. August can't handle it. He is too privileged. He never had to work for anything. You know what it's like to have nothing, and you'll work hard to keep everything you have. You're my legacy."

He handed a drink to West and they tapped their glasses as West thought of the power that came with his position. He was a black man in the energy business. That alone afforded him many enemies, but his business savvy made him a commodity. He was already vice president of the company; but to hear Senior had plans to hand it all over made him wary of the potential conflict that lay ahead with August. The last thing he wanted was to take August's birthright, but he had worked for it. Most little boys from the hood dreamed of being king of the streets. That had never been West's plan. When he had lost his shot at playing professional ball, business became his passion. He didn't want to run a block, he wanted to control an industry. He wanted to be a tycoon and oil gave him the resource to control the world.

• • •

"Senior, it's our anniversary. I sit quietly and I let you put this company before our marriage every other day of the year. I only ask for one day, this day, to be your priority. This is unacceptable."

August Sinclair stood in the mirror knotting his necktie.

He didn't speak. He let the words of his wife go through one ear and out the other until his appearance was perfect.

"Senior! If you're going to attempt to mask business and call it an anniversary dinner, I'll pass."

"Abigail, darling," Senior said as he pulled his sulking wife from the bed. She was stunning. Age hadn't detracted from her beauty one bit. Her ginger hair was curled in voluptuous waves and her fair skin was complemented by matching freckles. He had fallen in love with her at first sight and the Louisiana Southern belle had made him work hard to win her over. "Trust me. Tonight is all about you. We have thirty years to celebrate, my dear. I just need to make one stop and then you'll have my undivided attention." He stared into the greenest eyes he had ever seen, and it felt like he could see the history of their life in the depths of her gaze.

Abigail's reluctance was buried beneath submission as she sighed deeply before following her husband out of the room.

"Looking good, Senior!"

Senior paused for his youngest son, extending a hand, and the two shook firmly. At ten years old, Brandon "Beamer" Sinclair was the youngest of the bunch and Abigail's miracle baby. He had come well after her childbearing years should have passed; but when she was forty years old, he had blessed them all. He was their pride and joy, and their anniversary was also his birthday.

"Thanks, son," Senior said.

"You throw on a suit real fast and you can join us for dinner," Abigail proposed.

"He's old enough to stay home alone," Senior said. Abigail smiled at her son. He was the center of her entire world. He was diagnosed with high-functioning autism, and she doted on him more than she should, but she couldn't help it. He was her baby. He needed her. No matter how much he thought he didn't.

"But why should he have to? It's his day too," Abigail insisted. "Go get dressed, son."

Beamer raced up the stairs and Abigail smiled at Senior. "Now you can do all the business you like. My baby will keep me company when the inevitable phone call comes that will pull you away from dinner," Abigail said.

Beamer was dressed in ten minutes flat and the threesome departed. A Rolls Royce awaited them outside their plantation-style Texas mansion. Senior had afforded Abigail a wonderful life. Her every wish had been fulfilled over the years, but he was aware of the one thing he owed her—time. It took an understanding woman to marry a man of his caliber. The world expected pieces of his day. Early mornings and late evenings were the routine, but he had built them quite an estate.

Their driver took them out of the city toward Galveston and Abigail grew disgruntled instantly when she noticed the direction they were headed.

"Senior, you said no work," Abigail said.

They pulled up to the port where a boat awaited.

"I just have to check something out on the rig, and we'll be on our way. I promise. It'll take an hour tops," Senior stated.

"Senior, you're blowing it big-time," Beamer snickered.

Senior chuckled. "Watch and learn, son." He waited for the driver to open the door and then he went to open his wife's door.

Abigail took his hand and stepped her expensive Dior heels on the cement.

The rig was twenty-five miles offshore and the disappointed look on Abigail's face made Senior chuckle.

"You would think this rig didn't fund our entire lives the way you dread coming out here," Senior said as he moved a tendril of hair out of her face and they stepped onto the boat that would take them to the rig.

"I don't hate it, it just consumes everything, Senior," Abigail said.

"Nobody consumes me like you," he whispered in her ear. He kissed her ear and then her lips, causing Abigail to giggle. It didn't matter how long they had been together, he made her swoon.

"Dude, gross. I'm right here," Beamer said without looking up from his phone.

Abigail and Senior laughed harder as they settled in, letting the boat carry them out to the rig.

A half hour later, the boat dropped an anchor portside of the rig and Beamer hopped up out of his seat in excitement.

"Careful, buddy, the rig isn't a playground," Senior said as he watched his son board his pride and joy.

"Senior, you've got one hour," Abigail said.

"Right this way," Senior said as he led the way to the top deck. Abigail complained the entire way and Senior didn't utter one word.

"I could have worn jeans and boots if I knew I would be on a dirty . . ." She stopped speaking when she saw the candlelit table that was in the middle of the deck.

Senior turned to her and extended his hand toward the display. "Happy anniversary," he said.

"Surprise, Mom!"

Abigail looked at Senior and Beamer, stunned. "You knew about this? You sneaky snook, you! We don't keep secrets!"

"But this was a good secret, right, Mom?" Beamer asked.

Abigail's eyes misted because her son was so innocent. To another mom, having an autistic son would be a challenge; but to Abigail, it felt like a gift. He was extremely intelligent, possessed a photographic memory, and was the most empathetic kid she had ever met. He sometimes seemed like he was younger than he was, and other times, he seemed like a young businessman. All the time, she loved him.

"A really good secret, Beamer. Your father did really, really good," Abigail said.

"Beamer's going to be our waiter for the evening," Senior said. "Will you join me for dinner, Mrs. Sinclair?"

"You really put me first?" she asked. Beamer pulled out his Bluetooth speakers and connected them to his phone, turning on a playlist Senior had curated. Sinatra crooned through the air.

"I'm going to put you first for the rest of my life. Can an old man have this dance?"

Abigail blushed as she grabbed Senior's hand, taking a twirl beneath his arm as they swayed under the starry sky.

Senior held his wife close, cheek to cheek, his hand securely on the small of her back.

"I love you, Abigail. If I could give you all the stars in the sky, I would. I'd gift them to you."

Abigail pulled back to stare into his eyes but before she could fix her lips to respond . . .

BOOM.

· · ·

Sutton's phone rang incessantly, and she silenced it as she sat in the dark room. Almost as soon as she pressed the button, it rang again.

Gadget.

Sutton silenced it again.

A text.

Gadget
Answer the phone. 911.

Sutton didn't respond. Her heart clenched. She could hear it beating in her ear. Her pulse raced. Every sense she had was heightened. Her phone rang again.

"What?" she shouted as she tapped her earbuds to answer the call.

"Sutton, what did you do?" Gadget asked. "You don't decide alone. I told you it wasn't a good idea. What the fuck are you thinking!"

"I did what needed to be done. Ain't no free licks around this bitch," Sutton responded.

"Turn on the news," Gadget stated.

"I don't need to," Sutton replied. "I know what went down."

"You don't know shit, Sutty," Gadget replied. "Turn on the news!"

Sutton hung up on Gadget and powered off her phone. She knew Gadget wouldn't understand. She hadn't run it by Honor and Ash at all. She was the oldest. She felt she had the right to call the play.

She reached for her remote control and turned on her television. The chyron that ran across the bottom of the screen was like a punch to the gut.

TWO DEAD, ONE CRITICALLY INJURED IN OIL RIG EXPLOSION

"It was supposed to be empty," she whispered. "There's a strike; there weren't supposed to be people on the goddamn boat."

Sutton grabbed her laptop in anguish and opened it, Googling the explosion. She gasped, covering her mouth in horror when she saw the pictures of August Sinclair Sr. and Abigail Sinclair on her screen. She clicked the video on the news story and she felt like she would throw up.

"The ten-year-old son of the billionaire oil tycoon, Brandon Sinclair, was pulled out of the Gulf of Mexico after being found clinging to a piece of debris from the explosion of the Sinclair oil rig. He has suffered burns on fifty percent of his body and has been transported to—"

Sutton slammed her laptop closed and rushed to the en suite bathroom. Her body betrayed her as she vomited her regret.

"Why were they on the boat?" she whispered. "No, no, no, no, no!" Guilt weighed her down so heavy, she couldn't pull herself from the floor. She sat beside her toilet, back leaning against the wall and elbows resting on her knees as she looked at the ceiling. There would be no forgiveness for this. Two people had been killed. A little boy had lost both parents, and that was if he survived.

The knock on her door pulled her to her feet. She was terrified. Creating scandal and committing murder were two different things. She was smart, cunning, and always willing to push the envelope for a dollar, but a cold-blooded murderer she was not.

She half expected the police to be her guests, but logic told her they weren't. The news was reporting the explosion as an accident. She was in the clear, but her conscience was being dragged through the mud.

Sutton pulled open the door to find all three sisters standing before her. Even Ashton had climbed out of bed, interrupting her healing to show up.

"What did you do?" Gadget asked.

Sutton's mouth fell open, but nothing came out.

"What she had to do."

Ashton entered Sutton's condo, walking by Sutton. The other girls followed suit as Sutton turned on her television. The report was on every channel.

"Ashton, this is serious. People were hurt," Honor said.

"I was hurt," Ashton shot back. "Karma don't always hit you directly. I hope August Sinclair feels every bit of this shit. So, we created the problem, now let's make them pay to fix it." Ashton looked at Sutton. "That was the point of the explosion, right?"

Sutton cleared her throat and gathered her bearings, pushing her guilt aside. She looked at Ashton, then at each of her sisters.

"Sutty?" Ashton pressed.

Again, eye to eye, she focused on Ashton. Her baby sister was silently begging for her to do something. To make it right.

Sutton nodded. "We're going to add tax on this one."

CHAPTER 9

"You're lying! You're lying! I don't believe you!" Beamer shouted as he kicked and flailed in the hospital bed.

"Beamer, I'm sorry," August said, sniffing away his own grief as he delivered the news to his baby brother.

"I want Mom! Where's Senior? They were right there! Then boom. Then boom. Then boom!" Beamer shouted. He repeated things in threes when he felt anxious, a tic caused by his condition.

"Calm down, Beamer! Mom's not coming! I need you to chill out!" August said, his frustration mounting as he looked at Beamer. He had burns everywhere. He was in so much pain, but the emotional anguish was killing him. August couldn't stomach it. He was high out of his mind in an attempt to numb the pain. He couldn't reassure Beamer. He couldn't even contain his own grief. He was spiraling.

"Beamer! Cut it the fuck out, man! Give me a break! You're not the only one who's fucked up over this!" August shouted.

"Hey!"

The voice came from West as he entered the hospital room. "Fuck is wrong with you, bro?" West barked.

"He won't stop crying!" August shouted. "What the fuck am I supposed to do? We're all sad! It is what it is! I can't deal when he gets like this!"

"When he gets like this or when you get like this?" West asked, removing his suit jacket and hanging it on the back of the chair before approaching Beamer. He could always tell when August was high. West had been pulling August out of situations he couldn't handle since they were kids. Today, he lacked patience. Today, he had buried two people he loved. They all had, and Beamer hadn't even been well enough to attend his parents' funerals.

"I don't need this shit today," August said.

"Go for a walk, bro," West said. It was an order. His tone left no room for interpretation.

"Beamer, my man, I need you to listen to me, okay?" West asked, sitting on the edge of the hospital bed. Beamer was over-stimulated. His body hurt unimaginably, his heart was ripped in half, and his mind was racing with the realization that his parents were gone. He was stuck in a fit. He had them some-times. Usually, no one would be able to tell he was autistic; but when he felt overwhelmed, he couldn't control himself. He just had to scream.

"I want my mom. I want my mom. I want my mom," Beamer shouted.

"I know you do, man, me too," West said. "I know, but you're not alone. You still have family who love you. I know you're scared, but I'm not going anywhere. No matter what happens, I'm going to make sure you're okay." It was so hard to look at Beamer. He was covered in bandages. He was burned everywhere. His arms and legs were so badly singed that he would need skin grafts for years to come. West had never seen anything like it. It almost seemed like surviving the explosion was worse than the quick death the blast had delivered to their parents.

"It hurts," Beamer whimpered.

"Close your eyes, kid," West said.

Beamer's tears squeezed out of his eyes and his lip quivered as a nurse walked into the room.

"We have him on the highest pain medications we can administer. I'm going to up his dosage," she said as she hooked a new medication up to his IV. "We're doing everything we can to make sure his burns don't get infected," she said.

"I don't want him to feel any of this. He's the last of us who deserves it," West said.

"Are you a friend of the family?" the nurse asked.

West looked up at her, brow pinched, glowering. The question didn't surprise him. He had gotten it most of his life. His black face among the Sinclair family's, him sitting in the family Christmas photo, him showing up at Mass, all appeared out of place. "I am family," he said.

"He's my big brother. The best big brother ever." Beamer groaned as the pain medication pulled him into a haze.

August cleared his throat and West glanced behind him.

An awkward beat filled the air and West saw the injury behind the weight of Beamer's words.

"The attorneys are at Sinclair Enterprises. The press is all over the oil spill. We've been summoned," August said.

West stood to his feet and leaned down to kiss Beamer's forehead. "I'll be back, kid," he said. "Take care of him."

The nurse nodded as West slid into his jacket and walked out of the door, leaving the scent of expensive cologne behind him.

"August," West said when he entered the hallway. August's eyes were bloodshot from the mixture of cocaine and crying that had consumed his day. West wasn't sure if August would even remember where Senior and Abigail rested. He was out of his mind with grief and the grief pushed him to test the limits. West knew whatever sadness lived in him was multiplied in August. Blood counted for something in that aspect. West's loss was great but incomparable to what August was feeling. West lived on without regret. He had told Senior and Abigail how much he loved them often. Not a day went by when they were unaware of how grateful he was for them. August, on the other hand, was a man who spoke his affections rarely. Unspoken sentiment had been buried today because in death, words left unsaid went forever unheard. It was a tragedy felt most by August Sinclair.

August turned to him, reluctantly, unwilling to lend his eyes to West, instead opting to scroll through the unimportance of his Instagram timeline. "I know this is rough. I need you to tighten up though. Senior would have wanted you to be at your best."

August nodded but didn't reply. West pulled him in for a brotherly hug.

"I can't do this right now. I don't care about the press, the lawyers, none of it. Not today," August said. "I think I'm going to stick around, make sure Beamer's straight."

West reached into August's inner jacket pocket and pulled

out a small baggie of powder cocaine. He pocketed it discreetly. "You take care of Beamer. I'll handle the company. Sober up, a'ight?"

West departed, sliding into the awaiting black Escalade, a company-chauffeured vehicle. West's phone had been ringing nonstop for days. The blowback from the explosion was devastating. He knew the Sinclair legal team was trying to minimize the damage. They had set up meetings with potential PR firms that could help their company recover from this. He would have to put on a strong front for the Sinclair family in order to preserve the legacy that Senior had left behind.

• • •

"I'm sorry, how much longer will the meeting be delayed?" Sutton asked.

"Please accept our apologies. The Sinclair family funerals were today. This meeting is very important to Mr. Sinclair, however. It's his top priority to establish a relationship with a good firm that can help the company navigate through this trying time. The LaCroix Group is the best. It's imperative that this meeting take place."

Sutton cleared her throat and nodded. "Considering the circumstances, I can extend a bit more patience." Before she could go on, the door to the boardroom opened and Sutton placed eyes on West. She faltered, stunned, as he rounded the table.

"Tim, I'm sorry to keep you waiting. As you know it's been a trying day," West said. Sutton's throat tightened. She wasn't even breathing as he finally turned to face her. His shock matched hers and they stood there staring as the night they shared pulled a seat up to the table. An elephant in the room.

"Mr. Sinclair, this is Sutton LaCroix."

The introduction wasn't necessary, but she played along, extending her hand. She was thrown off. The temperature in the room seemed to be on hell as she stood under his stare.

She saw the amusement in his eyes as he reached for her hand, holding on to it a second longer than appropriate.

"Timothy, give us the room, please," West said.

"I really should sit in on these . . ."

"That wasn't a question," West stated. The finality in his tone sent the older white man from the room.

"Ms. LaCroix," West said, finessing the sides of his mouth as he sat on the edge of the table, placing shiny Prada shoes around her so that she was standing between his legs.

She took a step back. "Mr. Sinclair," she countered. "This is so inappropriate," she whispered.

"Or fate, depending on how you look at it," he snickered.

"I don't think fate leaves a $25,000 check as payment for services," she snapped.

"I told you, it was too good to get it free," West answered. His eyes took her in, and Sutton raised an eyebrow.

"You're so arrogant," she said, shaking her head. "I had no idea you were affiliated with this company."

"I'm not affiliated. I'm a Sinclair," West added.

Sutton's brows lifted, stunned.

"The adopted black son from the hood," West explained.

The guy from the jet that Ashton was trying to tell us about, Sutton thought.

"I thought you owned a sports agency?" she said, confused. "Or is that what you say to get women to sleep with you."

He stood, closing the space between them. Sutton was cornered by masculinity. He smelled so damned good that she wanted to taste him. He looked even better.

"That's not why you slept with me," he replied. "But I own that too. That wasn't a lie." He bypassed her and took a seat at the head of the table. "Now, do you want to tell me how our paths crossed again?"

Sutton took a seat at the other end. "You have a PR problem; I have solutions," she said. "The explosion of your oil rig has resulted in the damage of the underlying wellhead. Every day, thousands of gallons of oil are leaking into the Gulf of Mexico. Wildlife, water quality, and food sources are all being tainted. Your company's stock has declined. You need the LaCroix Group to spin this story for you and to help you take the steps to repair your company's image financially and publicly as you work on stopping the leak."

"I want to take you to dinner," West said, interrupting her.

She sat back in her chair, offended. "Is that all you see? A pretty face? You didn't hear one word that I said," she accused.

"I heard every word," West said. "I'd prefer to continue the conversation over dinner."

"I don't mix business with pleasure," Sutton stated.

"If there's a choice in the capacity I'd like you to serve me, I won't choose business. A nigga ain't had pleasure like what you was giving out before. I'm trying to double up."

His hood slipped out effortlessly and Sutton's body revolted.

"Mr. Sinclair." His name came out clipped, a warning.

"Say yes to dinner."

She didn't know why it sounded like he was ordering her around. He wasn't the boss of her. She didn't even know this nigga, but somehow her heart raced anyway.

"I'm not interested in that. You can hire another firm for this job, and they'll fail you. I have a strategic plan ready for implementation that will . . ."

He stood from his seat, rounding the table as he approached the window that revealed the rest of the office. He closed the blinds.

"What are you doing?" she asked, voice trembling as he clicked the lock on the door before approaching her. He spun around the chair she sat in and Sutton stood. "Mr. Sinclair."

"You didn't cash the check," he stated. He was so off subject. Sutton just wanted to steer the conversation back to her agenda because he was too close and her stomach was somersaulting.

"It wasn't a transaction," she whispered, flustered as he loomed over her. It was like her body was betraying her, yearning for this man, as she remembered the ways he had made her cum. He had been so good. It had been a long time since a man had been anything more than a disappointment in bed.

"Can we just keep this . . ." She paused, blowing out a deep breath before swallowing the lump in her throat. "Professional?" she finished.

"I don't come across women like you often," West said. "Women are easy. They're shallow, too willing, chasing clout, fame, money . . ."

"Mr. Sinclair." Sutton was basically pleading at this point. Her panties were destroyed.

"We're past formalities," he stated, taking a finger to the curve of her jawline and then lifting her chin so she was forced to stare in his eyes.

"West," she whispered.

"Just like that," he said, his voice dripping in authority, soaking with seduction, like he was losing restraint. "You said it just like that and suddenly I can't hear it any other way."

The finesse was top notch. She was sure he had his pick of women all over Houston. He was almost hypnotizing. Sutton could barely gather a thought in her head she was swooning so hard, but she was too stubborn to let it show.

"A smile won't make you less tough," West said, smirking. She rolled her pretty, stubborn eyes up to him. "Have dinner with me, Sutton."

"I can't," she whispered. "The only thing I have to offer you is a business relationship."

"So, a business dinner it is," West said, stepping back, allowing her to breathe air that wasn't tainted with his scent. "Leave your address with my receptionist on the way out. I'll send a car for you. Eight o'clock."

He didn't even look at her as he headed toward the door. His focus had already shifted to the phone in his hand. He didn't even look back at her before he left her standing in his conference room alone.

· · ·

Honor's feet wouldn't move. She stood in the threshold of the hospital room door, frozen as she stared at the small body in the bed. The fact Sutton had done this, ordered an explosion that had left this young boy so badly burned, brought tears to her eyes. They had run long cons on many entities before, but this was the first time it felt malicious. Normally, they were on the side of right; but with an innocent kid injured and his parents dead, this con hit her conscience differently. Yes, they had been wronged, but Ashton was an adult. Kids were supposed to be off-limits. This felt cruel.

Honor placed a stilettoed foot inside the room, taking timid steps toward the bed. The medication dripping into his veins from the IV made him sleep, but even in his unconsciousness, he still moaned out in pain from the injuries he had suffered.

"I'm really sorry," Honor whispered as she placed the "Get Well" arrangement full of candy at his bedside.

"Who are you?"

Honor turned to the door, startled, placing a hand to her chest. She stood face-to-face with the man who had beat her sister and left her to die. Not until she saw him did she remember how badly Ashton had been hurt.

"I, um . . . I'm sorry, you scared me," she said. She stared into the eyes of August Sinclair.

"Who are you?" he asked again. He stood there in an Armani custom suit with a blond Beckham haircut, demanding answers.

"I'm . . ." She paused. There was no point in lying. Sutton was already in the makings of forming a fiduciary relationship between the LaCroix Group and Sinclair Enterprises, so August would see her around eventually. To lie would bind her hand so instead she told the truth. "My name is Honor. I am co-owner of the LaCroix Group. We heard about what happened to your family. We wanted to express our condolences. Our president is meeting with someone from Sinclair Enterprises right now, actually. I just thought it would be more heartfelt to deliver this personally." She prayed he didn't put two and two together, connecting Ashton to their company. The silent stare he gave her unnerved Honor and she felt the need to say more, explain further, defend her reason for standing in this room, but she knew better. Guilty people talked too much. Rambling and elaborating on what she had already said would only make her seem like she was lying, so instead she said nothing.

"I'm sorry, I don't mean to stare. My head is all over the fucking place right now. Everybody has to have their day. We all know that. We're all preparing for the same thing eventually but when it comes . . ." August stopped talking as he shook his head, swiping both hands down his face. The sigh that followed was heavy, burdened. Any worries she had of him recognizing her affiliation went out the window because she was sure he didn't even recognize himself right now. Death had introduced him to a version of himself he had never met. "I'm having a hard day. Shit is rough," he finished.

He was undone. Gone was the arrogance. Grief had stripped him of it. All Honor saw standing before her was sadness. Her chest tightened. His anguish was like another presence in the room. It sat on his shoulders, pressing down so hard that August's normally perfect posture was hunched. She remembered that feeling. She had felt it when her father had caught his bid. She was sure August's sorrow was worse. He had lost both people who made him.

"I'm really sorry," she said, meaning every word. August swept a tattooed hand through his hair. He didn't look like a monster. He didn't seem like the type of man who could beat a woman and leave her for dead. "I'm going to give you some privacy. I didn't mean to intrude. I hope he'll be okay."

Honor walked out of the room and August moved aside as she passed him.

She stopped when they stood shoulder to shoulder. "I went through this phase in my life after I lost someone special to me. I drank a lot, had sex with random men." Honor closed her eyes as she recalled moments in her life she wasn't proud of. "I popped pills, started doing lines every day," Honor said. "All because I didn't want to feel anything. I get why you're high. You don't want to feel the pain, but that little boy . . . your brother. He's feeling everything. Every single burn on his body he has to endure. He has to heal from them. Doesn't seem fair for you to take the easy way out, now does it?"

Honor walked out, leaving August with a heavy heart.

CHAPTER 10

"You killed two people. I don't know how you're this calm right now." Luna shook her head in disbelief as she watched Sutton apply her makeup to perfection.

"Stop saying that," Sutton snapped. "You know that wasn't my intention. I didn't know anyone would be on that rig. Panicking does nothing but get me locked up. The plan is still the plan."

"You didn't know a lot, Sutton. You didn't do the research. You didn't put us up on game. You just decided. You made the choice for us all and now a little boy is laid up in the hospital while you pick out fancy dresses for a date," Honor added.

"It's not a date," Sutton defended.

"Bitch, then why you putting on your good bra?" Honor asked.

"Because she's gonna let that nigga hit if it comes down to that," Ashton answered.

"It isn't a date," Sutton reiterated. "We're discussing the

arrangements of our deal. By the end of the night, I'll have Sinclair Enterprises contracted."

"Don't you think we've caused enough harm, Sutton?" Luna asked. "Two people are dead. Isn't that payback enough?"

"You don't have to keep reminding me. I know what happened," Sutton replied.

"And revenge isn't yours to measure," Ashton added. "I lost a baby. Look at my face, Gadget." Ashton still bore bruises from the beating she had endured. Her pretty face was swollen and marred with black and green marks; there was a red clot on the white of her left eye. She was in bad shape. The indentation of August's hands was left on her thighs, bruising in the shape of his fingertips. Ashton couldn't even recall exactly what had occurred. Everything else had been a blur. There had to be a price to pay for that violation. People only got so much time in one lifetime. It wasn't unlimited. August had taken a bit from Ashton. A little life was reduced, a little self-respect, a little dignity. He had done the unforgiveable and all because he felt entitled. Sutton and Ashton felt justified; they didn't care Luna and Honor held reservations.

By the time Sutton finished, she was the picture of perfection. The nude-colored, high-waisted, wide-leg pants she wore were high fashion, but the cropped baby T-shirt she accessorized it with gave it some edge. She wore a matching nude blazer on top. Big earrings and slicked-back short hair that gave her an effortless look finished off her ensemble.

"I've got to get to the office. He's sending a car for me. I'll

FaceTime you guys when I get home to fill you in," Sutton said, as she leaned over to slip into her heels. "Lock up on your way out."

Sutton took the expressway and was downtown in half an hour. On the elevator ride from the parking garage to the lobby, she felt butterflies fill her. Dating was something she hadn't done in years. She was a pretty face with ugly scars inside and the trust issues she held were emotional baggage. She hated to even play this cat and mouse game. The chase, the hunt. She wasn't in it for that. If she had known who he was when she had originally met him, she would have never let him sneak between her thighs. Now lines were blurred. West had one goal and Sutton had another. She knew he didn't take her seriously because all he could see her as was the woman who had been willing to sleep with him after an hour's interaction on a rooftop. It wasn't the best first impression and not her finest moment. Tonight, she would remedy that.

As promised, a car was waiting at the entrance to her office building. She pushed out of the revolving door and headed toward the black SUV.

"Ms. LaCroix?" the driver asked as he stepped out and rounded the front of the car.

She nodded. "Good evening," she greeted. The driver opened the back door and to her surprise, West stepped out, unbuttoning his jacket. Gray suit, Oxford shirt, wheat-colored shoes. He was always so well put together.

Fine ass, Sutton thought, slowing down her stride as she neared the car.

"I thought you would meet me there," she said.

"So, you thought I was a man with no home training, basically?" West asked, rubbing the back of his neck and wincing as he stared down at her.

"I mean, this is business. It's not exactly required. I didn't expect a personal escort."

"Your firm is hired," West stated.

"What?" Sutton was taken aback.

"You have the job. Now that we have business out of the way, I'd still like to take you to dinner. I see the businesswoman. I respect it. I'm confident that you're capable. I've done my research on your firm. I'm entrusting the state of Sinclair Enterprises to you. But the woman, the one who threw caution to the wind and let me have my way for one night, is the one I haven't really been able to stop thinking about. No lie, the image in my head has been a beautiful distraction."

"What image is that? Me naked in your bed?" Sutton asked.

"You standing underneath the stars on that rooftop."

His answer surprised her, warmed her even. "I'll give you two hours," she said.

He nodded. "You know, I don't think I've ever encountered this much pushback from a woman," he said as he slid inside the back seat. Sutton moved over to make room for him.

"I'm sure women make it real easy for you," she replied, blushing. She thought about their first encounter, how she had made it easy too. Too easy. The easiest. He had to be judging her. He had to have a misconception of who she was and what she stood for. She was positive he thought this night would end the same way.

"I don't sleep with men on the first night," she said,

staring him in the eyes. "I don't even know how I allowed it to happen."

"'First night' is still a thing? Women still think about shit like that?" he asked, scoffing.

"I don't speak for all women. It's just something I don't go around doing," Sutton stated.

"Guess it's a good thing that tonight is night number two," West said. He looked out the window and Sutton's mouth fell open at his frankness.

Who the fuck does this nigga think he is?

"That's so forward I don't even know what to say," she said, laughing.

"So, she laughs," he noted, turning toward her.

"When it's funny," she replied.

"It ain't that funny," he said, joining her amusement. Sutton focused on his teeth. They were beautiful and his lips were full. She knew firsthand they were soft. He had used them in places that made her weak. The pulse in between her legs made her turn her gaze elsewhere.

"It's hilarious," she teased.

They pulled up to the restaurant and West helped Sutton from the car.

It was a Friday night so the popular, five-star venue was crowded but West bypassed the line.

"Mr. Sinclair, it's nice to see you. You and your guest can follow me right this way," the hostess stated.

West's hand to the small of her back steered Sutton through the restaurant. Their table was lit by one candle in a private section. West pulled out her chair and Sutton sat as he got comfortable across from her.

"Tonight's specials—"

"We'll take one of everything on the menu," he said.

Sutton smiled. He was used to being in charge and he carried the power well.

"So, tell me how you ended up with the Sinclairs," Sutton said.

"Is that a question or a demand?" West asked.

She smiled. "A demand. I'm a little bossy. You'll get used to it."

"To get the opportunity to get used to Sutton LaCroix," he answered, chuckling as he pondered the idea for a bit. "Hmmph."

West sat back in his chair, folding one leg over the other. Normally, Sutton hated men who sat that way. She had always deemed it a weak man's tell, but West made it look like money. Like he had been around groups of men who retired for brandy and cigars at the end of a social night. He sat with such confidence and prestige. The nigga's aura screamed important.

"Are you going to answer the question?" she pressed.

"They adopted me when I was young. Took me out of a real bad situation and welcomed me with the purest intentions. Gave me the same opportunities as their blood-born children. They were real good to me. . . ." West said, voice lowering and trailing off.

"I'm sorry. I shouldn't have asked," she said. "You just lost them. I didn't realize you were that close to them. You're their son and I'm prying."

"It's all good," West answered. "I'm used to people being curious. You know, I buried them today. The two people who changed my life. Doesn't even feel real."

"And it was right back to business for you? You didn't want to take time off?" Sutton asked.

"I wanted to do what Senior would have done, and that's make sure this company recovers. He poured everything into it. So will I," West declared.

Sutton understood that. She admired that. She functioned the same way. She didn't know how to turn off her desire to build. All she ever did was work. She hadn't even missed the company of a man because she barely had time for herself, but sitting with West felt overdue. She hated to admit it, but he was excellent company.

"What about you? Tell me something. I'm not gon ask you no wildly intrusive shit like you did me, but I'd love to hear something intimate. Something that explains who you are," West said.

Sutton tensed and he noticed.

"I don't use people's weaknesses against them, Sutton."

She looked at him in shock. The sincerity couldn't be mistaken for anything less than honesty. She let out a breath of angst. "Fine, umm let's see," she started. "My favorite color is black."

"That's the starter kit of getting to know someone." He chuckled. "You're going to make me work for this, huh?"

Sutton rolled her eyes. "Okay, fine, I'm afraid of failure," she said.

"You want to come a little deeper with me?" he asked.

Sutton's foot tapped against the floor. "That was something, right?"

"Barely," he answered, licking his lips, eyes sparkling.

"You like to see me uncomfortable," she said, twisting up

her mouth as she bit inside her lip. "How deep do you want me to go?"

"Drown," he answered.

She looked him in the eyes.

"What's the worst thing you've ever done?" he asked.

Sutton's heart felt like it stopped beating. He had no idea her greatest sin was tied to his hurt. Her eyes prickled. She didn't know what to say. She couldn't even think of a good lie because guilt was holding her tongue hostage.

He stared at her and Sutton cleared her throat as she looked down to avoid eye contact.

"I don't even really know how to answer that," she said.

She was grateful when his phone rang. The grip on her heart eased some as West switched his focus. It was a welcome interruption.

"I wouldn't normally take this but . . ."

"No, please, go ahead, I understand," she replied. He stood and stepped away from the table as he talked into the phone. Body language spoke volumes and Sutton didn't miss the change in his temperament.

She saw the look of horror cross his face in a flash before anger settled onto his brow as the person on the other end of the phone delivered a message.

"I'm on my way," he said, ending the call as he approached the table. "I've got to go. You can take the car home. My driver will get you where you need to be." He removed his wallet and motioned for the waitress, asking for the bill. The night was coming to an abrupt end.

"Is everything okay?" Sutton asked as she stood and gathered her handbag.

"I'm telling you this because you now work with Sinclair Enterprises and this will affect your ability to do your job. The explosion wasn't an accident. The police have confirmed that there was foul play involved. It's now a homicide investigation."

Sutton's stomach bottomed out. This was the last thing Sutton needed. If they knew the rig was blown purposefully, they would open a criminal investigation. The stakes had just been raised and Sutton feared the worst.

"What exactly did they say?" she asked.

"They found evidence of explosives in the debris and the body of a diver floating miles from the wreckage," West said.

"What does that mean?" Sutton asked. Her heart sank and her stomach hollowed with guilt. Fear made her grip her wineglass too tightly. Her ass was on the line. This was bad. She had left a trail of bread crumbs behind and this dead diver was a sure way to get caught. She watched his disposition change. With her, he was a finesser. He was smooth, a gentleman. After receiving this news, he had transformed before her very eyes. She saw his brow dip in discontent, the anger flaring in his eyes, and his shoulders bricked. He went cold. He motioned for the check and then fingered his goatee. He was no longer on a dinner date. He had disappeared into his mind, trying to piece together the puzzle of this attack on his family. He was declaring war and had no idea he was sitting across from the general of the opposition.

He pushed back out of his chair. "It means my parents were murdered. I don't mean to cut this short, but my head is all over the place. Can we—?"

"Of course," she said, voice trembling, hands shaking.

She was trying her hardest to keep her composure. Her mind was spinning. She needed to get to her office, to her sisters, so they could figure out what the hell had happened. Something had gone wrong and Sutton had to cover her tracks to avoid being discovered.

CHAPTER 11

"We want to warn our viewers beforehand that the visuals and graphics you are about to see may be disturbing to some at home. Sometime early this morning, a huge explosion erupted near the shore of the Atlantic Ocean. The images you see are the remains of the sharks and sea animals that were direct victims of this catastrophic explosion. As you can see, various animal rights activists and organizations are there trying to help save as many survivors as possible. Local authorities have confirmed the three bodies and one survivor who was airlifted and transported to Texas Medical Center. Apparently, a Latino scuba diver was one of the people pronounced dead. The names of the deceased have yet to be released as officials try to figure out what exactly went wrong. The only news that we know as of now is that the rig that caused the spill belonged to Sinclair Enterprises. More details are to follow about this devastating incident. You can find out more about this on Houston's own News 12 . . ."

Sutton quickly turned off the television that sat in her office as they all sat there in disbelief. It was in the early morning and their office had just opened for business. All of the girls were silent as worry and fear took a seat at the table. Shit had gone left quickly. The news of one of the divers being killed had taken them all by surprise. This plan had gone from bad to worse. Gadget had her phone set for Google alerts surrounding all their clients. As soon as another report came in regarding the rig explosion, she found out in real time and quickly turned on the television. This discovery was troubling. This mistake could lead back to them.

"Were you careful?" Honor asked.

"I think so," Sutton answered.

"You think so or you know so?" Honor pressed.

"I was, but I can't control how careful these divers were. They fucked up," Sutton hissed. She quickly went to her desk and grabbed her burner phone, dialing the number to the original SEAL she'd hired. The call went straight to voicemail.

"What the fuck is going on?" Honor asked as she crossed her arms and looked at the news report in total confusion.

"Everything is so fucked up. Sutton, I thought these guys were professionals. What the fuck? They talking about bodies? This is not what I signed up for," Gadget said as she nervously paced back and forth, trying to process everything that was happening. Ashton sat back and watched closely as her sisters were visibly shaken up by the unexpected news. It was nothing she was proud of, but death wasn't foreign to her, so she wasn't moved.

"See, the problem is y'all stepping into a dirty game and scared to get muddy hands," Ashton said.

"What the fuck is she talking about?" Honor said as she snapped her neck and looked at Sutton in confusion.

"I don't know; that's what I'm trying to find out," Sutton said as she smoothly folded her arms and looked at Ashton who leaned against the wall nonchalantly. "Why don't you enlighten us, Ash?"

"Y'all stepping into a game that you know nothing about. It's amateurish, to be honest. Bringing knives to a gunfight is going to get us all fucked up," Ashton said as she shook her head in disbelief.

"This bitch talking in codes," Honor said.

"You've been here a whole five minutes and trying to put in your confusing-ass two cents," Luna spat.

"Right. Just say what you're trying to say," Sutton added, slightly offended by Ashton's blatant patronizing. Ashton walked toward the television and shook her head in disgust.

"Look, I know I haven't been around lately, but you all have no idea what I've been through. I'm not the same girl that y'all knew before. I know a thing or two and was taught by the best. I know one thing for sure and two things for certain. No amount of money or clever scheme is going to save us if the police traces this back to us. We have to cut all ties connecting us."

"What do you mean 'cut all ties'?" Honor asked.

"We have to get them three remaining divers hit. We have to get to them before the police do. Because like I said before, ain't no amount of money going to keep them from pointing their fingers back at us once the heat is on. They're going to sing like birds given the chance. I'm not going back to jail for none of y'all bitches. We gotta hit," Ashton said with confidence. Her time under Miamor in prison taught her much more than what met the eye.

"Hit? Oh, now we're killers, huh?" Sutton asked as she

frowned and snapped her neck, totally dismissing Ashton's reckless suggestion of murder.

"We are not killers. What type of bullshit you on, sis?" Honor asked.

"Speak for yourself," Ashton said as she reached for her phone in her pocket. She scrolled through her contacts, placed it to her ear, and held up her finger for the conversation to pause while she made the call. She placed the phone to her ear and hoped the number hadn't changed since the last time she spoke to her friend.

• • •

Niggas sayin they outside
Send the addy . . . we gon slide
Air it out when we arrive

The song's strong 808 drums resonated throughout the venue and the vibrations were felt with each thud. The energy in the building was electric. Charisma, also known as "Ris," sat in the front row of the show with the long runway a few feet above the audience. It was the world-famous New York Fashion Week. One of the most sought-out urban designers held a star-studded private event. All of hip-hop's finest and all the social media influencers were in attendance. Charisma was brown-skinned with flawless skin. His five-o'clock shadow beard was perfectly lined up on his face. Cartier frames sat on the brim of his nose and his neatly twisted braids were pulled back tightly. He wore the latest Louis Vuitton silk shirt, which was open and exposing his impeccable physique, as well as the waistband of his Versace underwear. A number of gold chains were around his neck and diamonds flooded his Medusa's head charm. His Rolex sparkled in the light as the cameras flashed away, and the rumbles of chatter began to get louder and louder. Ris had been personally invited by the new designer. As Ris sat front row, his goons were scattered throughout the venue as they always were. Ris and his crew were like wolves because they traveled in packs at all times. Ris was the leader of the notorious crew called "Zoo," a young pack of savages that had made a strong name for itself. As youngsters, they had been known to stick up everything moving in New York. Ris had smartened up and transitioned his crew from stick-up kids to party promoters. Ris had a dominant presence in the streets of New York and now with his new move to Miami, he was growing more powerful there as well. One wouldn't guess he was a homosexual. However, Ris wore his sexuality differently than what society was used to. He had no feminine energy whatsoever. He was one hundred percent man, but his sexual preference was men. Ris was as rough as they came. The world had just made him cold on females and he didn't have an interest in them. Ris was an alpha male with a deep, raspy voice and a calm about himself that instilled fear in his opposition. Ris was different . . .

"Yo, you got a call coming in," Dirt said as she handed him the phone. Dirt was slim with short golden hair. She had golds in her mouth and seventy-five percent of her body was covered in tattoos. Her childlike face was the only part of her body not riddled with artwork. Her bright green eyes and high-yellow skin gave her a bizarre, weird look. She was so awkward looking that it was beautiful. She was also being courted by some of the biggest fashion agencies in the country. But that was the least of her concerns. She was having too much fun being a criminal with Ris. She was addicted to the rush of robbing . . . fuck the money; it was the criminality that she lusted for. She was one of one. She was also his best friend.

Ring!

Ring!

The phone continued to ring in Dirt's hand and she looked down at the name. It was a good reason she had Ris's phone. He never carried one because he hated to have the bulkiness of the device fucking up his Italian fitted clothing. Everything was always smooth and neat with him—from his appearance to the way he talked to the way he executed anything he did. No wrinkles. No flaws. The only thing he made an exception for was the gun he always kept discreetly tucked.

"Send 'em to voicemail," Ris instructed nonchalantly as his eyes stayed focused on the runway and its models.

"It's Ash," Dirt said with a look of concern in her eyes, knowing what she meant to him. Almost instantly, Ris put all his attention on the phone screen, confirming his friend's name on display. He had been worrying about her after the last time seeing her in Miami. Ris immediately grabbed his phone and walked toward the restroom where he could hear her over the loud music.

"Hello?" Ris said in his deep, raspy voice.

"Ris . . ."

"Where have you been? Are you okay?" Ris asked with genuine concern for his friend.

"Hey, yeah, I'm good. I had to leave Miami. Shit was getting too crazy," Ashton said, explaining her unannounced disappearance.

"I'm just glad to hear your voice. I didn't know what to think."

"It's a long story . . . but check this out. I need you to come see me," Ashton said, clearly wanting to get straight to business.

"Say less. Where you at?"

"Houston," she answered.

"Oh, so that's where you disappeared to?"

"Yeah, had to shake Miami . . . long story. But I need you here. Something came up. You hear what I'm saying?"

"Yeah, loud and clear. I'll be there in the morning. I'mma jump on a red eye and I'll be calling you in the A.M.," Ris said, immediately agreeing to come and see about his dear friend. There were no questions on his part. Ashton felt relieved on the other end of the phone knowing that if all else failed, she always had one killer on her team. Solid.

"Nah, I need you to drive, bro," Ashton said, dismissing the option of traveling by air. Ris immediately knew what time it was. He had to drive there because he had to come with artillery.

"Copy. Be there in a few days. Call you when I'm a few hours out." Ris smiled and ran his tongue across his perfect, pearly teeth. Nothing got him more excited than gunplay.

"See you soon," Ashton said just before she disconnected the call.

Whenever Ashton called, he would come running. She was the only woman who could make him move like that. Ris didn't play about her and he already knew something needed to be handled by the tone of her voice. Whatever it was . . . he would handle it.

Ris returned to his seat, but now he was disinterested in

the runway before him. He wondered what Ashton had gotten herself into while in Houston. He knew he couldn't ask
over the phone, so he would be hitting the ground as soon as
possible to get to them. He was willing to shake the whole city
of Houston up on behalf of his love, Ashton.

Back at the office, Sutton watched Ashton sit her phone
down.

"Ashton, who did you just call?" Sutton asked.

"Our problem solver," Ashton replied with a smirk. She
was bringing her sisters into her world, where she was comfortable dwelling.

• • •

Forty-eight hours later, just as promised, Ris was pulling
up to the LaCroix Group's offices. The sisters were all, once
again, in Sutton's executive suite. Honor was looking out
of the window at two black Sprinter vans pulling into their
parking lot. All the windows had smoked-out tint and the
faint knocking of the speakers sent vibrations, making the office windows slightly rattle. Honor watched the sliding doors
open. Immediately, men began to hop out and she noticed
that they all looked fly. It looked like a rap video was about to
happen. The only things she saw were designer threads, gold
chains, and weed smoke flowing from the cars. As the wolves
exited the vans, they began to shake out their legs and arms,
stretching their limbs. The effects of the long drive obviously
had everyone tight.

They all stood around as if they were waiting on something or someone; and after a few seconds, out came a tall,
well-built man with two big braids neatly twisted to the back
of his head. He wore black Ferragamo loafers, black slacks,

and a black mock turtleneck. He looked like a model rather than a stone-cold killer.

"Oh Lord," Honor said as she placed her hand on her chest and studied the specimen of a man stepping out of the van. Her heart fluttered. She hadn't seen a man so beautiful in her entire life. His rugged face totally contradicted his stylish attire and it immediately turned her on.

"That must be Ris," Ashton said while smiling, knowing the gravitational pull of her close friend. She walked over to the window to peek out and saw the circle of wolves talking among each other while Ris stood over to the side and straightened his clothes and fixed his collar. She smiled at his smoothness and effortless charm.

"Charisma," she said under her breath.

"Sutton, Gadget . . . come look at this tall glass of water right here. Goddamn," Honor said as she felt a tingle between her legs. The girls walked over to the window to get a glimpse of what Honor was gushing about and they immediately understood where she was coming from. Once they reached the window, it was clear who Ris was out of the bunch without Ashton having to tell them. He looked like he'd stepped directly out of the pages of *GQ*. The big, black rose tattoo on his neck gave him thug vibes that were appealing to any woman with a pulse.

"Oh my . . ." Gadget said as she tilted her head to the side and crossed her arms.

"Y'all some hoes," Sutton said playfully as she glanced out and shook her head. They all burst out laughing at her remark and watched as the crew entered the office.

All of Ris's crew stayed in the lobby. Only Ris and Dirt came to Sutton's office after the receptionist directed them there. They heard Ris walking down the hall, his chains swinging back and forth, making jangling sounds echo through the hallway. His hard-bottom loafers clicked on the floors, creating a movie-like entrance to the office. Dirt was two steps behind him wearing a distressed-denim outfit and oversized designer shades. She had no undershirt on, so her small breasts showed at some angles. She was definitely a fashionista like her big homie and it showed. They were dripping with swagger and had young energy that couldn't be described as anything more than . . . fly.

"Hello, ladies," Ris said as he stepped in the door and scanned the room. His confidence took over the office and Honor was mesmerized. She then understood the window view did him no justice. Up close, he was much more handsome, and she was lost for words. His six-foot-something frame made him loom over them and his perfect smile seemed to lighten up the room. His Cartier frames had a light tint to them, but they were still able to see his big pretty eyes and bushy eyebrows.

"Ris," Ashton said as she lit up and approached him. He opened his arms and embraced her, slightly picking her off her feet.

"Hey, baby girl," he said and hugged her tightly, rocking side to side. His shirt slightly rose, exposing the black Glock on his waist secured tightly by a black Ferragamo belt. He then slowly placed her back on her feet and looked around at the other women.

"These are my sisters," Ashton said as she focused on her sisters who stood around the desk. "Sutton, Luna, and Honor," she said, pointing to each of them individually. Ris calmly walked over to each lady and shook their hands, giving them all his undivided attention and eye contact as he shook each one of their hands. Honor was the last one he greeted, and she gave him bedroom eyes and giggled as he scooped her hand.

"I'm Ris. It's a pleasure to meet you, beautiful," he said smoothly as he ran his tongue across his top row of teeth and grinned. Honor immediately felt her pussy begin to get wet and it was obvious that she was flirting. As they shook hands, she ran her thumb over his knuckles and held on for an extended amount of time.

"Oh, you didn't get the memo?" Ris said smoothly as he stared in Honor's eyes. He looked back at Dirt and Ashton and they all began to laugh together, obviously sharing an inside joke.

"Memo?" Honor replied, not catching his drift.

"I like what you like," Ris said as he gently pulled his hand back. Dirt and Ashton were having a good laugh as they waited for Honor to catch on.

"Wait, huh?" Honor asked.

"I'm gay, love," Ris said confidently with his raspy tone.

"Get the fuck outta here. You're shitting me," Honor said as she stepped back, crossed her arms, smiled, and looked him up and down. She couldn't believe this hunk of a thug was homosexual. Ashton smiled and stepped forward with her arm entangled with Dirt's.

"Nope, Ris is on our team," Ashton said playfully. She turned her attention on Dirt and introduced her. "This is Dirt."

Dirt stepped forward and pulled off her big glasses, exposing her beautiful eyes. She gave them her gap-toothed smile and all their attention went on her openly displayed nipples, which were pierced. Her boldness was foreign to the sisters.

They all shook hands and then Ashton invited her friends to sit down. Dirt stood by the door and Ris and the other girls all sat at the board table.

"Listen, my sister said that you could be of assistance to us," Sutton said, cutting straight to the point as she sat directly across from Ris. He was hesitant before responding, not used to talking this openly about criminal activity. He looked at Ashton before he responded.

"She's good. You can trust her," Ashton assured him as she nodded her head in confirmation as she spoke.

"What do you need?" Ris asked as he focused his attention back on Sutton. She pulled out a file and placed it in front of him. Sutton opened it, exposing pictures of three gentlemen and their whole profiles. That's when Gadget interjected.

"These are the entire rundowns on each person involved. This person to the far right," she said as she pointed to the middle-aged Caucasian male pictured. It was a headshot of him in a Navy SEAL uniform, obviously while serving. She continued, "He died two days ago, by way of an explosion in the ocean. These other three are our targets. These are their home addresses, personality profiles, and social media direct messages," she said, giving him candid access that he had never seen before.

"What the fuck? This crazy impressive," Ris said as he looked closely and was shocked by the intel that they had.

"My sister Gadget is a beast," Ashton added, giving praise to her tech-savvy genius of a sister.

"Gadget?" Ris asked confusedly, the name not sounding familiar.

"Oh yeah. That's Luna . . . we call her Gadget sometimes," Ashton explained.

"I see," Ris replied.

Sutton stood and slowly paced the floor as she began to speak. "We have connections to these people and shit's about to hit the fan. We need to cut the cord that connects us with them. We cannot let the authorities get to them before we do."

"Say less. Give me a day or two to get the drop on them and it'll be taken care of." Ris smoothly closed the file and held it up. Almost on cue, Dirt walked over and grabbed the file and Ris stood and fixed his clothes.

"We will pay fifty per," Sutton said as she walked over to her desk and grabbed the white envelope filled with money. She picked it up and gently patted it in her palm. "Half now and half after the job is complete," she said.

"Nah, your money is no good. Ash is my family. This one is on me," Ris said as he tapped his chest, causing his rings to bang against his gold chains, causing a clinking noise. Sutton looked at Ashton and playfully frowned as if she were highly impressed.

"Is that right?" she said with a grin. For the first time, she understood her little sister had connections that she was unaware of. She was charmed.

And just like that, Ris pecked Ashton on the cheek and swiftly exited. You could tell by the look in his eyes he was now locked in. He was there to handle business and his focus instantly shifted to those three people inside of the folders. They had work to do.

• • •

The sun was just rising, and birds were chirping. The morning dew was on the leaves and on top of the blades of grass.

A modest, midsized home sat on a corner in a quiet neighborhood. It was a peaceful, serene sight from the outside. However, hell and total chaos were about to ensue inside.

Ris sat patiently on the floor of the front closet near the home's entrance, waiting for the owner to return. Some would be uncomfortable in the small space, but Ris was used to it. He had laid in bushes for hours to get a job done. This one was no different. He was determined to tie up this loose end for Ashton.

He looked at his watch. It was almost showtime. He stood and comfortably leaned against the wall with his gun in hand, waiting for the last target to enter. He had been keeping a tail on the three men for the past three days and within that time, he had learned their patterns and discovered this man was a jogger. He ran every morning at 7:00 A.M. Ris had carefully timed his entry into the man's home while he was temporarily away. Ris had paid the other two divers visits earlier that morning. Needless to say, they were no longer of this world. Ris had been on a killing spree that day, knocking them off one by one. He couldn't wait to take care of this last one so he could go back to New York and catch the last few days of Fashion Week. He decided to do this final hit solo because the target lived in a gated community and multiple people entering would have thrown up red flags. Ris was high on moving smartly, so he had left the wolves at the hotel.

Ris wore all black and a ski mask was rolled on top of his head. Even in crime, he made it look fashionable. His tight-fitting sweater and slacks were YSL and the slacks were by the same designer. It was accented by a gold belt buckle that showcased the company's logo. Ris didn't care if he was on a runway or a murder run, he would always be chic. It was a guilty pleasure/addiction, but it was also his signature.

Ris heard the doorknob turning and quickly tightened up. He gripped his gun hard, holding it up as he peered through the crack in the closet's door. With his free hand, he rolled his ski mask down, hiding his face. Only his brown eyes and full lips showed through the openings. He slowed his breathing and remained still as he watched the man enter the home. As expected, the diver was in jogging attire and sweaty. Ris closed his eyes and said a prayer as he always did before a hit. The man began to lock the door behind him and that was when all hell broke loose.

Boom!

A loud thud sounded, and the diver flew back as the front door swung open. Two intruders forced their way in, guns high. Without hesitation, the first gunman put a bullet through the diver's chest. The muffled sound of the gunshot meant a silencer. There was only a grunt from the diver as the bullet pierced his sternum. The two men moved swiftly to stand over the dying man gasping for air. Ris watched closely from the closet, trying not to make any noise. *What the hell was going on?* Here he was in the middle of a hit and he had stumbled into some other shit.

There were two more muffled shots, the diver's body jerking with each one before the life left his body. The shooters didn't say anything, using hand signals to talk to each other.

Ris watched as the two young black men stepped over the body and began to slowly move through the house, guns still drawn. Suddenly, he understood. They knew someone else was in the house; they just had to find him. Ris instantly began plotting his next move. If they were thorough, it was only a matter of time before they checked the coat closet he was camped in.

Stay calm . . . breathe . . . breathe, Ris thought as they searched the house. He was cool under pressure, even when he smelled death in the air. He heard footsteps on the second level of the house and thought about making a dash for the door, but he quickly dismissed that notion. They might have people waiting outside. No, he would stay where he was and prepare for the worst. He wanted to make a phone call to his team, but the hotel where they were waiting for him was across town. They wouldn't get here in time.

Fuck . . . think . . . think, he thought.

As Ris listened closely, he noticed the house had grown silent once again. It seemed as if the two other intruders had stopped moving completely. Ris could hear himself breathing as he slowly raised his gun up and gripped it tightly once more, slowly moving his finger to the trigger. His killer's intuition told him something was about to go down.

Suddenly, the closet door swung open. Before he knew it, he was pointing a gun in a man's face while one was pointed right back at him. Ris and the other man stood there, guns pointed, fingers on the triggers, staring into a stranger's eyes.

Ris slowly stepped out of the closet, backing the other gunman up, never taking his eyes off the man's. They slowly began to circle one another, neither of them saying a word. They just breathed heavily, almost in unison, both recognizing the stone-cold killer in front of him. A wolf always recognized a wolf.

The sound of the other man approaching distracted Ris, making him turn and break the staring contest that he was having. The man that was approaching him from the rear was Sire. Sire had his gun drawn and pointed at Ris's head. Wasan, who was the man standing in front of Ris, saw the opportunity and took it. Wasan squeezed the trigger, but it jammed, making a clicking noise. This prompted Ris to let off his gun as Wasan dove into the next room for cover. Ris sent a bullet straight through Wasan's forehead, killing him instantly. Sire fired back as Ris tumbled across the floor. Everyone had silencers so this was the quietest gunfight in history. Muffled thuds and bullets whizzing through the air created a beautiful and deadly symphony. Sire shot wildly as he tried to take cover from the bullets shooting from Ris's gun. Sire shot until his clip was empty and watched Ris sprint out the back door, leaving a bloody trail. Sire knew he had hit Ris but didn't know exactly where.

After a few seconds of calm, he looked across the room and saw his brother bleeding out from his head as his eyes stared into space. Sire hurried over to him and cradled him in his arms as the brain matter leaked from his skull. Sire began to cry, rocking his brother like a baby. He ran his hand over Wasan's eyes, closing them. Whoever had killed his brother, he vowed he would pay them back tenfold.

CHAPTER 12

"Thank you all for your time this morning. This company has taken a devastating blow. Our founding CEO and his wife, two beautiful people who I was very fortunate to love, parents who chose me, have left us behind. It's an honor to be left this legacy. This is a birthright and I'm humbled to be chosen to steer this ship into the future. It is with the partnership of my brother August that I take over as CEO. Together, August and I hope to be half as successful as Senior was. We have big shoes to fill and starting out, we have some major challenges to overcome. We need to rectify this rig situation and remedy this strike. I need all ideas on the table," West said. He looked around the table at the board Senior had chosen. Most were twice his age and had been with the company for decades. August sat at the far end of the table and Sutton, the only new addition to the group, sat across from him.

"Both stories in the scope of the media at the same time is disastrous. We need to rely on temporary workers, offer them full-time positions but at a lower pay rate than what we're paying our salaried employees. Once they see that someone else is doing their jobs, the salaried workers will be less likely to stick to this imposed strike."

West ran a hand down his goatee, nodding as he bounced the suggestion around in his mind. "Senior planned to be agreeable with the workers on strike," West reminded.

"That was before this rig fiasco. We can't afford to accommodate them now." Tim Rogers was the chief operating officer of the company. West respected him greatly, but he also knew Rogers was an old-school Texan with little empathy for the working class.

"We can't afford not to accommodate them," West objected. "They've already been out of billable hours too long. We want to be the company that takes care of our lowest-tier workers, not the one that takes advantage of them. The oil spill doesn't change that. So how do we please the workers and get them back to work to fix this spill? Not only are we losing money, but we're leaking oil in the middle of the ocean. The environmentalists are all over this."

The table was silent, and West knew it was because they didn't have a solution. In all their years of operation, they had never faced anything this detrimental.

"So, you all are sitting here telling me that you make millions of dollars per year in salary and benefits and bonuses, but you have nothing to say to save this company?"

Again, silence.

"Get out," West said. "Go to your plush offices and do your jobs for once. Actually earn those company cars you're driving around in, then report back to me with solutions for an afternoon meeting. Tisa, let's get it on my schedule at three P.M." His assistant nodded in obedience and exited the room as the men and women of the board stood from the table. They didn't dare speak as West's disappointment chased them from the room.

Sutton gathered her things and as she rounded the table, he discreetly touched her hand, catching her fingertips, preventing her from passing him.

"Stay back for a minute?" he asked in a low tone.

She paused, pulling her hand away quickly because no way should his touch cause her heart to race. She took a seat at the corner nearest him. August grabbed his jacket from the back of his chair.

"August . . ." West knew change wasn't easy. It would take time for them to get used to this dynamic. West was the smart choice, but he wasn't the emotional one. Senior had operated on logic alone when selecting his inheritor. He had left all three of his sons with wealth, but he had handed down the power to West. There was tension in the air.

"The thing about a birthright, you got to be born into it, bro," August said. "I'm out of here. Beamer's expecting me."

"I can't help that Senior entrusted me with this. I want us to do this together. As brothers," West said.

"Sure, whatever you say." August walked out, slamming the door behind him. West finessed his temple, massaging the stress away. He hadn't asked for this, but it had been placed in his lap. He would have to find a balance with August. Blood didn't make them brothers, bond did, and he didn't want their relationship to suffer behind business.

He took his seat and turned his chair toward Sutton. He leaned over, elbows meeting knees as he rubbed the top of his head.

"That was rough," Sutton said.

"Extremely," West answered, lifting his head to focus on her. "I wanted to apologize about the other night. I didn't mean to run out on you like that. I appreciated your time."

"It's okay. I understand. It's the cost of being the boss, right?" she asked. West had so much on his shoulders. He had lost so much over the past week and the lack of answers about who was behind it scratched a nerve. He had no idea that the root to his problem was sitting in front of him.

"Expensive as fuck," he mumbled. "What do you think?"

"*Abouuutt?*" Sutton sang.

"I would like to hear your take in repairing things. Your firm is known for fixing the impossible. Where's your head at?" West asked.

Sutton crossed her legs and tapped the arm of the chair with her stiletto nails. "First thing you need to do is fire everybody who just left this room," she suggested.

West's brows hiked and he sat up. "That's a bold move. These people have worked for Senior for as long as I can remember."

"Exactly. Their alliance is with the old king, not you. Transition of power needs a transition of leadership. They're old and rich and comfortable and too fucking white," Sutton said.

West found the laughter in that.

"I'm serious. You need some new blood in here. Some young, hungry, educated execs that can help you clean up this mess. I have some suggestions to help clean up the environmental issues as well. You need to back an organization, pour money into it, and then get out and help clean it up. The media needs to see you hands-on with this. A donation to an animal charity of course, a public statement about the commitment to cleaning up the biohazard caused by the spill. People need to see that you are going to help reverse the damage for years to come."

West nodded, impressed.

"I had a whole presentation. You got the ghetto version," Sutton said, smiling. "I'm usually way more professional."

"I'm not mad at this version," he replied. "It's good to see a more relaxed side of you. It suits you."

Sutton scoffed and smiled a bit. West sensed her discomfort, so he changed focus. "I do think you're right, though. Your approach may work. Take a walk with me?"

"Sure," Sutton said, as she pushed back out of her chair.

They strolled out of the office. The headquarters sat on one hundred acres of land. It seemed endless as they stepped out into the humid Houston heat.

"Where are you taking me?" Sutton asked.

"This place sits on protected wetlands. I come out here to think when the office walls start closing in on me," West said.

The company's land was landscaped beautifully; but the farther they walked away from the buildings, the wilder the land became. Sutton hesitated when West stepped off the paved path and into the tall grass.

"So, another thing to know about me. I'm kind of afraid of bugs," she said.

The smirk that crossed his face embarrassed her.

"Oh, that's funny?" she asked. "Fucking Texas boy," she scoffed.

Before Sutton knew it, he scooped her in his arms like she was a new bride. She yelped and wrapped her arms around his neck.

Her hand to the side of his face forced his stare on her.

"You're too tough to have such an irrational fear," West said.

She turned her head away from him, smudging her lipstick as she folded her lips to stop herself from laughing.

"I got bit when I was a kid," she admitted.

"From what I remember you like a little bite," West said.

"Don't you get fresh!" Sutton said, laughing aloud as she hid her face in his broad chest. It wasn't exactly professional, and he knew she was timid about blurring lines, but he held no qualms. She trembled and he knew visions of their one night played in her mind. He had eaten her pussy like he was starved, and he hadn't needed any instructions on how to heat the plate. When he was done, he had kissed her inner thighs, biting them softly, causing her back to arch off the bed. He was magnificent. A species of lover that was going extinct and Sutton had been lucky to experience him.

"You will not bring up that night again." Sutton blushed as she spoke.

"Yes ma'am," he replied.

She looked up at him. "Good ol' Southern boy, huh?"

"Oh, you got jokes," West asked, snickering.

"No jokes. I'm very pleased about that part," she said, beaming.

He stopped walking and placed her on her feet. A small wooden rowboat sat on the edge of a lake.

"West, I can't swim," Sutton said, a tremor of concern sneaking up on her as she watched him climb into the boat. "If this boat flips—"

He held out his hand to her. "Trust me, Ms. LaCroix."

She stepped out of her heels and bent down to pick them

up before pushing out an anxious breath. She grabbed his hand to climb aboard.

She sat at one end of the boat, facing him, and he sat at the other. He removed his expensive jacket, rolled up his sleeves, and then handed the jacket to her before taking the oars in his hands. They were silent as he worked overtime, carrying them across the water. He could see her anxiety about being out on the lake, but the farther he took her through the channel and out into the bountiful water reserve, the more at ease she became.

"It's beautiful out here," she said, dipping her hand in the water. "I can't believe you own all this."

"I kind of can't believe it myself," West admitted.

"The crown has been passed to you. This is your kingdom," Sutton said. "I get why you come out here to think. It's peaceful."

West rowed until they were on a different side of the property and when Sutton got on dry land she gasped in wonder. A field of colorful trees stretched as far as she could see. Their purple and white blooms painted the tall green fields.

"Wow," she whispered.

West reached for one of the purple flowers, plucking it from the tree and holding it up for her. She took it, smiling, before lifting it to her nose. It smelled so good.

"You live to give me a hard time, Sutton LaCroix. Can't give a woman like you a bouquet. You got to bring her the field so she can see you do the work yourself." He walked over to the grass and picked up a wicker basket. Sutton strapped her heels on and climbed from the rowboat. Her heels sank into the grass.

"Might want to keep those off." West smirked. "The grass

out here soaks up the water from the lake. It's a bit beneath sea level. Good for the trees, not so good for the Louboutins. I'll buy you more."

"I wear thousand-dollar shoes. You don't want to buy my shoes," she snickered.

"I want to buy you everything," West stated.

"I can buy myself everything, West. I'm not that girl," she added.

"Just because you can doesn't mean you want to," West stated. "You deserve to slide a nigga's card when you feel like it, Sutton. Let a man do what he supposed to do. It's a lot more fun."

Sutton smiled, teeth breaking through stubborn lips as she looked off. "You make it really hard to stay professional," she said.

A sexy chuckle filled the air. "You want to show me which ones you like?" he asked. He handed the basket to Sutton and she removed her shoes before following him.

"I want all of them. A flower from every single tree," she said, taken aback by the natural beauty of it all.

"Let's get started then," he said. He bent down to grab an extra basket. "We'll need more than one."

"Is this what you do? To impress women? Because it is definitely kind of hard to resist," Sutton said as they strolled.

"Nah, it ain't like that. I don't think anyone else besides me and August have even ventured out this far on the property. When our mom was sick, we used to come out here to pick flowers for her. Some of the days got real bad. She said they made her feel better."

"They're beautiful, I see why," Sutton said. West pulled a flower from the tree and placed it in her basket.

"Wait! Look at that one!" Sutton pointed to it.

West looked up and plucked it from the tree, placing it in Sutton's basket.

"I've had some bad days lately. Lost a lot of people. Right now, I don't feel it too much. It's the first moment in the past two weeks that my mind hasn't been clouded by death."

"It's the flowers," Sutton said. "It's hard to be down around something so beautiful."

Sutton reached for a flower, standing on her tiptoes. West bent down a bit, gripping her under her arms and lifting her so she could reach her target. He lowered her but didn't place her on her feet. Instead, he held her in front of his face so they were level, eye to eye.

"We should go back," he said.

"We should," she agreed. "We really should."

He put her feet on the ground, but she didn't move.

"This is literally the only place I'll ever let you kiss me again, so you might as well shoot your shot," Sutton said.

"You play real tough, Sutton LaCroix," he said.

"Only I'm not playing," she replied. West took a knee in front of her. "What are you doing?"

He rolled her dress up her thighs and hooked her knee over his shoulder. "Shooting my shot."

Sutton quivered as he slid her panties aside and kissed her lips. Sutton sucked in air. She wanted to protest, but she had given permission. All she could do was let him lead.

Her taste was delicate, feminine, sweet, and he sucked on her like his favorite piece of candy.

"West, *sssss*." Sutton gritted her teeth as he devoured her slowly. "We can't keep doing this."

"You can go back to professional when I'm done," he groaned.

He loved to weaken this woman. He had never encountered anyone like her. Women were easy. Sutton was hard. Sutton was a challenge. When she gave into him, it made him feel kingly. Submission from a queen was an honor.

West pulled an orgasm out of her effortlessly and then rolled her dress back down. He came up her body, subtly biting her belly, then her nipple through the fabric, before coming up and landing in the crease of her neck. Sutton didn't even protest. Her head fell to the side and a moan escaped her. It was swallowed up as he made his way to her lips. He planted a single kiss to her mouth and then pulled back.

"You can't keep doing this to me." Her voice was weakened. Defeated. Like she was disappointed in herself for letting this happen again.

"Apologies," he said, his smile lifting in one direction. A smirk.

"So arrogant," she said, smiling as she pulled on his chin, gripping it between her fingers and pulling his face to hers again.

The ringing of her cell phone was like a reality check. She pulled back and he finessed his lips. He could still taste her there. She was a flavor he didn't know he had an addiction to. A craving. He had developed a craving for Sutton LaCroix.

Sutton pulled her phone out of her purse and read the notification on her screen.

Ashton
911

"I've got to go," she said, almost panicking. "I won't be able to make the afternoon meeting. I have to take care of something."

West nodded, his fingers still on his lips, where the taste of her lived. "Let's get back."

Sutton was preoccupied on the boat ride back. When they reached the buildings, she paused. "I'll miss your meeting, but I'll have my office send over—"

West snatched her by the waist, interrupting her, his lips covering hers. Sutton melted into him.

"Take my company car. My driver will pull around to take you wherever you need to go," he said. "I don't want to hear from you secondhand. I want to hear your plan from your mouth, in person. I'll have my assistant call your office to check your calendar."

He didn't even give her time to respond before he headed back toward the office. He didn't know what it was about Sutton, but ever since he had met her, she had become a welcome distraction. Today, he appreciated the energy they'd exchanged because it had given him a few hours of reprieve, putting a little life back into his world where nothing but death surrounded him.

• • •

Sutton pulled up to the location that her sisters had sent a pin to. It was a seedy motel. Sutton frowned as she peered out the window.

"Should I wait, Ms. LaCroix? I was instructed to be available to you as needed," the driver said.

Sutton glanced at the driver in surprise. "Just for today?" she asked.

"Indefinitely," the man replied.

Sutton's brows lifted. She didn't know how to react to that. "What's your name?"

"Leslie," he answered.

"Thank you for the ride, Leslie. You don't have to stay. I can find my way back to my car," she insisted.

Leslie pulled out a card and handed it to her. "In case you need to call for the car," he said.

She tucked it in her handbag and then gave a friendly smile as he climbed out to open her door. She approached room B, looking around, frowning.

The closer she got to the door, the more commotion she heard. She was glad she was the only person around. The screams from the other side of the door were audible from the outside.

Sutton knocked urgently. "It's me!" she called out.

The door swung open and Gadget stood before her covered in blood.

"Gadget, what the fuck happened?" she asked, rushing into the room. "How the fuck did this go wrong?"

"Aghhh!" Ris shouted at the top of his lungs as Ashton pressed a saturated towel to his bloody stomach.

"I can't stop this bleeding!" Ashton hissed.

"He needs a hospital!" Honor shouted.

"No hospitals," Ris groaned. "I dropped a body at the scene. You take me to a hospital and that's my ass. You got to fix me up here." Ris lifted his neck slightly and then let his head fall weakly against the bed. "I'ma die in this bitch if you don't plug that hole."

"I'm trying!" Ashton panicked. "This is bad, Ris!"

"Shut the hell up! Let me think!" Sutton shouted. "Put

something in his mouth for when he screams. They can hear you all outside! We have to bring a doctor here. Honor, did you drive?"

"Yeah," she said, eyes pooled with tears of fear. She had never seen so much blood before.

"Let's go. Y'all keep him up and alert and keep putting pressure on that wound," she ordered. Sutton was terrified but someone had to be in control. She and Honor rushed out of the room.

"You know someone?" Honor asked.

"No, but we're going to find someone. Everyone has a price. Go to Memorial City," Sutton instructed.

Honor hit the freeway. She gripped the steering wheel. "What if he dies?"

"He won't," Sutton said, voice shaking.

"What if he does!" Honor was shouting.

"Just drive!"

Honor was making her panic. She had gone from a fairy tale to fear. If Ris died, she would have more blood on her hands. That couldn't happen. She didn't know if she'd be able to bear the weight of more sin. She wasn't a killer. She was a businesswoman, but lately her hands seemed to get dirtier and dirtier. It was like once she'd started down that path, it got more slippery. Even if she wanted to, she couldn't turn back now. The divers had to be taken care of to erase any chance the explosion could come back on her. She was too far in. She told herself Ris would be the last crooked thing she indulged in, but she had no idea that she was a queen pin in the making.

They pulled into Memorial City Hospital's parking lot and Honor turned off the ignition.

"I can't go in there like this. I have blood all over me," Honor said.

"Okay," Sutton said, eyeing the entrance to the emergency room. "Okay, okay. Turn on this car and keep it running. Be ready to drive when I get back."

"What are you going to do?" Honor asked, eyes wide.

"Whatever I have to do," Sutton replied.

Sutton slammed the car door and hurried across the parking lot and through the sliding doors of the ER. Her eyes scanned the room. There were nurses and doctors everywhere. Sutton's eyes danced around. She didn't have time to waste. If Ris bled out, things would take a turn for the worst. She couldn't leave this building without a solution.

She didn't know which of these people were skilled enough to help. She just had to roll the dice. Women and men in scrubs and Crocs were all over. Mostly white, some Asian, one black. A woman in gray scrubs. When Sutton saw the red-bottom soles beneath the shoes of the Hispanic girl who emerged through the double doors, she knew she had found her girl.

Sutton rushed up to the woman. "Please, help me? Are you a doctor? My sister is in the car and needs help. She's about to have a baby." Sutton pleaded with the woman like it was a true story.

"Calm down. I'm going to help you. Show me where she is," the woman said.

Sutton rushed the woman out of the hospital. "Please hurry. There's a lot of blood," Sutton exclaimed. She opened the driver's door and the woman got down on her knees.

"Are you okay? Where is the blood coming from?" she asked.

Sutton pulled a hairbrush out of her bag and stuck the handle into the woman's back.

"Don't move," Sutton said, praying the woman didn't test her because she wasn't armed with a damn thing. Nevertheless, the handle of the brush held the threat of a gun when paired with her menacing tone.

"Oh my God, please, please. What do you want?" the woman asked as she stood slowly.

"Don't turn around," Sutton said. "We just need your help. I have a friend who's hurt, and we need a doctor."

"I'm not a doctor. I'm just a resident! Please, I have a new baby. I don't want to die," she said.

"She's not even a doctor!" Honor exclaimed. "Fuck are we supposed to do with a nurse?"

"Walk around the car and get in the passenger seat," Sutton instructed. She sounded calm. She seemed in control, but inside she was freaking out. "You turn around and I'll blow your head off. Are we clear?"

"Yes!" The woman's terror was measurable, and Sutton felt like shit. She got in the rear seat behind the resident and put the brush to the back of the woman's head. "You move and I'm going to put a bullet through your head. Put your hands on the dashboard."

"Please, please," the woman begged.

"Drive," Sutton ordered. Honor's hands shook violently as she sped out of the parking lot. "Do the speed limit!"

Honor slowed down and kept her eyes on the road.

"What's your name?" Sutton asked.

"M-m-maria Ramos," she stammered. "Please don't do this."

"Nobody's doing anything. We just need you to help our

friend. If you do what we ask, you'll be back at work tomorrow."

The woman whimpered the entire way to the hotel and Sutton kept her apprehended with the threat of a pretend gun.

"I'm going to put my gun away because I need you to be able to do your job. If you scream or if you do anything to get attention, I'll kill you."

Honor turned to her, looking at her like she was crazy. Sutton shrugged. She was improvising as she went.

They climbed from the car and Honor led the way to the hotel room. She used a key to enter.

"About time! He won't wake up!" Gadget said.

"He just passed out," Ashton said. "What are you just standing there for? Get over here and help!"

Maria looked back at Sutton. "We need your help," Sutton said. "Please just do what you can."

The malice in her voice was gone.

Sutton and her sisters watched anxiously as Maria went to work, assessing the damage.

She had no surgical tools. Sutton had to make a second trip out to meet Maria's colleague who snuck a medical bag from the hospital. Through it all, Ris never woke up, but Maria assured them he was still alive. She pulled out the bullet, wrapped him up, and ran a makeshift IV, setting him up in the motel bed as if he were in a hospital room.

"Why isn't he waking up?" Gadget asked.

"The body can only tolerate so much pain," Maria explained. "The next twenty-four hours are most critical. If he makes it through that, he should wake up. Until he does, please keep these bandages changed. I'm authorized to write prescriptions. If you take me back to the hospital, I can give you something for his pain because when he wakes up, there will be a lot of it."

"Then you need to stay at least through the night," Ashton demanded.

"Please let me go," Maria pleaded. "I swear I won't say a word. I promise."

Sutton pulled out the hairbrush she had used to trick Maria. "There's no gun," she said. "We just really needed your help. I'm sorry that I scared you but I'm grateful that you helped him. If you check your bank account, fifty thousand dollars has been wired into your account. It isn't dirty money, so you don't have to worry about not spending it. It's a gift. From me to you. Honor, take her back to the hospital," Sutton instructed.

Maria wore a look of relief and shock as she stared at Sutton. She bypassed Sutton and headed toward the door. Before exiting she stopped to face Sutton once more. "If you need help again . . ." Maria paused and glanced around the room. She was full of uncertainty, Sutton could tell, but the money was attractive, it made her fear ease. "I'd be willing to help," she finished. "You can't come to my job, though. If you take my number, you can call me whenever you need something like this again."

Sutton sat there in shock, but she took down the number just in case. Maybe West had been right. *Every woman has a price.*

CHAPTER 13

West looked around the Fifth Ward of Houston as his driver navigated the streets of his old block. He remembered everything about this neighborhood. It had been home for a long time. As grateful as he was to be adopted by the Sinclairs, this still felt organic. He hadn't been back in years and he hated that the circumstances of death had become his motivation to do so.

His Escalade stopped in front of a one-story bungalow. Green paint and brown shutters decorated the small house. It was the ugliest combination on the block but one of the most beautiful women he knew lived inside.

Leslie idled the car and got out to open West's door. There was a porch full of young wolves eyeing them.

"I won't be long," West stated. He reached for the leather bag that sat on the seat and then approached the house.

The men on the porch moved inward, closing the pathway so West couldn't pass.

West scratched his temple, wincing, because he hated when he had to pull out a piece of his past.

"This is entertaining. I guess you're the keeper of the steps or something," West said as he rubbed his thumb across his jawline.

"Who you here for? You don't just pull up in your fancy car 'round this bitch. Niggas need permission, you feel me?" the man said, pulling up his shirt to expose the handgun on his waist.

Without thinking, West grabbed the man up by his neck, squeezing so hard the goon couldn't breathe. "You on the block I own, nigga. You never know who you addressing, so you speak with respect always." West removed the gun from the man's waistline and delivered a vicious blow across his face before tossing the man to the ground. He discharged the gun, blowing a hole through the man's foot before removing the clip from the gun and tossing it aside. He was calm. He wasn't flexing. He didn't tolerate disrespect. The bullet to the foot was a fair warning. "Next time, I'ma blow your fucking head off."

The other men fled at the sound of the shot and the front door was pushed open.

"Man, get yo' ass off my mama lawn bleeding and shit!" Sire said as he emerged from the house. "Aye, Zo! Get his ass to Doc so he can patch him up. You teaching expensive lessons today, ain't you?"

Sire slapped hands with West.

"Nigga think cuz you wear a suit you won't put in work. Fuck is wrong with these new mu'fuckas around here, man?" West asked.

"You don't come around. You mainstream now. Corporate

thugging. These lil' niggas don't know you 'round here, bro," Sire said.

West adjusted his lapel and followed Sire into the house. "Where's Ma Dukes?" West asked.

"She's in her room. It's bad. She won't even go down to the funeral home to make the arrangements," Sire said.

West paused at the bedroom door. Sire delivered a knock and West waited for permission to enter.

"Ma, West is here," Sire announced.

"Come in," a soft voice called through the wooden door.

West entered the room and the smell of incense permeated the air.

West's heart ached when he laid eyes on Ms. Sheryl. He had spent so much time at her house as a kid. She had mothered him, fed him, wiped his tears when he was afraid. She was the strongest woman he had ever met but looking at her now broke his heart. She was a shell of her normal self.

West hugged her, wrapping her in a strong embrace.

"I'm sorry, Ma," he said, kissing the top of her head. Wasan had always been her pride and joy. A mother should never have favorites, but the entire neighborhood knew Wasan was her baby. Losing him had extinguished a light.

"We ain't seen you around here in a while," she said.

"I'm gonna change that. I've been real busy at work," West stated.

"I know. You work hard. You've done good for yourself. You made it out of here. You don't apologize for that. If Wasan had made it out I wouldn't have to bury him," she whispered. She squeezed his shoulders in support. "Let me fix you something to eat. You hungry?"

He knew it was a way to pull her out of her bedroom so despite the meal he had just eaten before arriving, he agreed.

Everything about the house was nostalgic, including the white gas stove that she had to ignite with a lighter.

He took a seat at the kitchen table with Sire and set the bag down on the floor beside his chair.

"I want to give you something, Ma," he said. He reached down and unzipped the bag. He knew he had to come with cash. Ms. Sheryl didn't believe in banks.

"Oh baby, bless your heart," she said, pausing to sit at the table. West could see she was overwhelmed.

"It's five hundred thousand dollars. It's enough to cover funeral expenses and enough to get you out of here," he said. "Buy you a house, live anywhere you want. If that's not enough, let me know."

Sheryl reached out for West's hand and gave it a squeeze as tears came to her eyes. "You've always been a good boy," she said.

He placed a hand over hers and squeezed back. "I don't mean to run, but you think you can put my plate up for me?" West asked.

Ms. Sheryl nodded. "Yeah." She swiped her runaway tears. "You go. I know you're busy. Thank you for thinking of us, baby. I'll see you at the memorial."

"I may not be able to make it," West said.

Ms. Sheryl sat back in her chair, stunned. "Oh. Okay." West could hear the disappointment in her tone, but she nodded reassuringly. "You were always smart enough to keep your hands clean. Good for you, West." She stood and they hugged once more.

"Aye, Ma, go get dressed. We need to go see Was," Sire said.

Sheryl left the room and Sire stood to his feet.

"You just walk in here and put your money on the floor like we need charity? I'm taking care of this whole block. We ain't short on paper. Nigga, my brother died putting down a move for you and you too good to come to the funeral?" Sire asked.

"You know it ain't like that. Every move I make is being scrutinized right now. I just took over the company. The rig explosion has all eyes on me. What you think going to happen if the press catches me in a photo with you? I got to move smart. It's not personal," West said. "What about the diver? Did he say who hired him? I need a name, Sire. I put two people I love in the ground. I need to know who to see about that."

"Nigga, my blood brother got his head blown off on behalf of you and you back to business already? Don't come around here talking business, throwing around paper, talking about it ain't personal. It don't get more personal than that, businessman," Sire said. He couldn't believe how far life had separated them. West had helped Sire make his first million dollars. He had fronted him the money to cop bricks back in the day and Sire had flipped it effortlessly. They were silent partners, fifty-fifty. Sire even had a stake in the sports agency. But the more West submerged himself with the Sinclair family, the more he seemed to forget where they started. "Better get out of here before somebody see you with one of us."

West nodded and bit his tongue. Normally he wouldn't have tolerated the tone, but he knew emotions were running high. He knew his pain couldn't compare to what Sire was feeling.

"Tell Ma I'll be back for my plate," West said. He patted the side of Sire's face sternly, brotherly, remorsefully. "I'm sorry about Was," he said.

"Me too," Sire answered. "Remember where you came from. Don't get too big, my nigga. Don't want none of these little niggas around here to feel like they got to bring you down a notch."

"It would be a shame to leave mothers sonless, so I pray they know better," West replied.

. . .

"Thank you for helping us," Honor said. "You were never in danger. I just want you to know that. We were just desperate."

"She put a gun to my head," Maria replied.

"It was a hairbrush," Honor admitted.

"A hairbrush!" Maria exclaimed. She was in such disbelief that she laughed hysterically, infecting Honor with the giggles as well. "A goddamn hairbrush."

Honor pulled curbside and parked valet.

"Next time, just ask. Come inside; I'll send you with medication to manage the pain and stop infection," Maria said before opening the door and rushing back inside. Honor handed the keys over to the valet and followed Maria.

"Wait here," Maria instructed.

"How do I know you aren't going to call the cops?" Honor asked.

"I like money. Consider our relationship doctor/patient confidentiality," Maria said. "I'll be right back."

Honor waited anxiously, half expecting to be arrested at any minute.

"You like hanging out in hospitals, huh?"

Honor turned to the sound of someone's voice. She was caught completely off guard when she saw August on the opposite side of the circular reception desk.

"Just picking up a prescription from my doctor," she said. "How's your brother?"

August looked behind him and then back at Honor. "Why don't you see for yourself? He loves the toy he found inside the basket. He owes you a thank-you."

"Oh I . . ."

Honor was grateful for Maria's interruption.

"Every six hours take these," she said, holding up an orange medicine container. "Take this one once daily until they're gone. And call me if you need anything."

Honor nodded. "Thank you."

"Now I've got to try to go save my job," Maria said with a wink before rushing off. Honor stuffed them into her bag and then glanced at August. His shoulder-length hair was pulled back into a ponytail and tapered on the sides. He had a single tattoo on his face at his temple, but his neck and forearms were covered in ink. White Boys weren't Honor's thing, but this white boy had a little extra flavor in his juice. She understood the hype surrounding him.

"I'm headed up now if you want to pop in," August said. "We've hired your firm. You might as well join me. You can tell me how you and your sisters plan to fix this mess."

Honor squinted as she took him in. Charming Southern boy with money and legacy. He had to have an alter ego because she could not fathom this man in front of her maliciously raping and murdering anyone. He had, however. He had left her sister to die. She and her sisters were working Sinclair Enterprises from the inside out. She had direct access to the perpetrator himself in this moment. No way would she not take advantage of it.

"Sure, I can stop in for a few minutes," Honor said.

"I'll walk you up," August replied.

"It says a lot that you made the time to personally drop off that gift for Beamer," August said as they traversed the hospital hallways.

"He's just a kid. He didn't deserve what happened to him," Honor said.

August led the way onto the elevator, and they took opposing walls.

The silence between them was awkward and she breathed a sigh of relief when they reached the children's floor.

"After you," August said, holding out his arm. Honor was positive he let her go first so he could look at her ass. To her surprise when she glanced back at him, his eyes were focused on his phone. She paused at Beamer's room and August went in first.

"Beamer, I've got a surprise for you. Remember that nice gift you got the other day?" August asked.

Beamer was covered in bandages but the ones on his face had been removed so his burns could breathe. He was so red. So badly burned. Honor's eyes prickled.

"This is who got them for you," August said. "Her name is Honor LaCroix."

Honor glanced at him, shocked. He had remembered her name. She supposed there was no harm in that. Their companies were in business with one another. Of course he remembered.

"Thank you. That was nice. You didn't have to," Beamer said.

"A lot of people are rooting for you," Honor said.

"People at school thought I was a freak before. They'll destroy me now," Beamer said, looking away in embarrassment.

August rubbed the back of his neck. "I'm sorry. He hasn't been feeling the best. The burns bother him, but I told him he's lucky. He's not even supposed to be here."

"I wish I wasn't," Beamer huffed.

Honor's chest caved. "You're a miracle," she said. "I know it feels really bad right now, and I know it seems like your burns will never heal, but they will. And no matter what scars they leave behind, you should be proud of them. Scars are beautiful. They remind you of how strong you are. You survived something that those kids at your school never could."

Beamer still didn't turn to her.

August blew out a breath of frustration. "Beamer, bro, you're being rude."

"It's okay, he's not," Honor said patiently. "You want to see my scar?"

That got his attention. Honor pulled a makeup wipe out of her bag and handed it to Beamer. She pointed to her hairline. "Go ahead, wipe it off," Honor said. She tapped her temple and Beamer took the wipe to her face. A long scar ran from her ear to her chin.

"Whoa!" Beamer exclaimed.

"I was shot when I was a little girl," Honor explained. "It was much worse back then. It's taken years to fade but it made me feel strong. It made me feel like I could survive anything."

"It's really cool," Beamer admired. "It looks like a ladder on the side of your face."

"It's from the stitches," Honor said, smiling. "Guess what?"

"What?" Beamer asked, intrigued as he rubbed her scar.

"Yours are cooler," she said. "Get better, Beamer. You're a fighter."

She stood upright and smiled at Beamer then waved to August as she made her way out.

Honor made it to the door before he stopped her.

"I'd like to see you outside of the walls of this hospital," August said, finessing his lips as he stared at her. "You're fucking beautiful."

Honor scoffed, ignoring his invitation and walking out of the room.

• • •

"I swear you be cheating, Beamer," August said as he tossed the Xbox controller onto the hospital bed.

"I'm just better than you," Beamer bragged. It felt like old times. The smile on Beamer's face was worth the time August was missing from the company. West was holding down the crisis while August spent time at the hospital. After all the pain Beamer had been through, it was good to see his little brother smiling.

"Hang tight," August said as he stood from the chair and retreated to the bathroom. He popped three percs, washing the pills down with water from the sink, and then ran his hands down his face. He hadn't slept well since the explosion.

Grief was a bitter bitch and he couldn't shake the emptiness he felt without his parents. They were all he knew. They had provided for him his entire life and although they left behind a fortune he would never be able to spend completely, it wasn't worth their lives. Knowing the blast was intentional had him searching for answers. He needed to know who had a target on his family's back. His soul would be unsettled until he got them.

"Hey, Beam, how you feeling?"

August heard West's voice and he cleared his throat, straightening the lapel of his suit and running a hand through his disheveled hair.

He stepped out of the bathroom.

"What up, bro?" August greeted, slapping hands and embracing West before taking a seat. "You heard any news on who might be behind this shit? What Sire saying?"

West dismissed August's questions, focusing on Beamer. "You excited to come home, kid?"

"Yeah! I can't wait! I'm tired of being here." Beamer grimaced as he sat up in bed, making himself more comfortable.

"You're healing good. You're strong. I knew you would," West said.

"Where am I going to live when I come home? Mom and Dad are gone," he said, his sadness dripping off each word.

West glanced at August. "We're going to figure that part out, Beamer. You don't have to worry about that. You can come stay with me or August. Wherever you want to go, that's where you'll go."

"I want to go home," Beamer said.

West nodded. "I know, buddy," he said. "We got something real fly planned for you to celebrate you getting out of the hospital. A welcome home party. Everybody is real excited to see you."

He glanced at August. "Let me holler at you," he said.

They walked into the hallway and West said, "Don't talk about the explosion in front of Beamer. He don't need to know it was intentional. It'll just scare him."

"What do we know?" August asked. "The diver that Sire shot. Did he talk?"

"Didn't say a word. That's a problem because it means whoever hired him is official. Whenever a man will rather die than switch up on his boss, the boss is powerful. We need to know who the fuck we're up against," West said.

"They took my parents." August sneered. "I will spend every dime I got to find out who's behind it. Somebody has to pay for this."

"They will. We just have to play chess. Move silent," West said under his breath. "If we talking about murder, we have to move smart. Put the right people in place. You're not thinking straight. You're high right now. You got to leave the pills alone and move correct so we can find whoever's responsible."

"They were my parents," August stated. "Excuse me if I don't have enough patience in finding out who killed them. Fuck being a Boy Scout. I want revenge. If you don't get it, I'm going to make sure it's taken care of myself."

CHAPTER 14

It was a sad day for Houston's Fifth Ward as the mourners filed into the small church to celebrate the life of Wasan Hart. The fallen soldier was respected in the streets and the untimely murder was felt by the entire community. The ceremony was held at the corner of Lyons and Bring Hurst, and the sky was full of clouds blocking out the sun. An already sad day turned out to be a gloomy one as well. There wasn't a dry face in the building. Wasan's brother, Sire, carried the biggest burden because he'd had to explain to their mother how he hadn't protected his younger brother from an early grave, which broke a promise he had made to her years ago once she finally accepted their way of life. Being younger, Wasan had followed in the footsteps of his older brother and whatever Sire would have been . . . Wasan most likely would have been as well. The sad part was Sire chose the streets, but Wasan did not. He was just trying to be like his big brother and that got him to where he was ultimately—in a pine box.

As the middle-aged African American woman sang her

heart out, people stood in line as her powerful voice flowed through the chapel. They were all waiting their turn to pay their final respects to the fallen soldier. Sire looked down the row and saw his family members grieve, but the worst feeling was seeing his mother crying. He had never seen her cry like she did on that morning. Her entire spirit was broken, and she was crying like a little baby. Although he rubbed her back and tried to tell her it would be alright, deep inside of his heart, he knew that it wouldn't be.

"I need to see my baby," his mother whispered in between her sobs. She was zoned out and not focused on one particular thing.

Sire immediately stood and then reached down to help her get up as well. They made their way to the front of the church. He walked up to the casket and looked down at his brother who seemed as if he were sleeping. He then turned his head away, not able to accept Wasan was gone. On the other hand, his mother hovered over him, kissing his forehead as she wept. She spoke incoherently as her tears flowed off her cheeks and onto the corpse. The sight was breaking Sire's heart and he reached down to help his mother. His mother's weight on the casket made it move slightly, which made people gasp in concern. Nobody wanted to see the casket collapse, so it was becoming an uncomfortable sight.

"Come on, Ma," he said as he carefully pulled her up. She began to cry even harder as she sunk into his chest and bawled.

"It's okay, Mama," Sire whispered. His mom finally looked up at him and he could see the pain in her bloodshot eyes.

"You did this to him," she whispered as she shook her head. A look of hatred began to form on her face.

"Ma, don't say that. It's going to be okay," Sire said as he felt his eyes begin to water. Witnessing his mother break down was becoming too much for him and he was about to break.

His mother frowned at him and gently began to pound her fist on his chest. "No . . . No . . . No," she yelled.

Sire finally let a tear of his own drop as he tried to bring his mother in for an embrace.

"It should have been you! You killed my fuckin' baby!" she yelled and pounded on his chest more rapidly and with more force. Sire tried to embrace her again, but he was stopped with a fierce slap to the face that caused everyone in the church to gasp again. She followed it up by clawing at his face, and the scene became chaotic.

"You killed my baby! This is your fault! This is on you!" she screamed as she went crazy on him. Sire just stood there and took it as the guilt burdened his soul. He knew she was right and now it was too late to do anything about it. Things were getting so wild that the deacon had to come and pull his mother away as she continued attacking him. Still, Sire did nothing. No facial emotion or any words could express the feelings he had inside. He watched as more church members pulled his clawing, kicking mother away and he just looked on in a daze. There were mumbles and chatter going on in the church, but the only thing he could hear was his mother's harsh words toward him. He looked over at his brother's body and bent down to kiss his forehead. The feel of his dead brother's cold, tough skin only reminded him Wasan was gone forever.

With his shirt disheveled and out of sorts, Sire walked down the aisle and could feel all eyes were on him. He felt alone in the world and that loneliness turned to rage with each step. He thought about seeing his brother getting murdered. He also thought about West bringing the bullshit his way. That was when he realized West wasn't even there for support. Sire became even more enraged, knowing West was the cause of this entire ceremony and he didn't have the decency to come kiss his mother and show his little bruh his proper respect before getting put into the ground.

As he pushed through the church's heavy double doors and exited the chapel, Sire had a fire in the pit of his stomach. He was headed directly over to West's home to get a few things off his chest.

. . .

"This feels fucked up, bro," August said as he sat on the couch and sipped a small glass of cognac. West was directly across from him pouring himself another glass as well. August continued, "We should have gone," just before downing the rest of his glass.

"You're not using your head. There are certain things that aren't in the interest of the company. We are all Sinclair Enterprises has since . . ." West said before he stopped mid-sentence, not wanting to bring up the death of their parents. The room grew awkward and West downed the cognac as he stood and took a deep breath.

"But come on, that's family," August said as he put his hands up.

"No, we are family! I don't want to hear any more about it. I made a decision on behalf of our family and that's that," West said as he slightly raised his voice, something he rarely did.

He stood and headed to the kitchen. They were in the den

of their parents' estate and the luxurious place didn't have the same feel as it usually had before their parents' deaths. It had seemed cold ever since.

As West approached the kitchen, he heard the doorbell. He and August looked at each other in confusion.

"You were expecting someone?" West asked, with a slight frown.

"Nah," August answered. West walked over to the door and looked through the peephole. It was Sire. West took a deep breath and opened the door. He immediately noticed the redness in Sire's eyes and knew he had been crying.

"How are you holding up?" West asked, a look of concern spread across his face. Sire didn't respond, just walked past him, letting himself in. He brushed shoulders with West, slightly rocking him to the side. Sire's aggression was crystal clear.

West shook his head and closed the door behind him. Sire was going through some hardship and West didn't hold the bump against him.

"What's up, Sire?" August asked as he walked up to him and embraced him. Sire simply gave him a head nod and a quick hand slap.

"Hey, man, sorry about Wasan. I sent flowers to the church," West said. Guilt was evident in his tone.

"Nigga, fuck them flowers. You should have been there," Sire said as he stepped close to West, standing toe to toe with him. He was breathing heavily, his chest visibly moving up and down. He was heated. West understood his anger; however, he didn't flinch or back down. He stared directly at his childhood friend while standing his ground.

"I couldn't be seen at the funeral of a known felon. You

know that! The media would have had a frenzy over that. You know how I gotta move. It's politics, Sire," West said calmly and firmly.

"I ain't trying to hear none of that 'politics' shit. My mother had to put my brother in the ground today and you were a big cause of that. You sending flowers didn't do anything for her. You shoulda came for support and to pay your final respect to baby bruh. My mom . . ." Sire said as his eyes began to water up. It wasn't because he was sad; it was the rage creeping out and escaping through his eyes.

"I would have if I could. At this level of the game, the rules are different," West said. August stood by and watched, knowing this conversation was deeper than his relationship with Sire. They had both come from the same neighborhood and had known each other since they'd been babies. He decided to stay out of it as they stood face-to-face. The tension was thick and the hostility was evident.

"This was your problem. Now it's my problem. I'm going to find out who is behind this and when I do, I'm going to make them pay. I need to know everything you know and then some. I'm right there with you every step until we find out who is behind this. Whoever it is . . . they started a fucking war."

Sire stepped back and around West as he headed for the door. "Don't forget who you are," Sire said as he reached for the doorknob.

"Nah, you make sure you remember who the fuck I am," West said in an indirect manner. He was telling Sire something without actually saying it and Sire got the message loud and clear. He nodded and disappeared out of the house.

CHAPTER 15

Sutton stood in front of the mirror hanging on the back of her office door as she worked lotion into her smooth hands.

"You can't fall for him. He's a Sinclair. He represents everything you hate," she told herself. West was so rich that he didn't even know how entitled he was. It wasn't his fault. He was guilty by association, but the power of the privileged sickened her. What had been done to her sister turned her stomach. No one had even uttered Ashton's name after her incident. Sutton hadn't heard from one detective. The crime had just been swept under the rug, like the almost-deadly assault of a black woman hadn't even occurred. Sutton was determined to strip August of that power. She was going to break their company down to its bare bones, bankrupt them, and then buy them out just because she could. She wished West weren't attached, but his presence didn't change the plan. There would be reckoning for the pain her sister had suffered and she knew the only pain wealthy people felt was financial burden.

She looked at the tweed Chanel business skirt and blazer she wore. The cameras would be present today. Every national media outlet in the country was covering the oil spill and the first efforts of the cleanup would be captured worldwide. West would be in attendance. At her urging, he was spearheading the cleanup initiative.

Ashton knocked on the door but pushed it open without invitation.

Sutton snickered. "No point in knocking if you don't wait until I say come in."

"It's just a warning, not me requesting permission. I'm barging in regardless," Ashton answered, smiling.

"Ever since you were a kid," Sutton replied. "How are you feeling?"

"My body is healing just fine; it's my mind that's killing me," Ashton admitted.

Sutton gripped her sister's chin. "Your mind is strong, Ash. You couldn't overpower the niggas who did this to you, but you can outthink them every time. I got us. You just stay out the way. I don't need August seeing you. You just heal and if I need you to come off the bench for anything, I'll let you know."

Ashton nodded. "You better go. Don't want to be late."

Gadget and Honor were already en route. Sutton rushed down to the lobby and as she walked out of the glass doors, she smiled. She didn't even mean to. The sight of West just made her giddy. He stood outside the black SUV. His suit was designer and fit his athletic build. He was such a man. Tall and strong. Sutton just wanted to climb him.

She walked directly up to him. "What are you doing here?" she asked.

"I need you next to me today. All day. Twenty-four hours of you next to me. It's going to be a lot of cameras, a lot of pressure, all eyes on me. When they see me, they should see you."

"Why?" she asked.

"So the whole world knows that's me," he answered.

The way her face heated she was sure she turned red despite her melanin.

"After we make it through today, we should talk," West said.

Sutton hated the way her heart raced around him. He was such a grown man. She wondered how she could separate him from August. She knew she couldn't, however. They weren't just business partners, but brothers. Ruining one would ruin both.

His hand on the small of her back guided her into the SUV.

"Hi, Leslie," she greeted.

"Ms. LaCroix," the driver replied, tipping his hat as he glanced at her in the rearview mirror.

Sutton was tense but West's hand on her thigh eased her tension some. He placed business calls the entire way as she sent off confirmation emails to the media, ensuring their attendance. By the time they pulled up to the Galveston pier, a full-fledged animal rescue event was underway.

Cameras flashed as West helped Sutton from the car.

"West," she said, gripping his forearm as she looked out into the ocean. "The water's black."

She had known the spill was bad; but seeing it up close was heart-wrenching.

West squinted as he looked out at the damage. He

grabbed her hand, shocking Sutton, and she looked up at him in wonder.

"Let's go do our part to fix this shit," West said.

"You don't actually have to get your hands dirty. Just make sure we let the media get some photo ops of you helping, make it look good, and let the real environmentalists do their job."

West came out of his suit jacket and handed it to his assistant, who approached him eagerly.

"Trenton, I'm going to need some of those mud boots and protective gear," he ordered.

"Right away, sir."

"You manage the PR for me? I'm going to dive in where I'm needed," West said. Sutton nodded as she watched West walk toward the chaos.

Not many people surprised her; but in this moment, the compassion West showed was mind-blowing. Sutton motioned for West's assistant.

"Yes, Ms. LaCroix?"

"Can you find another set of gear?" she asked. It was brought to her in minutes.

She quickly slipped into the protective wear and joined West beside the PETA staff as they washed oil from the feathers of hundreds of ducks.

"This is a real mess. You don't really grasp it until you see it with your own eyes, you know?" West said. "You want to give it a try?"

Sutton reached for a basket where one of the rescued animals lay covered in oil. It flapped its wings, causing Sutton to scream in surprise and drop the duck. She scrambled to pick up the frantic animal and West laughed. He walked up behind her, wrapping his arms around her body, invading her space with the scent of his cologne. He placed his hands on top of hers to help secure the duck.

"You've got to be gentle," he said. "She's already scared. You've got to show her that you won't hurt her."

His lips touched her ear as he spoke, and Sutton's stomach tightened in angst as she held her breath. She was sure they were no longer talking about the duck. She took the hose and began to rinse the oil from the duck's feathers as West held it still.

Her heart was beating so hard she was positive he could hear it.

"Mr. Sinclair, a picture?" A photographer aimed his lens before West had time to respond and snapped a photo of the two of them with the rescue duck.

"Thank you for this. For the game plan to salvage my family's company," West said.

"It's my job," Sutton answered. She had to say it aloud to remind herself this was, in fact, a job. She was there with a motive. Falling for West Sinclair was not her agenda. She had to rein in this emotion he brought out of her.

"Sutty!"

Sutton looked up to see her sisters coming across the parking lot. They maneuvered through the sea of people and Sutton took a step away from West.

"Let me introduce you to my partners," Sutton said. She hugged her sisters and then motioned for West.

"West Sinclair, meet the other parts of my firm. They're responsible for arranging all of this. This is Gadget and this is Honor."

"The infamous LaCroix sisters," West said. "It's a plea-sure. Gadget? That's an interesting nickname."

"I'm good with all things computers," Luna replied. "I've always been somewhat of a nerd."

"I don't know any nerds who look like you," West said. Luna was stunning. Honor too. The LaCroix sisters were a double threat. Beauty and brains.

"Let's get you to the stage. You should definitely make a statement. It's important that you control the narrative," Sutton said.

She already had reporters in the crowd on her payroll who were tasked to annihilate West once he stepped up to the lec-tern. She had given them all the ammunition they needed to ruin his image. After the press conference, West would have to step down as CEO. It would be the first of many bricks she'd underhandedly dislodge from the foundation of this company.

Sutton felt his hand on the small of her back as he led her through the crowd. She never missed how he secured her when he was around. She really wished they had met under different circumstances. Under this one, he was on the other side of the battlefield and Sutton was firing shots his way. She wasn't sure he deserved it.

Sutton ascended the stage first and approached the lectern.

"Ladies and gentlemen, if I could have your attention please," she said, smiling. "Thank you all for attending. I would like to bring Mr. West Sinclair to the forefront. He has stepped in as CEO after the tragic death of August Sin-clair Sr. and his beloved wife, Abigail. A lot of speculation has been spread through the media about where the future of Sinclair Enterprises lies. I'd like to invite him to say a few words."

West stepped up to the microphones and as Sutton started to step back, he grabbed her elbow, pulling her close and leaning down into her ear.

"At my side," he said. It was a command.

Sutton looked at him, shocked, and as their eyes met, she saw he needed her. Like he could handle this if and only if she were next to him. A king who needed a queen.

He turned to the lectern and Sutton stood at his side.

She felt like shit as the journalists she had given scoops to went in for the attack.

"Mr. Sinclair, do you still have plans to drill through American Indian tribe land? What about those tribes that rely on the water sources in the area?"

Before West could answer that question, another reporter fired off. "The investigation report from the explosion shows the blast was not accidental. What underhanded dealings led to the murders of Mr. and Mrs. Sinclair? Is there dirty money tied into the history of Sinclair Enterprises?"

Sutton watched West stiffen. He cleared his throat and finessed his goatee before finally speaking.

"I can't account for any decisions that were made for this company before I took this seat. I can only speak on ways I plan to make it better. The footprint I leave on the world through the power I have at Sinclair Enterprises will be a positive one. Whatever ill deeds that have gotten us here will not carry us further. I'm not into misplacing or destroying natural ecosystems on anyone's land. I want to work with the people of the native communities. If a pipeline benefits anyone, it should be the tribe it disrupts. If it isn't equitable, it won't happen. That's my word. The reality is we need oil to fuel the comforts of our everyday lives, but the drilling can be done responsibly and with consideration. If we haven't done that in the past, we will in the future. This oil spill is heartbreaking. It's a disaster. It's something we didn't ask for; but as CEO, I won't leave it undone. We are holding ourselves accountable. We only get one planet and we all must share it. I don't want to do anything to destroy it."

Who the hell is this man? Sutton thought, amazed at how well he'd handled himself under pressure. Those two questions would have destroyed anyone else. West, however, had the media eating out of the palm of his hand. He couldn't have answered the questions better if she had written the responses herself.

"Mr. Sinclair, can you speak on your partnership with the LaCroix Group?"

Sutton's neck swung right as that question came from a reporter she had never seen before.

West glanced at her and rubbed the side of his face bashfully. "We're very lucky to have the LaCroix Group on our side as we begin to repair the damage that was inadvertently caused."

The sound of subwoofers knocking interrupted the press conference as three old-school cars pulled up behind the crowd. Candy paint on the body, big shoes on the feet, tints so dark she couldn't see the drivers. The first car had bullhorns attached to the hood. Sutton looked on, taken aback as a gang of men climbed out of the cars. It was clear who was in charge. Wearing jeans, a fitted white T-shirt, Yeezy sneakers, and enough jewels to open a jewelry store, he leaned against the body of his car with folded arms across his chest and looked up at the stage.

Sutton eyed West, who clearly knew this man. If she didn't know any better, she would have thought she was looking at a standoff. Was this a threat? Were these people in danger? Was he an ally? Opposition? Sutton was at a loss for words, but her fight or flight reflexes were causing tension to build in her.

Okay, what the hell is this? she thought.

Her eyes found Luna next, who stood looking from the front of the crowd. She gave her a single nod and Luna knew Sutton wanted intel.

Sutton removed her phone and sent a text.

Sutton
Find out who that nigga is and put Ashton on him.

Sutton focused her attention back to West, who had returned to answering questions, but she was distracted. She watched Luna maneuver through the crowd and walk between the parked old schools. She already knew her sister was snapping pictures of the license plates. Within the hour, Sutton would have the man's entire existence at her fingertips. Perhaps she had underestimated West.

He's not as straitlaced as I thought if he's running with them. It's time to dig a little bit deeper into who he was before he came into contact with the Sinclairs.

• • •

"I'm not sure if you're washing the duck or if the duck is washing you?"

Honor turned to find August staring at her.

"You want to help?" she challenged.

August looked down at his three-thousand-dollar suit and chuckled. "I think I'm good. I'm gonna watch you."

"How's Beamer?" Honor asked.

"He's doing well, coming home tomorrow actually," August said.

Honor smiled. She was glad to hear that. He was a Sinclair, but he had no dirt on his name. He was an innocent bystander.

"We're having a welcome home party for him, at the big house."

"The big house?" Honor repeated, frowning. "A little distasteful, don't you think?"

"I'm sorry, I've called it that since I was a little kid. I guess you're right," he said. "I don't mean it like that. It's literally a big-ass house."

Honor lifted her brows and nodded. "I'm sure it is."

"I say stupid shit when you're around," August said, grimacing as he rubbed the back of his neck.

"You sure it only happens when I'm around?" Honor asked.

August laughed. "Pretty sure, yeah."

"Beamer asked me to invite you."

"Wow, you're really using your injured baby brother to get me to come to the big house, huh?" Honor asked, laughing. "That's terrible."

"I'm desperate," August replied, smiling.

"I'll come," she said, as she placed the duck back in its holding pool and removed her gloves. She turned to August. "For Beamer."

• • •

Sire pulled up to his house and hit the alarm on his car as he made his way up his walkway. He had always respected West's wishes to keep their worlds separated, but after the disrespect of missing Wasan's funeral, Sire was no longer playing by anyone's rules. He had shown up to the press conference just to let the world see what type of company West kept. West liked his dirt tucked away in the closet like he was too good to claim where he was from. Sire thought West could use the reminder. He hadn't needed permission to pull up. He'd dropped the same half million West had gifted his mom back into his lap during a public forum to prove a point: they didn't need his money, and he couldn't deny his roots. The move would cause much speculation, but Sire didn't care. He operated off principle. If West was his brother, he should claim the relationship all the time, not just when it was convenient.

He unlocked his front door and pushed his way inside. He turned to close the door but paused when the scent of perfume hit him. He didn't bring women to his home. Nothing feminine should exist inside.

He drew his pistol, turning to find the silhouette of a woman sitting with her legs crossed in his living room chair. She also had a pistol in her hand.

"Before you pull that trigger, I'll blow your head off," she said calmly.

"Small voice, big threat," Sire said.

"Bigger bullets," she said. She fired a warning shot, narrowly missing his head.

"What the fuck? Shawty, a'ight, a'ight!" Sire shouted. He

tossed the gun aside. "Your point is made. Who sent you? I'll double whatever they paying you."

Ashton reached for the lamp on the table beside her and flicked on the light. He stalled when he saw her. He recognized her instantly. His mask prevented her from identifying him.

"Sit down," she instructed. "I didn't come to kill you but if you make me, I have no problem doing so."

Sire squinted in confusion. He thought she was there for one thing, but apparently she was there for something totally different.

Sire inched toward the couch. "Don't reach for the one between the cushions, either, nigga," another woman said, lifting it out of the side of her chair. "I already found it."

"You a slick mu'fucka." He snickered. "Who would have thought?"

He sat down on the edge of the couch, staring at the woman. "What happened to your face?" Her bruises were healing but not gone. A ghost had walked into his life. She was supposed to be dead. Somehow, she was holding him at gunpoint.

"I encountered some bitch niggas who were never taught to finish their plate," she said.

Sire sat back in his seat, intrigued. "Is that right?"

"What's your name?" she asked.

Sire snickered again. "You polite with the pleasantries. Rude as fuck with the holding a nigga at gunpoint and shit, though."

"Who are you?" she asked.

"Sire," he answered.

"That ain't what ya mama named you," she replied.

"Sire."

Ashton already knew his full government name, aliases, and his mama's name. She just wanted to see if he would lie. He clearly knew the stakes were high because he hadn't. He was smart to not underestimate her because she was a woman.

"How do you know West Sinclair?" Ashton asked. She cut straight to the point. Sutton had asked her to get answers and she wasn't there to play games.

"Fuck you trying to piece together for?" he asked.

"How do you know him?" she repeated.

"We came up together," Sire answered vaguely. "You can get these answers without the gun, baby."

"The gun keeps you cooperative," Ashton informed.

Sire snickered. "No lie, the gun makes me want to fuck you," Sire said.

Ashton stood and walked into Sire's space.

"Pussy all in a nigga face . . . better put that thang up before I do something with it, shawty."

Ashton put the gun to Sire's head.

"Baby better pull that trigger. I ain't never let anybody point a gun at me and live to tell about it." He bit the front of her jean shorts.

"First time for everything," Ashton said, tapping his temple. Her cell phone rang and Ashton answered, putting it on speaker.

"I've got someone who wants to speak with you," she said.

"We have a common enemy. That makes you a distant friend." Sutton's voice filled the room.

"Friends don't hold friends at gunpoint," Sire said.

"Associates, then," Sutton responded. "I hear you're the man to see about guns and dope."

"Nah, you heard wrong, baby," Sire answered.

The knock at the door startled him. "You fucked up. She hates to have to do in person what can be handled over the phone. She's anti like that."

Ashton kept her gun trained on Sire and went to open the front door. Sutton stepped inside.

"Shit just got real interesting," Sire said, recognizing Sutton instantly. "You work for West."

"I work for myself," Sutton answered. "I think you and I can work together; however, I hear you move product. What's your game? Cocaine? Heroin?"

"This ain't the eighties," Sire snickered. "I move pills. Fentanyl. Question is, why are you and lil' mama over here interested in my business when you stand up at press conferences for Sinclair Enterprises?"

"I like money; doesn't have to be clean," Sutton lied. "I have a buyer. Sale is international and I want to use the new rig as the place where we make the drop. I want you to supply the pills."

Sire sat up and reached out to Ashton, disarming her without thinking twice. To his clear surprise, she pulled another handgun from her back waistline and pointed it at his head.

"A'ight, a'ight." He tossed the gun. "I wasn't shooting, baby, I just like to break bread in peace," he said. "Can you call your baby pit off?"

Sutton sighed and without looking at Ashton she said, "Put the gun away."

Ashton sucked her teeth but she did as she was told.

Sire stood. "Now let's have a drink and talk bi'ness," he said.

He poured three glasses and passed two to Ashton and Sutton. They didn't take one sip. He chuckled. "This some crazy-ass, gangster bitch-ass shit," he said in disbelief. He took a sip, proving the drink was pure.

"So y'all wanna move drugs off the rig," he said. "West will never go for that."

"West will never know," Sutton said.

Sutton had no intention of becoming a drug dealer. It was a ruthless game she wanted no part in, but orchestrating a drug bust on a Sinclair rig wasn't something West could talk himself out of. He might have been able to finesse the press and dodge tough questions today, but he couldn't shake a federal investigation and the IRS audit that would come along with a drug bust. Sire had no clue she was in it to sabotage the deal.

"What type of numbers we talking?"

"I don't speak anything under ten million," she said. "My buyer's trying to supply cities, not blocks. I don't deal in chump change. Can you handle that type of exchange?"

"Ten million ain't exactly major, shawty," Sire said.

"Per week," Sutton added. The lift of Sire's brow showed he was intrigued.

"It's not a problem," Sire stated. "What you need?"

"Xanies and fentanyl," Sutton said.

"Got you covered," Sire said. He reached for Ashton, pulling her into his lap.

"What are you doing?" she asked, pushing against him as he forced her to straddle his lap. He removed her cell phone from her back pocket and held her in place with a hand to the small of her back.

"What's your code?" he asked.

"I ain't telling you my code!" Ashton protested.

"0814," Sutton said.

"Sutty!" Ashton shouted.

Sire snickered and entered the numbers then dialed himself. His phone rang.

"Now you know how to reach me. Hit me with the time and date. I'ma do my part. Make sure you do yours," Sire said, staring at Sutton.

"Can I get up now?" Ashton asked.

Sire gripped her chin between his fingers. "I'm sorry about that face," he said.

"What you sorry for? You didn't put these bruises here," she said. She had no idea she was looking into the same eyes that had thrown her into that trunk. She snatched her phone and climbed out of his lap.

He snatched her back down into his lap.

"Next time I see you, we gone make a baby, shawty," Sire said.

"Not in your wettest dream, country boy," Ashton said, wrenching away. She walked out and Sutton smirked while shaking her head.

"You can't handle her, but nice try."

Sire was sure he couldn't handle these sisters at all. They were a different breed. He was getting money—good money—in the city, but this would be the biggest deal he ever made. He didn't have the inventory to supply a ten-million-dollar buy. He would have to go to his plug to convince them to up his load. These pretty girls were popping big shit and he knew he was playing a dangerous game because one of them he was responsible for hurting. For some reason, he had an overwhelming urge to know her. In order to do so, he had to step his game up.

He picked up the phone and called his connect. It was time to do more than reign over Houston. It was time to take over the South.

CHAPTER 16

The sun was beaming down, and towering palm trees lined the highway. The backdrop was a beautiful body of blue water with cruise ships in the distance. Sire drove in silence. He wanted to take in what was happening and how it could change his life. He had made a call to his friend he'd met on the underground gambling circuit. This friend wasn't just a regular Joe. Mo was an urban legend and with one snap of a finger, he could make any drug dealer a kingpin. Mo was a direct connection to cocaine heaven, which was also known as the Cartel. They had met at the historic Price Bash that was held in Houston every summer. An ex–music mogul who was well respected would throw this event annually and it was like the Super Bowl for hustlers. Dealers from all over the country congregated there to establish new plugs and relationships each year. Gamblers had a tendency to find other street gamblers when going to different cities. A good dice game was alluring and through these underground games, plugs were met. This was exactly how Sire met Mo Diamond, one of the heirs to the street royalty family known as the Diamonds.

After a smooth initial interaction during one of the dice games, Mo Diamond soon became Sire's coke connect. For the past few summers, they had done good business and built a good rapport. Sire never purchased more than two or three bricks at a time, but he was consistent. Sire always hinted for Mo to hit him with more weight on consignment, but Mo was wary, and it never went further than a few words. Sire knew he had to have a good proposition to demand the consignment that would take him to the next level. Sire smiled, realizing he finally had the right situation to request a sit-down with Mo. After a few calls and texts, Mo agreed to have him come to Miami to meet with his partner and him. Sire was excited about the endless possibility. Every hustler's top goal was to have a Colombian connect. Mo liked Sire and it showed through their conversations. The mutual love for sport betting and friendly wagers over the years got Sire in position to make his move.

The GPS notified Sire to get off on the upcoming exit and he smoothly veered off. He followed the directions and they led to a wooded area where houses were miles apart. The deeper he got into the drive, the more wealth he began to feel. The mansions got bigger and fancier with each block. He looked and admired as he passed homes he aspired to dwell in someday.

"Your destination is five hundred feet to your right," the voice from the GPS announced as he pulled up to the gated castle.

The tall steel gates of the Diamond estate amazed Sire. He had been getting money for a very long time, but the property he was approaching was on a different level. He had heard stories about the Diamond family for years, but now he was feeling the aura of the notorious street family everyone called the Cartel. He saw the intercom speaker to his left. He slightly hung out of the window and touched the red button. He looked up and noticed a security camera looking down on him.

"What up?" came a male voice through the intercom.

"Uh . . . I here to meet Mo," Sire said as he leaned forward.

"My nigga," a voice said from the other end. Sire instantly recognized it was Mo and smiled. There was a brief pause, then the clinking of steel sounded and the tall gates began to part. Slowly, the green grass of a spacious lawn appeared, and a long concrete driveway appeared leading up to the home. Sire slowly pulled forward and drove up. As he got closer, he saw a man standing at the top of the driveway. It was Mo with his shirt off and his tattooed body on display. His long hair was wild all over his head, but his hairline was perfectly trimmed. The crinkles were in his hair from the braids he had just recently unraveled. He smiled with his arms out as he saw his Houston friend approach. Sire hopped out of the car with a smile as well.

"Welcome to Miami," Mo said as he slapped hands with Sire and immediately followed it with an embrace.

"Thanks, bruh. Good to be here," Sire said as the smell of marijuana smoke filled his nostrils. The potent sour smell that came off Mo told Sire he had just got done lighting up. They ended their embrace and Mo put both his hands on Sire's shoulders, staring at him with his bloodshot eyes.

"So, I told my people all about you. My uncle and my

cousin are in the back. Come on," Mo said and led Sire to the tall front doors. A butler was there to open those doors for them, and Sire was impressed as he walked through, greeting the butler with a nod. This was a different kind of money and he could get used to the feeling. The whole vibe of the city gave him a rush and yeah, money was cool . . . but dope money was the best. It had a different feel. Sire was loving Miami and the way the city made him feel already.

As they walked through the spacious home, Sire was impressed by the immaculate structure. It reminded him of a museum more than a home. The paintings that lined the corridor and the high ceiling were artsy and nothing short of amazing.

"So, this is our grandfather's home and the house our parents were raised in," Mo said as he turned and walked backward, opening his arms up and giving him a tour of the property.

"This shit fly as hell," Sire said, nodding in approval as he looked around.

"I'm going to take you 'round back where the fam is at. I been telling them 'bout you. That setup you told me about is crazy," Mo said, referring to the Houston pipeline Sire had mentioned a week prior.

"Yeah, it's a win-win, my nigga." Sire smiled and rubbed his hands together, exuding confidence.

"What type of shit you got up your sleeve? How did you get a rig plug? We been doing this thing a long time and we never had access to a rig," Mo asked, knowing that game was for billionaires. It wasn't that his family didn't have rig money, but that was a white man's game outsiders and minorities rarely got into.

"I fucked around and stumbled on these bitches that's cold with it. I mean, I never seen anything like it. They move like bosses, all of 'em. They all smart, all beautiful, and know how to get shit done. They had connections that blew my mind. So, we put a play together," Sire said, repeating what he had been telling Mo that entire week.

"I want you to break it down to my uncle and cousin so they can fully understand, you feel me? We lose loads all the time dealing with highway patrol, planes, and UPS. This shit right here is next level."

"Yes indeed," Sire said, nodding in agreement and smirking.

"If it was up to just me, I want to green-light it. But the whole family has to be down for it to be a go," Mo said as they approached the kitchen. The smell of delicious spices and garlic filled the air. The sounds of sizzling food echoed through the air. An Italian male wearing chef's attire was moving about the kitchen and cooking on the industrial-style stove. Mo pointed toward the chef and added, "We got Tony hooking up some lunch. Hey, Tony! Say what's up to my man, Sire," Mo said nonchalantly as he smiled and steadily walked through.

"Hello!" the chef greeted joyfully and waved to Sire. Sire nodded and continued his way through the kitchen and out the rear sliding doors. The large glass led to the backyard with an Olympic-sized pool. An older gentleman was on a flotation device with a sun hat on. He smoked a cigar while leaning back and catching the sunrays. Sire looked to the far side of the pool and saw a muscular man with a clean Caesar cut swimming laps. His muscular arms swung ferociously and cut into the water with every stroke, causing small splashes. Sire followed Mo around the platform, and they walked to the edge of the water. The outside speaker system was lightly pumping out Griselda and the sounds of Benny the Butcher serenaded the area, which gave Sire a comfortable vibe. The cocaine talk sent chills up his back and he felt like he was in a dream, a dope boy's dream.

Mo placed two fingers in his mouth and whistled, causing the man to stop swimming and look toward them. The older man also looked.

"Yo, this my man from Houston I was telling y'all about," Mo said as he reached into his pocket and pulled out a pre-rolled cigar. The uncle didn't say anything, just looked at Sire with a stern stare. The swimmer did the same and Sire didn't like the awkwardness, so he spoke first.

"Peace, kings," he said, breaking up the silence.

"Hop in," the swimmer said as he made his way toward who Sire assumed was his uncle. The older man slid off the flotation device and joined the swimmer in the water.

Confused, Sire looked at Mo, trying to figure out what was going on.

Mo leaned over and whispered to Sire, the joint between his lips hanging out the left side of his mouth.

"Yo, they're not going to talk to you unless you get in the water," Mo said. He swayed back and placed the lighter to the joint, lighting it. "Just the rules." He shrugged his shoulders and inhaled the smoke.

"I didn't bring any swim clothes," Sire said as he looked down at his Gucci sweatsuit that cost a few grand.

"You got drawls on don't you, mu'fucka? Betta hop in that mu'fucka if you want to do business."

"Say less," Sire said as he began to pull off his jacket and then his gold chain. He stripped down to his Gucci drawls and hesitantly slid into the pool. The cold water made him shiver.

He made his way over to the older man and the swimmer. As he got closer, he recognized the young man instantly. It was the boxer Carter Jones. Sire was a fan of boxing, so he remembered when Carter was rising as one of the biggest stars in the fighting game. However, after a bad loss, he disappeared.

Sire approached them and joined in, creating a small circle of men in the water.

"I'm CJ," the swimmer said and extended his hand.

"Peace. I'm Sire," Sire answered.

"Nice to meet you," CJ said very humbly and welcoming. "This my uncle Polo," CJ said.

"Nice to meet you, young man," the older man said as he shook Sire's hand as well.

"Likewise," Sire responded and nodded in respect.

"Let's talk. Mo said you got a way for us to get in and out of Texas with no interference."

"Yeah, I do," Sire confirmed as he stood in the water, still freezing. It took a minute for his body to adjust to the water. It didn't dawn on him until that moment that he was dealing with the best. At first, he thought it was weird when Mo asked him to jump in the water; but after deeper thought, he became impressed. He realized they had him in the pool to make sure he wasn't wearing a wire or any type of recording device.

These mu'fuckas on point, he thought to himself as he rubbed his hands together and blew in his fists.

"So, you have access to a rig that can bring our packages

onshore with no police checkpoints?" CJ said, repeating step by step what Mo had explained to him during the week.

"That's right. I have the access and the ability to get 'em in and move 'em out," Sire said assuredly.

"How confident are you in your system?" CJ asked, looking Sire right in the eyes, as if trying to see if he wavered. However, Sire returned the stare and spoke with confidence.

"I'm locked in with the owner. It's a flawless system. Under the rigs are submarines that are used for cargo. We could put our joints in there. The transport would be underwater. There are no police patrols underwater, feel me?"

"What inside guy do you have on the rig?"

"The owner," Sire confirmed.

"The owner? If he owns a rig, why would he want to get into trafficking blow? Doesn't make sense."

"He's one of us. He from the hood. A childhood friend that fell into a position. But at the end of the day . . . he owes me."

"Oh yeah?" CJ responded calmly as his mind began to churn.

"Absolutely," Sire answered.

"And the logistics?" Polo chimed in, obviously wondering how this could run smoothly.

"I have a team of women that are sharp. We can take care of everything. We just need the supply and it can get there safely."

"Women? That's genius actually," CJ agreed as he nodded, impressed.

"Okay, so what about once the bricks get out of the water?" Polo asked.

Sire slightly smiled. "That's my game. I can handle as many as you can set on me. The streets have been dry for months. I have a Houston team and also a shop set up in Dallas. They just need me to come and push the go button. We can make 'em disappear."

"Mo," CJ said as he looked past Sire and focused on his cousin who was sitting on the edge with his feet in the water.

"Yeah?" Mo answered just before pulling the cloud of smoke into his lungs.

"You say he solid, huh?" CJ asked.

"My nigga right there a hunnid. I vouch for 'em for sho'," Mo said positively, nodding his head in confirmation.

CJ focused back on Sire. "A'ight, we gon to start light, just to see how it goes," CJ agreed. He reached out his hand and shook Sire's.

"Bet. You won't regret this," Sire said, feeling inspired. He was finally in.

"We gon start with one hundred joints," CJ confirmed.

Sire was blown away by the numbers.

"A hundred?" Sire asked, making sure he heard him correctly.

"You can handle that, right?" CJ double-checked.

"Yeah, I got it."

"Bet. Fifteen a joint. Bring me back 1.5 and we can go from there," CJ said as if they were talking about pennies. Sire felt like a little kid on the inside, filled with excitement. In all his years of hustling, he'd never seen more than ten bricks at a time or, better yet, been paid fifteen for each one. He did the math in his head and knew he had just become a street millionaire. It was time to turn the fuck up.

CHAPTER 17

Sutton lay in bed, tossing and turning as her mind ran wild. She hated that this was becoming personal for her. She hated that she thought of West, that worry about how the press conference had taken its toll on him was a concern of hers. She had set him up to fail; and once the drug bust on the rig happened, Sinclair Enterprises would come crashing down. She hadn't expected to care this much. She wondered where West would land afterward. Did he need his privilege to be successful or was he naturally cunning? Did he have any resilience left in him or had he attained everything easily?

She climbed out of bed and reached for her phone. She couldn't even stop herself from dialing him.

"It's two o'clock in the morning."

His drowsy Southern drawl was raspy, full of sleep, but she was happy he didn't sound irritated.

"You were brilliant today," she said.

"As were you," he replied, then groaned.

"The party crashers were interesting. A gang of hood niggas

from the Fifth Ward I'm sure will have the press speculating like crazy. I can't wait to see the headlines tomorrow." She wondered if he would be forthcoming about his involvement with Sire. "Did you know them?"

"The oil spill affects everyone, not just the white people in the 'burbs. The hood deserves to be informed too. They count. I was glad to see them there. They might not fit the narrative, but they represent an underrepresented community," West answered.

Oh, this nigga is good, she thought.

He had just finessed her with the most politically correct answer she had ever heard. West was smart. She understood how he had dodged the incriminating questions she had planted in the crowd.

"Where did you disappear to today?" West asked.

"Another client needed me," Sutton lied.

"There's no other client when you're working with me that takes priority over what we do together. They need to call someone else," he said.

"I can't just ignore my Rolodex for you," Sutton said, smiling.

"I'll pay your fee for whatever you'll miss out on, but all that's dead. I need your focus, Sutton," West said.

"You have it," she whispered. "More than you even know, and I particularly don't like it," she admitted.

"Slip on some clothes," he said.

"For what?"

"Leslie's outside," West said.

"You know where I live?" she asked.

"Human resources," West answered.

"That's a little stalkerish." Her tone was playful, but

she worried some. She had never made herself accessible to clients in the past. She always covered all her bases. She hadn't even used her home address on the tax paperwork she had submitted to Sinclair Enterprises when they partnered.

He's got some juice. He had me looked into.

The thought both flattered and intimidated her. She had a feeling she had underestimated him. He was powerful and from the likes of the company he kept outside the boardroom, she was learning his reach went far beyond business deals. He was connected to the streets. It explained his dominance in every situation, even over her.

The laugh they shared warmed Sutton and she shook her head because she couldn't stop smiling.

"I told you he's your driver. When you need him, he'll come, anytime."

"But I don't need him," she said.

"Yeah, but I need you," West replied.

"I'm on the way."

It had been a long time since she had subjected herself to a "spend the night" bag, but somehow, she found herself packing all her essentials inside a Saint Laurent tote. She was out the door in ten minutes. She didn't even put on clothes. She wore her silk robe beneath her trench coat with heels.

"Ms. LaCroix," Leslie greeted as he awaited her with the SUV door wide open.

"Hi, Leslie," she said. "Thank you."

She slid into the truck. Sutton tried to talk herself out of visiting this late the entire way to his place, but she never spoke the words. Thirty minutes later, they pulled up to a modern-styled home. "This is where he lives?" she asked.

"This is it," Leslie said. He exited and opened her door. "Shall I wait?"

"No, I'll call in the morning when I need you," she said.

She found herself at West's door, second-guessing, regretting, nervous as hell until she rang the bell. He pulled open the door and then picked her up. She squealed as he carried her through his home.

"West, put me down!" she shouted, laughing until he placed her on the kitchen counter.

He placed fists on either side of her hips and leaned into her. Eye to eye, he admired her.

"You have the worst staring problem," she said.

"I need you to help me out with something," he answered.

"What's that?"

"You're the only woman I've ever met that I've had to pursue," West stated.

"And that's a bad thing?" she asked.

"I can't lie. It's rather frustrating," he replied truthfully. "I'm a man that's used to having what I want, when I want it."

"What do you want?" she asked.

"You," he replied simply.

"When do you want me?" she pressed.

"All the time," he said, pulling at the belt to her coat and leaning into her neck, planting kisses that made her thighs spread wide open. West slid into place. "I want you on this counter, in my bed, in the shower." He groaned as he removed her coat, revealing the silk robe. Its sash came off next. "In the back of my car with the partition up, in my office on the desk. I want you everywhere, Sutton."

His hand slipped inside her bra. He flicked her nipple,

rolling it between rough fingers, before lowering his lips to her areola.

Her body anticipated the pleasure to come as he picked her up and carried her up the stairs toward his bedroom. They were locked in a kiss. Her trench coat and robe created a path on the floor.

"West?"

"Oh my God!" Sutton shouted as she jumped out of his arms, hiding behind West's body to hide her lingerie. She thanked God he hadn't gotten to that part yet.

"Beamer, I thought you were asleep, kid," he said as he thumbed his lips. Sutton wasn't sure if he was wiping off her kisses or rubbing them in, but the way he pulled his bottom lip into his mouth told her he could taste her there. "You're kind of breaking bro code right now."

"How was I supposed to know you were about to get laid?" Beamer asked.

"Oh my God," Sutton whispered again, mortified.

"Are you going to introduce me?" Beamer asked.

"Sutton, this is my little brother, Beamer. Beamer, this is Sutton," West introduced.

Sutton peeked from behind West, waving in embarrass-ment. The bandages stabbed her straight in the heart.

"It's nice to meet you, Beamer," Sutton said.

"Hey, Sutton and I were about to . . ."

"Have sex?" Beamer asked.

West snickered. "Before you broke up the vibe? Proba-bly so, kid." Sutton slapped West, reprimanding him, and he and Beamer laughed. "I think the moment has passed, however. I'm going to put on a movie. You down?"

"Yeah!" Beamer shouted.

"A'ight, cool," West said. "Meet us in the theater room in ten minutes."

Beamer retreated to his room and West pulled Sutton into the master.

"Why didn't you tell me you weren't alone?" she asked, covering her face.

"He was supposed to be asleep," West said, shaking his head and fighting the grin on his face. He moved to the drawers and pulled out a white T-shirt for Sutton. She slipped it over her head. "He just got out of the hospital. I picked him up after the conference," he explained.

"I'm glad he's okay," she whispered. Beamer was evidence of her sins and facing him only made it worse. "He will be okay, right?"

"He's been through three surgeries for skin grafts already. He has a lot more to go. The worst burns are on his back and legs. The burns on his face aren't as severe. We're paying the best doctors," he explained.

Sutton's stomach hollowed out as she heard about the battle Beamer was fighting.

"Beamer's strong. He's a fighter and whatever he can't beat, I've got covered. He'll be okay. He was really attached to his mom though. Losing her has been the hardest of it all," West said. "It's been hard on all of us. It's a lot of death being handed out lately."

"Will he live with you, now?" Sutton asked.

"I don't know," West answered. "August and I have to figure things out. Neither of us have lifestyles that accommodate a kid, especially one like Beamer. He's autistic."

"Is he, really?" Sutton asked.

"High functioning, but he has his moments where he has a hard time. When he's overstimulated or overwhelmed. Abigail was the best with him during those moments. August and I have some adjusting to do, but we have to make it work. We're all he has," West said.

"You really do love them, don't you?" Sutton asked.

"They're my family," West said.

"And your biological family. Where are they?" Sutton asked.

"That's a discussion for another day," West replied, diverting away from the subject. It only made her more curious. How had this black boy from the inner city come to be so indebted and in love with this prestigious, rich, white family? Sutton had to know.

Her brow dented and her heart heavy, she reached for his face with one hand. "I really am sorry," she whispered.

"What is it about you?" he asked.

She looked up at him, adding a second hand to the other side of his face. "It's you. I'm only this way with you," she replied.

His hand slid down her back, gripping her ass as he stole her lips.

"Hey, Sutton! You like chocolate or strawberry ice cream?"

She turned to find Beamer there again.

"What kind of question is that?" she asked. "Why choose, when you can have both?"

"You're a genius!" he shouted.

Sutton laughed and followed Beamer out of the room, descending the stairs to the media room.

She eyed him curiously. He eyed her back as one made assumptions about the other.

"West, is this your girlfriend?" Beamer asked.

West froze as he walked into the room.

"We're just friends, Beamer," he answered as he took a seat beside her.

Sutton wasn't sure why she was disappointed with the response. She expected him to say more, despite the fact friendship was an overqualification for what they were.

Sutton was a snake in his grass.

Her disappointment was reflected in her eyes.

"Is that the wrong answer?" West asked.

Sutton shook her head. "No."

She settled in beside him, folding her hands across her chest.

She was so irrational because she was here for all the wrong reasons, but still, she wanted to mean more to him than "friends." She felt sorry for all the men who had ever tried to figure her out. She couldn't even figure herself out.

"Beamer, buddy, go get the snacks," West instructed.

Beamer nodded and as soon as he was out of earshot, West placed a finger to Sutton's chin.

"Hey," West said, commanding her stare. "This thing can be as casual or as complex as you want it to be. You just got to let me know what time you're on." His kisses were like emotional Band-Aids, healing cuts he didn't put there, injuries she had collected from years of dating the wrong men. It felt like she had stumbled across a good one and it turned out she was the one who was going to ruin it. Life was a bitch that way. To give her something she couldn't keep, something she shouldn't have even entertained, was worse than not ever having it at all.

"This is more than friends, West," she whispered.

Beamer came back with as much junk food as he could carry and then he broke up their party, sliding his body right between them.

Sutton laughed as he handed her a big bag of Cheetos.

"Thanks, handsome," she said. "What are we watching?"

"*Remember the Titans.*" Both West and Beamer said it simultaneously and Sutton frowned in confusion.

"It's our favorite movie," Beamer said. "We watch it every weekend. Ever since West was in college. We would go to his games then come home to watch it while he did his ice bath. It's tradition. Right, West?"

"Wouldn't miss it, kid," West replied.

"You played college ball?" Sutton asked.

"A long time ago," he said.

"He was supposed to go pro!" Beamer exclaimed.

"Pro, huh? How'd you end up in a boardroom instead of on the field?" Sutton asked, reaching for the popcorn in Beamer's bowl. She popped a handful into her mouth and then frowned.

"Umm, Beamer, I think you spilled candy in there," she said, chewing slowly at the odd combination of gummy bears, chocolate, and popcorn.

"Nope. It's on purpose," Beamer said. West reached for a handful next, shaking up the contents in his hand like he was shaking a pair of dice before emptying the odd mixture into his mouth.

"Another tradition," he said.

Sutton nodded, laughing. "You guys are weird. Tradition is blueberry pancakes on a Sunday morning. Not this!"

"Can we watch the movie now?" Beamer asked. "We're missing it!"

Sutton snickered and settled in on her side of the plush sectional. Beamer leaned into her. Within half an hour, he was a goner.

West snickered. "He never makes it to the end. I don't think he's ever seen the whole thing."

He stood and carefully moved Beamer's bandaged legs to the couch as Sutton moved out of the way. She placed a throw blanket over his body.

"He's a really cool kid," she said.

"Yeah, he is," West said.

They crept out of the room and Sutton passed his office. She drifted inside where dozens of trophies lined glass shelves.

"Wow, you really were good, huh?" she asked. "I'm trying to picture you in those tight football pants and a jersey instead of thousand-dollar suits." She smiled.

"You think you would have thrown pussy my way on the first night if I was in the NFL?" he asked.

Sutton scrunched her face as her skin grew hot with embarrassment. "I would have fucked you on the rooftop," she said.

"I mean I got a rooftop deck. It's not too late to make that happen," West answered.

"You wish." Sutton snickered. "Why'd you stop playing?"

"An injury ended my career."

"That explains the sports agency," she said.

"I love the game, just can't play it anymore," West said. "I enjoy the mental chess with the owners, though. The corporate side is where the most money is made but the passion of suiting up? Nothing can compare to that."

"Sounds like you really loved it."

"For a long time, I thought that would be how I spent my life. The game was the love of my life."

"And now? What do you love now?" Sutton asked.

"In this very moment, you," West replied.

The answer might as well have knocked Sutton off her feet. It was unexpected and blunt and sudden. How the fuck was he feeling this way so soon? How was she feeling the same?

Bitch, you ain't shit, Sutton scolded herself.

She charged him, kissing him aggressively. He picked her up, turning her toward the desk and knocking everything off to lay her down on top of it. She was breaking so many rules, handling this job in all the wrong ways, but her heart ached to be touched by him. The ways this man delivered dick was a sin and a shame. He strapped up and pushed into her body like he was desperate to feel her. The power of a man like West—the way his back tensed in definition as he stroked her, the way he bit her ear, then her neck, then her shoulder as he damn near growled in her ear—made her body soak for him. It was as good as the first time.

"West," Sutton moaned. Her face was balled up, a mixture of lust, regret, and pleasure tearing up her pretty features as he served her body well. She placed her hands on the sides of his face. "West . . ."

He focused on her.

"If I ever hurt you, know that I'm sorry."

He ignored her, swallowing her warnings along with her tongue. Sutton closed her eyes and held on tight. There was no switching of positions this night. Just good fucking, sweet loving, until he heard her call his name as she came. He picked her up and she rested her head on his shoulder as he carried her back to the bedroom. When they were behind the privacy of the closed door, he placed her on her feet.

"I can't fall for you," she whispered, bowing her head into his chest.

"I'm not asking for that," West said. "We're just enjoying whatever this is. If you want more, I'm with that. If the moment passes, I'm grown enough to accept that too. One thing I don't want to fuck with is a woman that's going to hold back. If you got to put guards up when we're together, that's not my vibe. Lower the walls, Sutton." He kissed the top of her head and then headed out of the room.

"Where are you going?" she asked.

"To the guest room. You can have the master for the night," he said.

She frowned, confused. "You're not sleeping with me?"

"I don't stay the night with women, Sutton. I normally don't even allow them into my home," he said.

"So, you can have guards, but mine aren't allowed? We're either in the moment together or not at all, West. I don't give without taking something in return," Sutton said.

"If I climb in that bed, we won't be sleeping," West warned.

"So, let's do something else."

Exhaustion. Exhaustion glued Sutton to the bed. Sex until 3:00 A.M. had done her body well. West had fallen straight to sleep, but Sutton didn't sleep well in foreign places. She had showered, hoping it would ease her restlessness; but as she lay under him, she couldn't quite doze off. She touched his face, admiring his features. He was so handsome. Brute, manly, and powerful. He was a king and Sutton was going to topple his kingdom. In a different world, she would sit beside him and help him rule. Her heart battled with her mind, trying to convince her to call it off. She wouldn't, but she wanted to.

She slipped into her robe and walked out of the room, searching for the rooftop terrace. She just needed a bit of fresh air. She crept through the halls silently until she passed Beamer's room. The sound of Beamer screaming alarmed her and she pushed open the door to find him tossing and turning in a full night terror. She turned on his light, but Beamer's eyes were closed as he panicked, fighting in his sleep.

"Beamer, hey, Beamer, wake up. You're just having a nightmare," she whispered softly as she rushed to his side. "It's just a dream." His pajamas were wet from the cold sweat of panic and he panted as he came to, looking at her in confusion.

"Hey, it's just a dream," she said, pulling him back to reality.

It took him a minute to recognize who she was before lying back down. Sutton pulled the covers up to his chin. She turned to leave.

"Sutton?"

She doubled back to his side.

"My mom used to stay until I went back to sleep. Can you just stay for a bit?" he asked.

An awkward beat passed as anxiety filled her. She was the reason his mom wasn't here to do the job herself.

"Yeah, I'll stay," she said. "You want to throw me a pillow?" Beamer passed her a pillow off the bed and threw in an extra cover. "I'll be right here until you go back to sleep, okay?"

"Thanks, Sutton," Beamer said.

"No problem."

Sutton didn't realize she had fallen asleep until she awoke the next morning. She smelled breakfast and she pulled herself up from the floor. When she entered the kitchen, she saw Beamer giggling as he flipped pancakes on a griddle.

"Tradition," West said, winking at her as she stood in the doorway, speechless.

"Blueberry pancakes coming right up!" Beamer shouted.

This time, Sutton didn't want to stop her smile. She crossed her arms and looked at them in amazement as she leaned against the doorframe.

West crossed the room to her. "How'd you sleep? Imagine my surprise when I woke up to find my baby brother took my girl."

"Is that what I am? Your girl?" she asked.

West didn't answer. Instead, he kissed her, gripping ass in one hand and pressing her into his body. It had been a long time since Sutton had allowed herself to feel like this. Girly and submissive and giddy for a man.

"August is on his way to come get Beamer. I want to do some things to you he can't be here to overhear," West said. Her body tensed at the sound of August's name. It brought a harsh reality washing down over her.

"I, um, I can't stay. After breakfast, I need to go. I have brunch with my sisters on Sundays. It's something we never miss," she said.

She was really looking for an excuse to leave. August was a reminder that she and West were aligned on two different sides of a war he had no clue was taking place.

He cocked his head back, lifting her chin between his fingers. He clearly felt the energy shift in the room.

"Are you good?" he asked.

"Yeah." Her voice was small, but her body was tight and

tense. Sutton LaCroix was back to business. Whatever wall he had broken down the night before had been restored.

"I had your assistant bring you by some clothes," he said.

"You did what?" Sutton asked.

"You need clothes, or did you plan to walk out of here naked?" West asked. "She went and grabbed something from Saks. I have an account there."

"You can't put my business out in the streets like that, West. I don't mix business with pleasure. My assistant doesn't need to know I'm sleeping with you," Sutton said. "You're a man. You can do what you want. It's different for women. It gets out that I'm sleeping with you, and it erases all credibility that I've earned in my career." Then again, Sutton didn't know if she was hiding it for business purposes or because she didn't want her sisters to find out.

"Understood. I respect it," West said.

The doorbell rang and West kissed Sutton's cheek.

"Grab some food, I'll be right back," West said.

Before he could even go to the door, August's voice echoed through the house.

"Aye, bro!"

"West!" Sutton whispered.

August appeared in the kitchen. "This is why you're not answering my calls. Good taste, bro," August said, smirking. "Really good fucking taste."

"August." West's tone was stern. A warning.

August lifted hands in defense. "Come on, Beamer. Let's go get you fitted for your big night." He slapped hands with West and then steered Beamer out of the house.

"I'll see you later, kid," West said. "Love you."

"Love you too! Bye, Sutton!"

"Bye, Beamer," she said softly.

West turned to her. "I'm a little old for secrets. I'm not really into worrying about what other people think about who I invite into my bed either. It's beneath me."

"My preferences are beneath you?" Sutton asked, insulted.

"I'm not out here acting boyish, Sutton. I want to know you. If I see you across the room and I want to touch you, I want to be able to touch you. If I want to taste you, I want to be able to kiss you. I've never done well with rules," he said. "Women bore me, but you . . ." He shook his head and kept the rest of his thoughts to himself.

"Me, what?" Sutton asked.

West backed her against the wall, stealing her air as he hovered inches from her face. He bit his lip as he wrapped a hand around her neck. Her chest rose and fell. She closed her eyes and felt his lips to her cheek.

"You're under my skin," he said in her ear, then pulled back. "You're either the best investment I've ever made or a distraction that I need to let go of. Decide what you want, Sutton. Beamer's welcome home party is tonight. If you don't show up, I'll know what it is. But if you do, you need to understand how I'm moving from here on out. It won't be in the dark."

West headed back to his room, leaving Sutton speechless. Before he disappeared from sight, he said, "Leslie will drive you home."

CHAPTER 18

"Gadget, how long does it take the US Coast Guard to get from shore to the Sinclair rig off the coast of Louisiana?" Sutton asked.

"About forty-five minutes, give or take," Gadget answered as she looked at the radar on her computer screen. "I've hacked their communication center. I'll know exactly when and where they are when they get dispatched. I'll be able to send in the anonymous tip about the drop as well."

"What happens after this? After the drug bust?" Honor asked.

"The company's assets are frozen while the feds investigate. They'll probably bring charges against August and West Sinclair, and the stock will be worth next to nothing. We'll buy it at its lowest and be owners of an oil company. That's real wealth, ladies. We'll be unstoppable," Sutton said.

The lust in her voice came from the thought of the power she was about to steal. She enjoyed West. She might even be falling for him. If any man were good enough for Sutton, it was him; but unfortunately, she didn't want to share a king-dom. She wanted to run her own. She wanted to wear his crown. Fuck a queen. Sutton wanted to be king.

Nevertheless, her gut nagged at her. The bond they were building didn't allow her to go into the play guilt free, but she ignored all her reservations.

"What makes you think another company won't try to buy Sinclair Enterprises before we get to it?"

"They will," Gadget said. "I've gathered dirt on the top three competitors. One built his money on the backs of Jews in Nazi Germany, the second has ties to Russian mobsters, and the third has no assets to leverage to acquire a new com-pany right now. We're in the clear. It'll come right to us."

"And what about Sire?" Ashton asked.

"What about that nigga?" Sutton asked, face frowning, because she didn't give a fuck what happened to him as long as she got what she wanted.

"He'll go to prison. For the rest of his life. He doesn't owe us a debt. Seems a little fucked up," Ashton said.

"He's collateral damage," Sutton responded.

"Honor and I will attend the welcome home celebration for Beamer. Gadget, you need to be somewhere near the pier. There is a restaurant there. You can sit at the bar so you can pick up the feed from the coast guard," Sutton instructed.

"And what about me?" Ashton asked.

"Stay out the way, Ash. I know you want to come off the bench, but you can't. It's not over yet, but it will be after tonight," Sutton said. "August can't see you. When he's in custody, you can move freely; until then, play the back."

"What if this is a mistake?" Honor asked. She had spent a little time with August. Her loyalty was with her sister, that

would never change, but August didn't seem like he was beyond redemption. She couldn't imagine him doing the things
that had been done to Ashton.

"It isn't," Sutton said. "The Sinclair family has done a lot
worse, I'm sure. Don't feel sorry for them."

Only Honor did feel sorry for them. Sutton could see it in
her eyes and deep down behind her walls, she felt the same.
She felt for Beamer and she felt for what she was destroying
with West, but it had to be done. Revenge was supposed to
be sweet, but somehow this time it was bitter.

. . .

Devil in a blue dress. Sutton LaCroix stood in front of the
full-length mirror admiring her reflection as she placed chan-
delier diamond earrings in her ears. Her stomach was hol-
low. She wondered how she had become this person. Her
moves had never been this underhanded. She had conned
her way through a lot of situations, blackmailed bad people
for good reasons, but this one . . . this one plan to destroy
the name of an entire family felt greasier than them all. Sutton slipped into her Louboutin heels and grabbed her clutch
as she headed for the door. West had given her a choice to
make. If she showed up, it would give every indication that
she wanted to be with him. If she followed her heart, that
much would be true, but her head was navigating this ship.
Sutton wasn't young anymore. She couldn't get sucked up
in whimsical love affairs. She had to keep her feet on the
ground and her eyes on the prize. She had to finish this. She
wouldn't show up at all if she didn't want a front-row seat to
the devastation that was awaiting the Sinclairs.

Before she did any of that, though, she had to meet with

Sire to ensure the deal went off without a hitch. If he didn't bring the right amount of product, it wouldn't be a large enough bust to make a federal case stick.

"Honor, are you ready?" Sutton called out as she headed to the living room.

"Yeah! Almost done!" Honor shouted back.

She stepped out of the room and Sutton gasped.

"Oh, bitch, I need to change. You didn't come to play, did you?" she complimented.

Honor snickered, shaking her head. "Sutty, I know it's too late to pull back, but the little brother, Beamer . . ."

Sutton smiled at the mention of him. "I know, Honor. I've already made arrangements for his care. The mother has a sister. A contact at DCS will make sure she receives custody if it comes to that."

Honor nodded.

"Let's get this over with," Sutton said.

They stepped outside and Sutton was stunned to find Leslie standing near West's black SUV. Sutton was speechless and stopped walking mid-step.

"Hi, Leslie. I didn't call for you," she said.

"I was given very specific instructions for you today," he replied. He reached inside the back seat of the car and pulled out a small gift-wrapped box.

"Mr. Sinclair hopes to see you tonight," Leslie said, handing the gift to her.

Sutton scoffed and opened the present.

A beautiful solid gold Rolex sat inside. A sixty-thousand-dollar Rolex to be exact. A handwritten note lay inside the box.

*Hoping to take up a bit of your time, Sutton
LaCroix. Leslie will lead you to the next gift. I'll see
you tonight.*

Faithfully Yours, West

"Sutton, what is going on between you and West?" Honor asked.

Sutton closed the box and wiped the lone tear that had escaped her eyes.

"Sutty?" Honor asked.

"I'll wait for you in the car," Leslie said. Sutton nodded, emotional as she turned to Honor.

"I think I fell in love with him," Sutton admitted. She had never said it aloud. It was wrong. It couldn't happen. Still, her heart told her it was true.

"Oh Sutty," Honor whispered. Sutton fell into her sister's embrace and gathered her composure.

"You know the rules. You made the rules, Sutton," Honor reminded.

"I know. I know what I have to do," Sutton reassured, quickly gathering herself because being vulnerable wasn't something she allowed herself to be. She was the strong sister, the leader, the one with all the answers. Her baby sister had been wronged, had been hurt, and Sutton was responsible for fixing it. Love didn't matter. West couldn't matter.

"I can't do this right now, the gifts and everything, but please go for me. Go with Leslie and go along with whatever it is that West has planned. Tonight, I'll meet you at the party. I have to catch up with Sire beforehand. I promise I'll meet you there."

Honor nodded. "Okay, but are you okay? Sutton, how long has this been going on?"

"Since the Draft party. I slept with him that night, Honor. I had no idea who he was and now I care. I hate that I care," Sutton admitted.

"We should leave, Sutton. Just take a job somewhere else. In LA. Pick someone new and start over. This one doesn't feel right," Honor said, trying to convince Sutton.

"It's too late for that. We already have resources invested. Let's just do what we're supposed to do so I can move on. Can you take care of this part for me? I can't be romanced by him today. It'll cloud my judgement. Whatever this is that he has planned for me, I can't; but if I don't accept it, it'll be an issue. I need him unsuspecting tonight. You can call me at the last stop and I'll meet you. Then we can go to the party together and watch this entire company burn to the ground."

Honor nodded and Sutton opened the car door.

"Be careful, Sutty," Honor whispered. Sutton pressed her forehead to Honor's. "I love you, sissy."

"I love you too," Sutton said. Honor ducked inside the SUV and as the driver pulled away, Sutton couldn't help but feel like something was going to go horribly wrong.

. . .

West stepped out of his AMG S-Class. He was uncharacteristically relaxed. Nike Sweat and a slim-fit white T-shirt hugged his athletic build. The LeBrons on his feet were a far cry from the Italian designers he normally opted for. He would slip back into the suit and tie later after he left the hood. He called Sire, who answered on the first ring.

"I'm out back," West said.

West made his way up the driveway and headed for the back door.

The young goon who answered the door stood in the threshold. A gatekeeper. He lacked patience today, however. No warning. No brakes. West came off his hip. A .45 to the middle. One pull of the trigger. The man dropped. Another finger curl sent a bullet through his head. West stepped over the body as he entered the kitchen where Sire sat.

"Hope you calling the cleanup crew through for that mess you just made," Sire said. He was unaffected by the body lying on the floor. Murder was a part of his everyday life as he sat back at the kitchen table. Tens of thousands of bills cluttered the table before Sire. They were wrapped in plastic shrink-wrap.

"Next time you lead these little niggas to my side of town, make sure you let 'em know you leading 'em to they graves," West said. He hated to get his hands dirty. He had removed himself from the ins and outs of the Fifth Ward when he was a college prospect. Any little scandal would have ruined his chances of going to the NFL, but he hadn't lost touch with the streets. He was Sire's silent partner on the drugs side too. He had gotten him started. Silent around these parts was misinterpreted for weak. So, West came loud.

"Fuck you think you were doing showing up to the press conference like that? You donated a half a million dollars in drug money. You associated that shit with my name. Have you lost your fucking mind?" West asked.

"I run this city. I go where I want to go, ain't no limits," Sire said.

"I love you like a brother, my nigga, so I'm going to shoot straight with you. Get out your feelings before I end all this street shit. The lines are drawn for a reason. You where you chose to be and I'm walking my path. I gave you an out. You chose to keep your toes in the sand. I can't play in it. I got too much at stake. It's love when it's personal. We're men. We chose our sides. An expired friendship don't make you my enemy, but treachery will, no doubt. You don't want it to go that way," West said.

"It can go whatever way you want it," Sire said.

West scoffed and nodded as he turned around, stepping over the body he had left behind as he walked out of the front door. He had seen it happen many times. Survivors of the hood became enemies of it. West hoped time would repair this misunderstanding, but what he couldn't repair he would erase, if he must.

• • •

August sat behind his desk swirling the aged whiskey in the tumbler he held in his hands. Four pills sat in front of him. He picked them up, putting them in his mouth and chasing them down with the bitter liquor. He had lost so much. His parents. CEO to his family's company. He had a part in Sinclair Enterprises, but the crown had passed him like he didn't even matter. His father had chosen West and it was a sting that never dulled. His parents' murders haunted him daily. The million dollars he had given the private investigator to conduct an investigation separate from the one West was pursuing had finally paid off. He stared at the white man in front of him. Boss Sparks. He was one of the most skilled hit men on the black market.

He looked at the picture in front of him.

"You're sure about this?" August asked.

"Sutton LaCroix hired the divers. Sutton LaCroix now works with West. You do the math. West is behind the murders of your parents. I don't believe he meant to hurt the kid. He didn't know Brandon would be on board that night. My guess is he wanted your parents out of the way so that he could acquire power of the company," Boss said.

August looked at the pictures of West and Sutton together. He was sick. West had been a brother to him. Blood meant nothing in comparison to their bond. He didn't understand this, couldn't quite come to grips with this type of deceit.

"My parents were good to him. They loved him like their own," August said, voice trembling, heart tearing, rage simmering. August's eyes burned and his vision clouded. This unexpected treachery tore him apart. He had never felt anything that hurt this bad. Not even the death of his parents. Learning that West had been the mastermind behind this took the strength out of him.

"I need it finished. Kill him."

"I don't offer half services, Mr. Sinclair. I take my job very seriously. The arrangements to eliminate the threat were arranged before I ever stepped foot inside this room. It'll be done by end of day," Boss replied.

August nodded and stood somberly to his feet. "Final payment has been delivered to your Swiss account."

Boss nodded and August closed the door as he exited. His chin quivered and one sob escaped him before he reined in his emotions. The ringing of his phone was a welcome distraction. He pulled it out to see Honor calling him. He wondered if she knew, if she was directly involved with the dealings between West and Sutton. He wasn't sure. He didn't think she could be. Not the beautiful, kind girl who had appeared in Beamer's hospital room after the blast. He prayed she had nothing to do with it because he liked her. He wanted to know her, but he would extend the job if he found out she had any hand in this.

August swept the contents of his desk to the floor and then leaned over the desk, placing flat palms to the top of the wood as he bowed his head and gritted his teeth. He had just lost a brother and it was agonizing.

• • •

"Bitch, whatever the fuck you have done to this man, you did it well because I'm staring at a truck full of gifts. Sutton, this is super sweet! His driver is taking me all over the city to pick up gifts for you with personal messages. He loves you, Sutton. Are you sure about this?" Honor whispered the last part as she glanced up at the closed partition.

She then stared at Sutton's face through FaceTime and she could tell that her sister was conflicted.

"I'm sure," Sutton said. "I'll see you tonight."

Sutton ended the call abruptly and Honor didn't press the issue. She knew when her sister was in her feelings. Honor didn't blame her.

The partition lowered and the driver looked in the rear-view mirror.

"Ms. LaCroix, we have two more stops before we have to pick up Mr. Sinclair," he announced.

"August?" Honor asked.

"No, young Beamer. I was instructed to bring Sutton and Beamer together. Since you have taken her place, I just wanted to inform you of our stops."

Honor nodded. "Thank you."

The partition rose and Honor reached for the champagne bottle that sat cooling in the ice bucket. She poured a glass as the city streets passed her by. It was a shame what was about to occur. She had a feeling Sutton was about to flush an epic love down the drain, but Honor loved her beyond measure because Sutton was doing it in the name of family. She was defending their sisterhood and Honor couldn't do anything but respect it. They had been taught at an early age that it was family over all else, but this sacrifice felt unfair. Her phone rang and her chest tightened as August's name popped up on her screen. She couldn't even bring herself to answer. Yes, he had done wrong, but Honor just couldn't see him raping anyone. The damage that had been done to Ashton was so terrible and malicious. She just couldn't marry the two thoughts together. It felt like they were reacting to half of the story. The entire situation felt wrong.

• • •

The one-story house was busy with action as Ashton pulled up curbside. She couldn't believe she was even there. She climbed out of the car and catcalls erupted as the fellas on the block took notice. Her eyes were hidden behind huge designer sunglasses, covering the remnants of bruises. Those bruises were footprints that led to the tragic night that was to come.

Ashton swung her hips and ass effortlessly as she took the steps up to the porch. She knocked on the metal-framed door. When it opened, Sire stood in front of her. In a black hoodie and black jeans, he was ready for tonight's drop. His eyes widened slightly at the sight of her because they both knew she had no business being there.

She didn't even know why she was there. She didn't know him. He was a pawn on Sutton's chessboard, but she had a feeling he had a board of his own and on that board, he was a king. She recognized a boss when she saw one. She wanted revenge but not at the expense of him. The only people she wanted punished were the ones who were responsible. She had no idea that she was looking the devil in the eyes.

"What you doing here?" Sire asked.

"Taking a risk that I shouldn't be taking," she whispered. "Can I come in?"

"I'm about to head out; got that thing, you know?"

"Yeah," she said, nodding as she turned to scan the block behind her. "I just need a minute. See something happened to me a while back, something bad."

Sire's back stiffened and his brow dipped. He didn't know where she was going with this.

"I just want to not think about it for a while. I need something just to help me sleep," she said. The no sleeping part was true, but Ashton would never run to pills for the remedy. It was an easy way to access his trap house, however.

"You want to cop something," he said.

She nodded and he pushed open the door farther.

"You do this on the regular?" Sire asked, feeling her out.

"No, but it feels necessary right now. I don't want to keep playing back these thoughts in my head. I'm walking around having nightmares while I'm awake. I just need . . ."

"To sleep," he finished for her. "A'ight. I'll help you out."

"I'm not asking for favors. I'll buy like everybody else," she said, pulling a roll of hundred-dollar bills from her Chanel crossbody bag.

"Don't nobody want ya small bankroll, shawty," Sire said. "I see you shining, though."

She shook her head.

"Let me get you right. You want a drink a'sum'n?" he asked.

"That would be cool," she said.

Sire disappeared to the back of the house and Ashton blew out a sharp breath. Sutton would kill her if she knew what Ashton was up to.

He returned with two short tumbler glasses, a bottle of Hennessey, and two small capsules. He placed the pills in her hands.

"What is it?" she asked.

"Just a little something for sleep. Nothing major. You came here. You must trust a nigga," Sire said.

She closed her palm. "I don't really want to take this with Henny straight," she said.

"I ain't got no girlie shit," he said.

"You got apple juice or something?" she asked.

"It's some Juicy Juice in there somewhere," Sire said.

Ashton snickered. "Juicy Juice? You have kids?" she asked. "In your trap house?"

"Nah, man, my niece be here sometimes," Sire said, giving up a lazy half smile. "She be here more now since my brother got killed a couple weeks back. We all doing our part so CPS don't take her. She be with my mama most of the time, but I have her sometimes, though."

Ashton already knew about his brother. She was responsible for Ris killing him. She had called Ris to town.

"I'm sorry about your brother," Ashton said.

"It's all good," Sire said.

"You gon get me the juice or what?" Ashton asked.

"I ain't no waiter, gorgeous, you better get that shit your-self," Sire said, sitting and nodding toward the hallway. "That way," he said.

Ashton made her way to the kitchen and poured two glasses of apple juice. She then split both capsules and emp-tied them into one glass and then mixed the drink up with her finger. She carried both drinks back to the living room and then grabbed the bottle of Hennessey.

"I'm going to put you on something new. Apple juice and Hen is smooth as fuck," she said, adding Hennessey to both glasses and handing one to him.

Sire looked at it skeptically and Ashton frowned. "It's just a drink," she said, taking it from him and taking a sip. She handed it back to him and Sire took a sip as well.

"My wettest dream, huh?" Sire asked.

Ashton blushed, rolling her eyes as she smiled. "Henny-thing can happen," she said.

Sire lifted her glass and he leaned forward to tap his against it. He swallowed down the drink in one gulp.

It took Ashton three gulps and accompanying grimaces to get her drink down. She climbed into his lap and wrapped her arms around the back of his head.

"I'ma fuck the shit out you, shawty, you better get out a nigga lap," he said bluntly.

Ashton kissed Sire. She needed to buy time, to give the sleeping pills time to kick in. He didn't seem like the type to waste time with a play on the floor, but she had never met a nigga who wouldn't get off track for pussy. He squeezed her ass and groaned as he sucked her entire tongue into his mouth. It was the sloppiest kiss she had ever received and somehow the best. She prayed he fell asleep before she wrote a check her ass couldn't cash.

"Aye," he said, pulling back to look at her. He gripped her face roughly with one hand, pushing in her cheeks as he looked at her. "I want to finish this, but I got bi'ness. Get your pretty ass out."

Ashton stood and adjusted her clothes. "Your loss, country boy," she said.

He stood and Ashton didn't move as he towered over her, wrapping her waist with one arm and staring down the bridge of his nose at her.

"I'ma holler at you, though," he said. She noticed the slur of his words and she placed a hand to his cheek.

"Do me a favor and don't," she replied. She walked toward the door and the step he took after her was off balance. He staggered.

"Oh bitch, I'ma kill you," he mumbled as he staggered once more.

"No, you'll thank me," Ashton said. She walked out with a clean conscience because she knew that Sire wouldn't make it to the drop.

• • •

Luna checked her Rolex as she sat in the coffee shop on the pier. She didn't like when things were off schedule. Things went awry when they weren't done on time and as she sat with the earpiece antenna in her ear, she knew something was wrong. She had tapped the US Coast Guard's frequency easily enough, but there was no activity. The drop was supposed to take place at 6:00 P.M. She had sent in the anonymous tip at 6:00 on the dot. A team had been dispatched to Sinclair Enterprises' Louisiana rig, but nothing had occurred. It had been forty-five minutes and the radio had been dead silent since.

Why haven't they called it in yet? Luna wondered.

When the static of an operator erupted in her ear, Luna perked up.

"Dispatch, we're at the Sinclair oil rig and there's nothing illegal going on here. The rig is clean," the voice said.

What the fuck?

Luna picked up her phone and sent Sutton a text.

Luna
Something's wrong. Boat is clean. No bust.

She quickly disconnected from the Coast Guard's communication network and packed up her bag. She had a six-hour drive ahead of her to get back to Houston. Whatever had gone wrong, it wasn't on her. She had done her part. She needed to link with her sisters to find out what the next move would be.

• • •

"Honor!" Beamer shouted as he ran out of the big house and into her arms. His nurse smiled a greeting at her too. Honor looked up at the huge Texas estate. It was massive, truly a big house, and she understood the nickname now. She couldn't believe her eyes as she gawked at its grandeur. Manicured lawns rolled perfectly for acres on end, fountains splashed, and three stories of luxury sat in front of her. It was like a castle.

"You must be Sutton. Beamer here has been so excited to see you all day," the woman said.

"No, I'm her sister, Honor. Nice to meet you," she greeted, shaking the nurse's hand. "Any special instructions for him? I know he's still healing. We're headed right to the party so his brothers will be there. I'm sure they know everything."

"Those brothers are the reason some of these burns aren't healing correctly. He really does need a woman's touch," the nurse stated. She passed a small bag full of medication. "His care instructions are inside. There is also a steroid cream, antibiotic cream, and something for pain inside. Fresh bandages too."

"I'll make sure I read everything and follow the instructions perfectly," Honor promised. She turned to Beamer. "You ready to go?"

Beamer nodded and Honor corralled him into the SUV. They pulled away from the estate.

"Welcome home, Beamer! I'm so happy you're out of the hospital. There are so many people who can't wait to see you!" Honor said, gushing over the resilience of this young boy. He was so special and she just wanted to make sure he had a good time. She knew his days had been hard lately and more hard days were to come as he figured out how to navigate through life without his parents. Today, however, should be fun.

"Is it a big party?" Beamer asked.

"Why do you think we're all dressed up? Of course it is!"

The smile that spread on his face warmed her. The driver headed toward the venue and Honor hooked her phone up to the vehicle's Bluetooth, turning on her favorite playlist.

Michael Jackson crooned through the speakers.

"Come on, Beamer," she said, smiling and snapping her fingers, dancing in her seat. "We've got to start the celebration now."

Beamer smiled and joined in as he moved his head and shoulders to the beat.

> *Keep on with the force, don't stop*
> *Don't stop 'til you get enough*

It felt amazing to see him so joyous. He deserved it. Beamer was a good kid, but life was about to get even harder. She had a hand to play in that, so this was the least she could do.

"Can you open the sunroof?" Beamer asked.

"Of course!" she said. "Nothing like dancing out the sunroof." She hit the button and they stood on the seats, sticking their heads out the sunroof as they pulled to a red light. They could see the venue up ahead and Beamer shouted, "There is West! West, over here!"

He waved his arms as the music blasted and Honor laughed.

"August!" Beamer shouted, seeing him from across the block. They lowered to their seats and the light turned green; but before Leslie could put his foot to the gas, a black car pulled up beside them. The windows seemed to roll down in slow motion. When Honor saw the barrels of the semiautomatic rifles, her heart stalled.

"Get down!"

She threw her body over Beamer as gunshots rang out.

RAT TAT TAT TAT TAT TAT TAT

Bullets pierced the vehicle, over fifty rounds. Leslie lost

control of the SUV and it went rolling into the intersection until a car from oncoming traffic T-boned it.

Honor felt her body as it was pulled from the back of the car.

"Call 911!"

It was August's voice. She couldn't breathe. She couldn't do anything and as the voices around her began to fade, she wished she could take it all back. She wished they had thought this thing out more because the cost was high. Revenge would be theirs, but it would cost them her life.

. . .

"What do you mean they didn't find anything?" Sutton asked. "I spoke to Sire. He was on his way to the rig."

"Well, something changed because the coast guard searched the boat and came up empty-handed," Luna said.

"Damn it!" Sutton shouted as she hit her steering wheel. "I'm on the way to Beamer's welcome home dinner. I can't miss it, especially if I still need to be on the inside. This didn't work, but I'm going to find a way to bring their shit to the ground. Meet me afterward, you and the girls, at Ashton's."

Sutton hung up the phone and took her eyes off the road for a millisecond as she put it on the charger. When she looked back up, red taillights stared her in the face as an all-white Maserati cut her off. She slammed on the brakes, abruptly stopping her speed.

"What the hell?" she shouted. When another car veered into her lane from the right, she turned the wheel hard, too hard, sending her car skidding off into a ditch. Her head hit the steering wheel as the vehicle made impact.

She reached for her forehead and blood greeted her.

She was so dazed she couldn't think straight. Her door was snatched open suddenly and she was jerked from the car. Before she could even protest, her mouth and nose were covered. Then a black pillowcase was thrown over her head and her hands were zip-tied behind her. Fear erupted in her body but all she could do was give into the darkness as she felt herself being tossed like a rag doll into the back of a trunk. The last thing she heard was the screech of tires before her eyes closed.

. . .

"I know you're afraid. I've been where you are. It's dark. You can barely breathe under there. Your heart is racing. You're panicking. The zip ties on your wrists and ankles are cutting into your skin. I always wondered what it felt like to be him. See, my weapon of choice is normally a gun, sometimes a knife or a razor blade when I'm in a position where I can't carry. But to beat someone to death? To use your hands to beat the life out of someone? That's a different type of kill. That takes a different kind of malice. You might want to start praying. It helps. The Lord's Prayer should suffice."

"Just tell me what you want!" Sutton shouted. She tried not to panic, tried to remain in control, but she was terrified.

When she came to, she was bound to a chair. She had no idea how long she had been out or where she was. Even worse, she had no idea who had taken her.

"You see the problem is you're too smart. I've done my research on you and your sisters. You find these men and you put down a corporate trap. I respect that part. It's genius, actually, but you fucked up. You crossed over into the streets, but you have no muscle to back you up."

Someone snatched the pillowcase from Sutton's head and Sutton stared into the face of a woman she had never seen before. She was beautiful, a little hardened by life it seemed, with eyes as dark as night and a tattoo of cursive letters on the side of her neck. A name. *Carter.*

Confusion flooded her. "Who are you?" Sutton asked.

"Ashton knows who I am. Why don't we call her so she can make a proper introduction?"

The woman produced Sutton's phone from her back pocket and then held it up to Sutton's face so facial recognition could unlock it.

She FaceTimed Ashton and kept the camera turned toward Sutton.

"Sutty?"

"Ashton, whatever she wants, don't do it. Just leave. Get the girls and leave town!" Sutton shouted.

"I swear to fucking God if you hurt my sister—" Ashton's threat fell short when the woman turned the camera toward her face.

"Oh my God! No, no. No! Please, I'll do anything," Ashton whispered as tears prickled her eyes.

"If that were the case, you would have done everything I asked you to do and we wouldn't even be here. Your actions led to this moment. Your betrayal."

"Ashton, leave town!" Sutton shouted. She let her head fall back and stared at the ceiling before closing her eyes.

The woman tossed the phone aside and picked up the long security chain that lay at her feet.

"If you're going to kill me, at least tell me who you are," Sutton said through clenched teeth.

"The connect you tried to set up tonight . . . the one who

295295295295295295295295295295295295295295295295295295 is son.295 is son. He's295 is son. He's all

295295

295295

295

Don't miss the next novel by Ashley Antoinette

BUTTERFLY 3

Coming soon from St. Martin's Griffin